No Faith in Justice

by Tom Barkwell

a Smoking Lamp Books
Publication

www.nofaithinjustice.com

I'm eternally grateful to my wife, Michelle, for her endless patience and support

Thanks also to Brenda Humphrey, for encouragement and assistance

Chapter One
October 06th, 2010

The contents of the envelope hit him like a two by four upside the head. His eardrums began pounding, and he struggled to breathe as the air was suddenly sucked from his lungs. He felt like he might retch, so he leaned over in the chair until his head was almost between his knees, and closed his eyes, face in his hands. His mind was racing. What the hell could this mean? Who could have sent it? After all these years, why is this happening now? After several deep breaths, he reached into the small private fridge under his large mahogany desk and pulled out a cold bottle of Pellegrino. He drank generic brand seltzer water at home. Half the price and couldn't tell the difference. But he knew his label conscious clients might get the wrong message from generic. And he was always careful not to let small things get in the way of business. There was enough to worry about with the big things. He chugged half the bottle in one long draw.

He picked up the envelope and examined it more closely. A standard plain white, the kind you could find in every home and office in the country. A computer printed address label was affixed: *Personal for Martin Mahoney C/O Prime Choice Properties*, postmarked locally in Englewood, Colorado, the day before. The return address was listed as *Peter P. Phoenix, 1313 Mockingbird Lane, Phoenix, Arizona*. An obvious fake. But it was the photo from inside that knocked him flat. The picture had been wrapped in a single sheet of standard printer paper, upon which the following message was typed:

Meet me thursday 6:30 pm on waterton canyon trail a mile south of mill gulch bridge. Ride your green bike, wear your red ball cap, come alone. I'll be watching. Tell no one, or I'll send additional incriminating evidence to police.

His skin crawled as he pondered the ominous note. How could this be happening? He studied the picture. A three by five print of himself and a girl he'd barely known, from thirty years before. He was about nineteen at the time, good looking and smiling, a half-drunken bleary-eyed smile, cigarette dangling from the side of his mouth, can of Milwaukee's Best clutched in his hand, leering down at the skinny, pleasant-faced young girl in her early twenties who was laughing, head tossed back, lying on a bed. She was wearing only pink bikini bottoms, and a midriff-exposing cut-off T-shirt with 'Road Hawgs' printed across the chest. Her hands were tied to the bedposts with what appeared to be neckties.

Fucking Radar. It has to be him. Who else could it be? The only other person in the world it could have been is long ago dead. As was the girl, Faith Cooper.

He had no recollection whatsoever of the event depicted in the photo. Not only was it from so long ago, but he'd been a habitual blackout drinker in those days. As a young Navy enlisted man, it'd been routine for him to go out with friends, then wake up the next morning to tales of their escapades, with only spotty or sometimes no memory at all of the goings on from the night before. On one occasion, he awoke in the morning, alone in his '67 Chrysler station wagon, parked at a convenience store in Richmond, Virginia, with no recollection of having driven the ninety miles from Norfolk the night before. And no idea why. Another time, he came to on a train bound for Washington, D.C. Again with no idea why he'd decided to board the train, and no memory of having paid for his ticket, or anything else. The last he could remember clearly from the night before, he'd been shooting pool in a waterfront dive near the naval base in Norfolk.

But he could vividly recall the moment he found out Faith Cooper had been murdered. Strangled, her body had been discovered in some dunes in the Oceanview section of Norfolk, near an apartment building on 23rd Bay Street. An apartment where he and his two best friends had lived and partied for a brief time in 1980, and the likely setting for the photo. The same apartment Faith had been with him in the night before her body was found, a fact he'd denied when questioned by an NIS investigator.

This whole thing was just beyond belief. For most of the past thirty years, he'd been building a life. A responsible life. A sober life. He'd worked so hard, against some pretty long odds, to put all those past mistakes behind and do something positive. And respectable. And now? What the hell could Radar want after all this time? And how did he find him, living under a different last name? And how long had he been watching him?

A sharp rap on his office door startled him out of his reverie. "The Mildenhalls are here, Mr. Mahoney," said Janine Estrada, his firm's new office manager, as she opened the door.

"Okay, thanks Janine. Please send them in," he said as he came around from his desk and buttoned his navy blue blazer. He was glad for the momentary distraction from this nightmare. He thrived on making the deal. It was a thrill not unlike betting a good poker hand, something he'd relished for as long as he could remember. But he knew that he would soon have to deal with this unexpected problem. The stakes were high. Far more than mere money was on the line. His freedom was in jeopardy. His life.

5

Chapter Two
April 28th, 1973

"You sure you should be drivin', Dad?", the boy said, hesitating before opening the passenger side door, a look of mild contempt mixed with concern on his face. It was a rhetorical question. The boy knew full well his father shouldn't be driving them anywhere in his current condition. Drunk driving was dangerous. He'd seen an episode of Perry Mason once where some guy killed a girl while driving drunk. He'd also been a passenger in more than one fender-bender in the past with his tipsy dad at the wheel. The same dad who was already half-in-the-bag, and would undoubtedly begin nipping on the bottle of Hiram Walker's Ten High bourbon he kept under the seat, soon after getting behind the wheel.

"What?", replied Harry Mahoney, incredulous at the idea that anyone would dare question his ability as a wheel-man. "I'm the best goddam driver in Kansas City, boy. Now get in the car."

The boy also knew that when his mother found out he'd been out running around town with his father, all hell was going to break loose, and the day would probably end in a brief scuffle between his father and the police, followed by all the neighborhood busybodies gawking and clucking on their front porches as his dad was hauled away to jail. Again.

They'd just left John's Fault tavern on 39th Street, where the boy had consumed six glasses of 7-Up, two bags of Guy's potato chips, three Slim Jims, played five games of fake bowling, nine games of pinball, four games of eight ball, and heard his father tell the same three stories and four jokes at least fifteen times each.

No Faith in Justice

After they got into the twenty-six year old '47 Plymouth his father so dearly loved, the boy began silently praying that his dad would take him back home and drop him off up the block, then disappear for another two years, just like he'd done after their last father-son visit, right before the divorce.

When his father instead said "Whaddaya say we go out to Peculiar and visit Uncle Ray and them," as they pulled out of the parking lot, the boy knew that his prayers were not to be answered on this day.

Still, he gave it a half-hearted effort. "I think you better drop me off at home, Dad. We were in the tavern a long time, and Mom's gonna get worried if I don't show up for supper at six. She probably thinks I'm still playin' baseball up at the playground."

"Your mom worries too goddam much. That's why I divorced her ass in the first place." He looked sideways at his son with that cockeyed half grin of his. "Besides, I might need you to drive later. So don't be a pussy."

The boy knew that it was his mother who'd divorced his father, not the other way around. And he also knew that he was probably not going to escape from this mess without enduring another visit with Uncle Ray and his half-wit cousins. If only he'd been thinking faster when he first saw his dad's Plymouth pull up near the Redemptorist Catholic Church playground, where he spent his evenings and weekends along with most of the other kids in their neighborhood, he might have been able to pretend he was chasing down an errant throw, then disappear into a nearby alley. There was no way any adult could find him once he had any sort of head start. But he was caught by surprise, and froze like a deer in the headlights.

"Isn't that your Dad?", his friend Marcel Blaine, whose mother was from France and used to throw dance parties and spin forty-fives for all the neighborhood kids, had said. The boy had just rubbed his eyes and stood there dumbstruck as his father got out of his car and started cracking wise with all the kids he hadn't seen for so long.

"What was your name before you got married?...If you ever hit me and I find out about it I'll kill you, you little son-of-a-bitch...You ever seen a nickel screw'n a dime?" The boy's friends had heard them all before, but they still loved cutting-up with the old man. He'd given them all nicknames, as he did with most everyone he knew. Lester Bennett became Luther. Ronnie Colazzo became Quasar. No one really understood why he gave them different names, or what the names even meant, but they all wanted one. They all liked Harry. More than the boy himself, sometimes.

Too bad the boy's big brother Danny hadn't been around at the time. He was quick on his feet, and might have been able to think of something on the spot. Danny had fast-talked them out of a jam over bb-guns and dead pigeons just the previous weekend with one of the railroad detectives down at Union Station. But he was off at some kind of Junior ROTC fascists meeting at Westport High School. His big sister Hollie was probably with one of her girlfriends somewhere, putting curlers in each other's hair or something. And his little brother Lee was only three, so he would've been no help at all, even if he wasn't two blocks away at home with their mother. Which left the boy alone to face the full brunt of his father, that force of nature known to one and all as "Hurricane" Harry Mahoney.

"Eleven might be a little young for city driving, Dad. I don't even have a permit yet. Maybe we should wait till I'm at least thirteen for my first drunk driving lesson. That'll give us something to look forward to for our next visit."

The boy's dad let out a big loud guffaw. Harry Mahoney could take a joke, or a jab, just as well as he could dish them out. There was little worth taking seriously in his mind. And if he thought anyone in his vicinity took themselves too seriously, they would be called out on it. Like one of their neighbors, a retired Army sergeant major named Jack Huddleston. When he stenciled *Sergeant Major Huddleston* in large black letters on the curb in front of his home, as if he wanted to keep anyone else from parking there, the boy's dad started parking in that very spot every day, even when no one else was in their own driveway, or in front of their house, two doors down. Then he stenciled *PFC Mahoney* in even larger letters on the curb in front of his own house, just to rub it in. His distinctive and loud booming laughs could be heard over the din of every bar in Kansas City. He made sure people knew he was there. Love him or hate him, you were going to have an opinion about Harry Mahoney. And he didn't care that much one way or the other which one it was.

"We'll have more fun than the law allows, you know it Marty?"

The boy knew there was no use fighting it. He was going to Uncle Ray's whether he liked it or not. And he was stuck with his dad until he was damn good and ready to take him home. It was probably going to end ugly no matter what, so he might as well make the most of it in the meantime. He figured there was a good chance he would end up with a nice chunk of coin for his trouble. His dad had been flashing a big wad at the tavern, and the boy had already pocketed almost five dollars in unreturned change from all the pop and snack purchases. So he decided to just give in and enjoy his Hurricane experience, and he smiled and nodded in reply.

"You know I miss you kids, son. But your mom doesn't want me to see you. Says I'm a bad example. Alcoholic, and all that shit. She doesn't trust me. But hell, I never hurt nobody. Poor little ol' Lee don't even know me. How's your brothers and sisters doin', anyway?"

"They're fine. Danny's on the wrestling team and Army ROTC. He's still got the paper route. He's gonna let me take it over next year. Hollie's trying to learn the flute, God help us all. And Lee's smart as a whip. He can already count to a hundred by fives. I'm trying to teach him how to play blackjack, but he always turns every hand into slapjack instead."

"Still playing cards all the time, huh? Maybe we can get Uncle Ray and them to pitch some nickels, or play some dominoes."

"I like poker, Dad. We could play silent partners. What should our high sign be? Pulling on our left earlobe?"

"Ha! We can't play silent partner poker against family, you little con artist."

"Yeah. I guess pitching nickels would be better, anyway. I been practicing a lot lately."

"You still doin' good in school?"

"Pretty good. After last year they skipped me up a year, so I'm in seventh grade now. Danny says if I keep it up I might be the only kid that graduates high school who's too young to drive. Said I might have to take a grade school girl to the prom."

"You could take your sister."

"Yeah, that wouldn't be weird or anything. And if she can't make it, I can always ask Grandma, if they'll let her out of the nursing home for a night."

No Faith in Justice

They were driving south on Troost, heading towards Peculiar, Missouri. There could not have been a more appropriately named place for the boy's Uncle Ray, his father's half-brother, and his family to live. Uncle Ray's kids were a bit odd, to say the least. And he was married to Aunt Linda, whose favorite story to tell was how one time she had to take a shit in the cat's litter box because her daughter Darla was hogging the only bathroom, and she just couldn't hold it anymore. That story, told with unrestrained gusto in excruciating detail, always made everyone howl with laughter, especially the boy's father. Apparently, the boy and the cat were the only ones not amused.

"Hey Marty, look at the fart box on that broad. If she pissed all over ya' it'd scald you to death, you know it?"

The boy had to agree that the lady his dad was ogling definitely was hot, as his father implied. He'd admired the finer female form himself from a very young age. His mom had found him completely engrossed in a stash of old Playboy magazines in their basement when he was only five, and he'd become even more interested in girls over the past year. He thought about girls even more than cards and baseball lately. He'd been hoping to see Cindy Dugan again tonight at the El Torreon skating rink. They'd skate-danced together during the "couples-only" segment of the previous Saturday night's public session, and continued holding hands long after the couples' dance song had ended. But his dad's unexpected intrusion had blown those plans out of the water. At least there was a chance he might see another girl he was sweet on, one Shelly Warner, who lived in a house near Uncle Ray's trailer. She'd played hide-and-go-seek with the boy and his cousins last time he'd visited Uncle Ray and them. They'd ended up hiding together in

11

the woods, and had a long conversation. The boy had sensed at the time that she was as interested in him as he was in her. And he hoped she might still feel the same.

A few blocks further South, and the boy's father suddenly shouted "*Hey Red*!" out the window. Then he looked at the boy and said, "Red-headed niggers are good luck, but only if you holler at 'em."

"I'll stick with my rabbit's foot, Dad." The boy's father let out another one of his booming laughs.

"That foot wasn't so damn lucky for the rabbit, now was it? Otherwise it'd still be attached to his leg."

The boy had never considered that. Good thing he also had a lucky penny for back-up.

As they turned on to Bannister Road, Harry pulled out the bottle for another quick snort. "Ahhhh, bluwee! You want a nip, son?"

"No thanks, Dad. I think I might've drank too many pops already. You don't want me to upchuck in the Plymouth do you?"

"Well, we're gonna have to stop and get some more pop and some beer before we get there, anyway. It's never good to show up empty handed, even with family." The boy's dad then broke into song, a favorite little ditty he'd been singing for as long as the boy could remember.

"*Did you ever go down to an Irishman's shanty*
Where food was scarce but whiskey was plenty
An old yella dog and a stool by the door
A three legged goat and a one legged whore."

They stopped at a liquor store on Highway 71, about a mile from the turnoff to Uncle Ray's trailer, and bought a case of

Budweiser and four large bottles of Coca Cola. The boy's dad joked with the liquor store clerk as if he'd known him all his life, as he always did with everyone he encountered. The boy could never tell if the people his father interacted with were lifelong friends or complete strangers. They were all the same to The Hurricane.

Uncle Ray's faded red and green trailer was situated on a dirt road several miles off the highway, among a cluster of three other mobile homes and two pre-fab houses. There was pasture land with horse stalls adjacent to the pre-fabs, and thick woods behind the trailers. A banged up '39 GMC pick-up truck sat in front of Uncle Ray's, with big green shamrocks near the doors, painted on by the boy's father using an airbrush. The hood was up and Uncle Ray was chest deep with a socket wrench as the boy and his father pulled in the driveway.

"Hurricane Harry! What the hell are you doing here? We ain't seen you in a coon's age. You ain't looking for bail money or somethin' are you?"

"Shit, I'd settle for that fifty bucks you've owed me since '61, you little son-of-a-bitch. Where's that sexy ass wife o' yers'?"

"Over at her mother's place, as usual. Don't tell me that's Marty. You better slap the milkman Harry, cause he's way too good lookin' to be your kid. Hell, let's go inside and put that beer in the icebox."

The boy's father and Uncle Ray settled into the kitchen, swapping the same old lies and jokes they'd been telling each other all their lives. The boy spotted his very strange thirteen year old cousin Dewayne in the living room. He had several catalogues spread out on the coffee table, from which he was carefully cutting pictures with a pair of scissors.

"Hey Dewayne. Whatcha' doin'?"

"Nothin'."

Dewayne was totally engrossed in his project, oblivious to everything and everyone else. Marty watched in silence as he cut out about a dozen pictures of women modeling bras and panties, then began gluing them onto pieces of cardboard. Once satisfied, he positioned the cardboard pieces in various places around the living room. Three were perched on top of the couch, leaning back against the wall behind. One was placed on the recliner. Two more were set on the end tables, up against the table lamps. When he had them all in place, he disappeared back into one of the bedrooms, and emerged several minutes later wearing only his jockey shorts and a white bath towel tied around his neck. In his hand was a broom. He leapt up on top of the sturdy coffee table and began to strum the broom as if it were a guitar while belting out the lyrics of "Hound Dog"' to the magazine cutout ladies.

The boy's father and Uncle Ray burst into hysterical howls of laughter as they rushed in from the kitchen. He'd never seen his dad laugh so hard in all his life. Dewayne ignored the laughter, and kept on crooning for all he was worth, intent on winning the hearts of his underwear model cuties. Once he was finished singing "Hound Dog," Dewayne informed his audience that he was indeed Elvis Presley, then flowed right into a spirited rendition of "Johnny B. Goode."

The boy's father was laughing so hard tears streamed out his eyes, and he could barely catch his breath. He stumbled back into the kitchen for a drink of his beer, then doubled-over again in more spasms of gut-shaking howls.

The boy didn't share in his dad's delight, however. He was completely dismayed and embarrassed at Dewayne's total lack of concern for his own dignity. He acted as if he didn't care one whit what anyone else thought about him. The boy had always known Dewayne to be slightly weird, but now he appeared to have completely lost his mind. That might explain why his other cousins were off somewhere with Aunt Linda, while their brother was preparing his one man show for the magazine ladies. Halfway through Dewayne's performance of "Johnny B. Goode," the boy had seen enough, and left the trailer, hoping to spot a particular neighbor girl.

He walked up in the pasture toward the barn. Its doors were open, and he spotted the imposing figure of a very large man inside. "Hey Mister Warner...is Shelly around?"

"She's off ridin' old Charlie back on those trails up yonder. But she should be back soon. Are you one o' Ray's kin?"

"Yes sir. I'm his nephew, Marty. Shelly played hide and seek with us last time I was here, and I was just wonderin' if she might want to play again, or somethin'."

Mr. Warner gave the boy the once over, and was apparently satisfied with whatever it was he saw. "I'm goin' back to the house, but you can wait in here for her if you want. She'll be along shortly, I expect."

The boy wandered around the barn as he waited for Shelly. He liked the smell of the hay, and some of the old-looking tools that hung on nails on the walls. After a brief wait, Shelly did indeed ride up on old Charlie, a rather hefty Welsh pony.

"Hey Shelly. Remember me?"

She looked unsure for a brief moment, then the light of recognition flashed in her eyes. She smiled as she said "Hey Marty, I ain't seen you in awhile. Whatcha' been up to?"

"About five-foot, last time I measured."

Shelly chuckled as they bantered back and forth for a few minutes, then they began working together at taking care of old

Charlie. After they had put away his saddle and replaced his bridle with a halter, she led old Charlie back to his stall and began carefully brushing him down.

"Dad gets mad if I don't brush him down every day. Sometimes I get tired of doing all this work just for a pony, but I feel guilty whenever I don't, so I've learned it's just better to do things right."

The boy worked on old Charlie's coat with a soft brush while Shelly used a curry comb on his tail and his mane. When they were finished, she made sure he had feed and water, closed up the stall, and they went back into the front section of the barn.

"Hey, you wanna sit on the haystack, Marty?"

"Sure." She picked up a blanket hanging over the edge of a stall, and they scrambled up on to a large stack of hay bales on one side of the barn. She laid the blanket over two of the bales, and they sat down side-by-side with their backs against the wall.

The late April weather was still a bit cool in the evening. It was about early evening, and there was a slight nip in the air. But the barn felt cozy, and the boy felt even warmer inside. Shelly Warner was "easy on the eyes" as his Aunt Millie liked to say, even more than he'd remembered. And he just might work up enough nerve to steal his first kiss tonight, if everything went right. Maybe his dad turning up at the playground wasn't such a bad break after all.

Remembering a piece of advice he'd received from his brother Danny long ago, the boy said "Hey Shelly. You ever seen a nickel screw'n a dime?"

She giggled. "No. Let's see."

The boy pretended to look around the barn as if making sure no one else was around, then reached into his pocket and pulled out a dime, a nickel, and a small sheet metal screw. She busted out with a good hardy laugh, and pulled playfully on his shoulder with one of her hands. The boy's brother had been right after all. Make 'em laugh if you can. Girls love to laugh.

The boy was just about to make his move when suddenly a fully dressed Dewayne came rushing toward the barn, shouting "Marty...Marty...Uncle Harry says to come back right now."

"Shhhh," Shelly whispered. "Get down. I don't want that ree-tard to see us. He's always trying to make out like I'm his girlfriend or somethin'. I can't stand him. He's so disgusting. I wish you lived next door instead of him."

They laid down as flat as they could so as not to be seen from below. But Dewayne wasn't fooled. Within seconds he climbed up the haystack. "There you are. Hey, Marty, you gotta go home right now. Uncle Harry said you gotta come right now so we can pitch some nickels. Right now."

"Okay, Dewayne. Gee-whiz. Hold your horses. I'll be along in a minute. Go on back to the trailer and tell 'em I'm on my way."

Dewayne looked at his cousin sitting so close with the girl. He decided to head the situation off immediately. "No. You gotta come right now. Uncle Harry said." Dewayne grabbed the boy's left shirt sleeve and began pulling him toward the edge of the hay stack.

"Let go, you weirdo," the boy said as he violently jerked his arm away from his cousin. Dewayne just stood there for a moment, unsure what to do next. The boy looked at the torn sleeve on his favorite shirt, then added "And by the way dill-rod, 'Johnny B. Goode' is a Chuck Berry song. Not Elvis Presley. And Chuck Berry is twice as good as Elvis ever thought about bein'."

"No it ain't. It's Elvis Presley. He's the king of music. It's Elvis Presley...you gotta come right now. Uncle Harry said. Right now." And with that he grabbed the boys shirt sleeve and began pulling again. The boy took one glance at Shelly, then slammed his right fist as hard as he could square on his cousin's nose. It was a pretty good shot which stunned Dewayne, and instantly started a strong flow of bright red blood. It also knocked him halfway down the haystack. The boy scrambled after his cousin in an attempt to press his momentary advantage. Unfortunately, Dewayne was bigger, stronger, faster, angrier, and a better fighter than his opponent. A very bad combination from the boy's perspective.

Dewayne began whipping the boy's ass up one side and down the other as they rolled all over the floor of that barn. The boy held on for all he was worth, and attempted to deflect as many of the blows as he could. The fight only lasted a couple of minutes, but it felt like hours worth of knuckles being pounded into his face from every conceivable angle. At some point, Shelly mercifully ended the one-sided beating by jumping on Dewayne's back, getting him in a vice-like headlock, and telling him if he didn't quit pounding on his cousin, she was going to have to go get her father. And no one, no matter how angry, wanted to deal with an upset Mr. Warner. Besides, Dewayne was so exhausted from throwing so many unanswered punches, he didn't have enough energy to continue, anyway.

As Dewayne sat with his back against a wall and his head tilted back in an effort to stop his nosebleed, the boy just lay on his side, groaning in agony. His mouth was bloody and swollen, and two of his front teeth were loose. But none were missing, thank God. His nose was bleeding, too. And there were scrapes all over his neck. One of his eyes was practically swollen shut already, and there was blood coming from a deep cut on his cheek. After several minutes, Dewayne got up and walked out of the barn without saying another word.

Soon thereafter, the boy got to his feet and stood unsteadily for a few moments, trying to keep from throwing up. He looked over at Shelly, who was staring down at the ground. His brother Danny had given him some good advice about getting a girl to laugh, but he hadn't mentioned what to do after the girl you're sweet on has just seen you get beaten to smithereens by an imbecilic Elvis impersonator. The boy couldn't think of anything clever to say, so he too just walked out in silence, and trudged back to his Uncle Ray's.

"You okay, son? We best get you cleaned up."

"I'll get you a clean shirt, Marty," Uncle Ray said as he headed to the back of the trailer. Elvis was nowhere to be seen. The boy's father reached under the kitchen sink for a clean cloth, wetted it, and began wiping the blood from his son's face.

"Quite a shiner you got working there. Any broken bones?"

"I'll be fine, Dad. I could use a couple of aspirin, though. I got a killer headache."

"Hey Ray," his father shouted. "Bring out some aspirin. And a band-aid"

After his face had been washed and band-aided, and he was wearing a clean shirt -- probably one of Elvis junior's -- the boy began to feel a little bit better. Maybe it was the aspirin, or the glass of beer his father had given him.

"Can I go home now, Dad?"

"Sure, son. I know your mom is gonna give me a bunch of static, so we might as well get it over with and face the music."

"Well, I was hoping you two would spend the night here," said Uncle Ray. "But under the circumstances…"

"We'll come out in a couple of weeks, maybe, when Linda and Billy and Darla are here too. I'll bring Danny and Hollie. It'll be like old times again, hey Ray?"

"Yeah. And we'll make these two knuckleheads put on some boxing gloves for the next battle royal. Less damage that way."

As they made the forty-five minute drive back to the boy's neighborhood, his dad took several swigs from the bottle of Hiram Walker's.

"Well...did you learn anything, boy?"

After thinking for a moment, the boy said "I guess Elvis really is the king."

They both had a good long laugh. After a few minutes, the boy said "Where have you been for the last two years, Dad?"

The boy's father thought about that for a minute. Then his mind flashed briefly back to his own childhood. Harry had been born and raised in Harrisonville, Missouri, a small town of less than ten thousand people. His father and mother had married young, then divorced in 1929, when Harry was only two. They both remarried, and each eventually had several more children with their new spouses. Harry stayed with his mother, naturally. But he had always known about his biological father, William Mahoney, and had seen him around the small community many times over the succeeding years. Once he stood directly behind his father in line at the A&P for almost ten minutes. Yet they'd never spoken a single word with each other, ever. The man had never so much as acknowledged the existence of his own son.

"Wyoming. Pretty country. Not so many goddam cops. You'd like it out there, Marty."

"What were you doing in Wyoming?"

"Worked on an oil-rig for awhile. Then we did some painting. High work, mostly. Smokestacks and bridges."

As they pulled up in front of the boy's house, where Harry's "PFC Mahoney" stencil had long since faded, Danny came bursting out the front door, followed closely by their mother. Her clenched jaw and forward lean were an unmistakable signal to all that she was on the warpath. One look at her son, who'd been beaten to a pulp, and you could almost see the smoke coming out of her ears.

The boy's brother Danny went straight to his father and grabbed him in a bear hug, and they began joking and cutting-up.

"What happened to you?" the boy's mother asked, her expression contorted, a mixture of concern and rage.

"Nothing, Mom. Just a little scrap with Dewayne out at Uncle Ray's. Everything's fine, now."

"Get your tail in the house, right now."

The boy knew better than to hesitate, and immediately went inside the house, but stood watching at the screen door as his mother began yelling at his father for all she was worth.

"You show up here out of the clear blue sky after almost two years, and take off with Marty without saying a word to anybody, then bring him back seven hours later with his face looking like that? What the hell is wrong with you? Are you out of your mind? Are you drunk again, or do I even need to ask?" And on and on and on.

At first the boy's father took his butt-chewing in stride, using his standard "aw shucks - I didn't mean to hurt nobody" defense. But eventually he too became angry, and pretty soon they were both screaming at each other at the top of their lungs, re-fighting all the ancient battles, where there were never any winners, only losers and prisoners.

"I'm calling the police," the boy's Aunt Millie, his mother's sister, said from behind him as she picked up the telephone receiver. The boy could hear her giving their address, and a description of the problem, as his parents went at it in the street. Aunt Millie also mentioned the fact that there had been previous instances of domestic violence, which had resulted in divorce and an expired order of protection from two years past.

Within a few minutes, a squad car pulled up in front of the house and two officers got out. The boy went out on the porch, along with Aunt Millie, while one of the officers took his father off to the side, as the other spoke with his mom. At first, they were all talking cordially. But it didn't take long for the situation to escalate, as the boy had known would be the case since he first saw his dad that afternoon.

Suddenly, the boy's father wagged a finger in the cop's face, and his voice took on a menacing tone. "I'm a combat veteran o' two wars, goddammit. And if I wanna see my fuckin' kids, ain't no son-of-a-bitch in this world ever gonna stop me...you savvy, kimosabe?"

That was all it took. The officer who'd been speaking to the boy's mother suddenly came up behind Harry, handcuffs drawn, and the fight was on.

There was one thing discovered by every policeman who ever attempted to arrest Harry Mahoney. A fight was guaranteed at some point in the process, and bonus charges of resisting arrest and assaulting an officer would be part of the bargain. Harry's policy was to always go down swinging. No exceptions. You could arrest him all you wanted. He was usually doing something illegal at any given moment. But there would be a price to be paid. The little Irishman was a natural born fighter, too, and had even boxed for a short time in the Navy. But he was no match for two burly police officers with nightsticks, blackjacks, and pistols. And within a few minutes, Harry was bloodied and beaten and handcuffed, sitting in the back of the squad car. The boy cried like a baby while Aunt Millie attempted to console him, and his brother Danny screamed about the "asshole" cops as his mother held him back, and did her best to quiet him down. One of the officers had a torn shirt pocket and a fat lip. The other a small cut on his chin. Both were disheveled and grass stained.

After everyone calmed down, the police finished getting the details needed for their report from the boy's mother. Then the boy looked at his father, sitting handcuffed in the back of the police car, and saw that he was grinning and chuckling as he looked back at his son. The sight of his father, smiling and shrugging at his own misfortune, laughing in the face of authority, made the boy feel better somehow, and even brought a smile to his face, too. The Mahoney's were zero for two in the fight department that night, but at least they'd both gone down swinging.

The boy would not have been smiling, however, had he known that he would never see his father again after that night.

Harry Mahoney was sentenced to serve eleven months on the work farm at Leeds, where he was a regular, and worked in the kitchen. By the time he got around to looking up his kids again after his release, his family had long since gone. His ex-wife had remarried, to a man named Jack Stillwell, and abruptly moved without telling a soul in the old neighborhood where they were headed, lest Harry find out and make trouble. Harry tried several times over the ensuing years to find them, without success. His ex-wife's relatives were tight-lipped as to their whereabouts.

He eventually gave up, and wound up back in Wyoming, where he died in a single car crash on a mountain road in 1984, at age fifty-seven.

The boy's new stepfather moved him, his little brother Lee, and their mother to the suburb of Liberty, Missouri, right after the wedding.

Danny remained in Kansas City, living with a school chum's family, so he could graduate from the high school he'd already attended for three years. Immediately after graduation, he enlisted in the Army, and was stationed in Stuttgart, Germany, where he met and wed a local girl, and ended up settling for good. They rarely came to the U.S. for visits, and eventually stopped coming all together.

The boy's sister Hollie didn't care for her new stepfather, and went to live with Aunt Millie on the North side of Kansas City. She eventually gave up on the flute, but ended up becoming a first rate pool shark, and once won a $25,000 eight ball tournament in Las Vegas. She promptly blew her winnings on the craps tables, but didn't really care, anyway. She'd had a good time.

Shortly after the family's move to Liberty, the boy's mother began using the last name Stillwell not only for herself, but also for her youngest child, Lee. She once brought up the idea of a name change for the boy, too, in the misguided belief it would help unify what was left of their family in spirit, but he resisted out of a sense of loyalty to his father. His resistance diminished, however, at age thirteen, when he got busted for breaking into a grocery store warehouse and stealing several cases of cigarettes, which he sold to classmates. His mother was so mortified and heartbroken by the event, her son a thief and conniver, that the boy offered to assume the Stillwell name in a desperate attempt to get back in her good graces. The grand gesture worked. His mother was pleased with him again for awhile. And so, just like that, Martin Mahoney became Martin Stillwell.

Several years later, when young Martin Stillwell dropped out of high school and enlisted in the Navy three days after his seventeenth birthday, the service only required a simple notarized statement asserting that although Martin Mahoney was his given name at birth, he was known throughout the community as Martin Stillwell, that his school transcripts reflected the name Stillwell, and he wished to enlist under the name Stillwell.

The boy's conversion from Mahoney to Stillwell would be short lived in the end. After three dead associates, a court-martial, and a Bad Conduct Discharge, Martin Stillwell would once again become Martin Mahoney.

No matter his last name, however, he could never really escape from his past, or from himself.

Chapter Three
August 10th, 2010

Another 0300 wake-up, unable to sleep. No use fighting it. A lifelong problem, getting worse each passing year. Occupational hazard, maybe.

Nick Maynard flicked on the reading lamp and pulled the huge book from the nightstand drawer. A biography of Teddy Roosevelt he was determined to finish, if it killed him. He would occasionally wonder if death might not be preferable. The biographer had insisted upon documenting every mundane event of the great man's life in excruciating detail, with seemingly little regard to its relevance. Nick had admired the former president before reading the book, but now found him more than a little loathsome. He wasn't sure if it was the writing, or because Roosevelt had been such a jackass. Either way, if this book couldn't put him back to sleep, it wasn't going to happen. Twenty minutes and eight painful pages later, he put the book away and got up to make coffee. Oh well, four and a half hours of sleep was better than nothing.

He did thirty minutes on a rowing machine, ate his usual breakfast of two boiled eggs and a bowl of oatmeal, and showered by 0445. He browsed some of his favorite websites; sports, business, news and political commentary mostly, and found little of real interest. BP oil spill. Corrupt governor on trial in Illinois. Mass murder in a workplace shooting. Too much joy first thing in the morning. Might as well make an early start for the office. But there was a stop he intended to make first.

Heavy sea air this morning. Thick and warm. It was going to be another hot one, like most August days in southern Virginia. Probably not unlike that morning thirty years ago, when Faith

Cooper's body had been found. He wanted to see the place. Breathe the air. Smell the smells. Besides, it was better to go now, when traffic was light and most people still slept. Nick hated traffic. And people? Some were okay. One in particular. But not many.

The beach where Faith had been found was a fifteen minute drive from his bungalow in Great Neck. He parked on East Beach Drive, and walked onto the beach. Looking around, he realized the terrain had changed somewhat since 1980. The dunes surrounding the spot where her body had been found, which had been photographed for the record, were gone. And some newer apartment buildings had been built. Beach areas were like that. Always changing.

The sun wasn't up yet, but it was beginning to get light. Almost high tide. He walked to the shoreline and stood for awhile, looking out to sea. A few gulls were squawking, and the waves gently lapped into the sand. He saw a lone figure a few hundred yards to the East, near the city beach, and began ambling in that direction. A fisherman sitting in a folding chair, with a surf rod stuck into a holder in the sand, a cooler, and a thermos of coffee.

"Morning. Any luck?"

"Just one flounder. Barely makes the minimum size limit, but it beats getting skunked." The fisherman gave Maynard the once over. "You ain't exactly dressed for fishing. Scouting out a spot for later?"

"No. I usually fish over at Lynnhaven. I'm here on an investigation." He handed his business card to the fisherman.

"NCIS? I bet it's just like the TV show. Hot babes and shootouts."

"Yeah. Those Hollywood producers are nothing if not pure sticklers about realism. No exaggerations or distortions. As a matter of fact, I just left the hot babe back in my bed, and I shot up a few bad guys just last week. With a gun that never needs reloading."

The fisherman chuckled. "In your dreams, pal...What're you investigating? Fishermen who fudge a tad on the minimum size requirements for flounder?"

"Naw. Don't worry. I don't care about that. I'm a cold case specialist. A girl was murdered about thirty years ago. Faith Cooper. A young sailor. Her body was found near here. I'm looking at the case to see if we might've missed something. Trying to breathe some life into the investigation. You ever hear anything about her, or the murder?"

"Not that I recall. I used to live near here in the early seventies, when I was stationed on the Plymouth Rock as a young swabbie myself. Seemed like there was always some kinda nasty shit going on in this area. That's why we moved out as soon as we could afford it, after I made second class. I live in Virginia Beach now. Retired from the canoe club twelve years ago."

"Gator sailor, huh? I was a tin can rider myself. USS Beauregard. One hitch as a deck-ape from '71 to '74. Didn't much care for hard work, so figured I better go into either law enforcement or politics. When I got back to Oklahoma, my pops said he'd rather see my sister in a cathouse than me in the statehouse, so I went to college, then signed on to NIS. Been at it over thirty years now."

The fisherman smiled. "I was a hole snipe. Boiled water for a living. Too ornery to do anything else. And too dumb to go to school."

The two men fell silent for a few moments, each looking out to sea.

"So why you fishin' here? I never figured this area was any good for anything but swimmin', and maybe crabbin'.

"Well, I caught a forty pound striper right here in this very spot in '74. Biggest fish I ever caught in my life. And every once in awhile I get to wondering if lightning might not strike twice, you know? Never has, though. Just an occasional flounder, or a croaker. But hey, nothing ventured, nothing gained. And I got plenty of time on my hands these days."

"Every fisherman's the same that way, I guess. A big one will always get you back to the same spot, even decades later."

The fisherman just nodded.

"Well, I guess I better get to work. Good luck with your fishin', Mr..."

The fisherman looked at Maynard, but didn't speak.

"I didn't catch your name."

"That's because I didn't offer it," the fisherman said, a slight smirk on his face.

Nick just chuckled, and started walking back towards his car. "Well good luck, anyway. I hope you catch another big one."

"Thanks. Good luck with your investigation."

Nick was sitting at his desk in the Norfolk field office by 0620. First one in, as usual. He preferred it that way. Made the coffee to suit his own taste -- light, not like that mud Jack Porter makes -- and used the quiet time to begin his work day.

The Faith Cooper file had recently made its way to the top of his working pile, due in part because of inquiries made by her sister, Joy Barry. Joy had written her congressman, who in turn rattled the NCIS brass. And now that the Lardner case was closed, Nick had more time to take on additional lines of inquiry.

The Lardner case had generated quite a stir. Jack Lardner had been a junior enlisted sailor who vanished from the USS Syracuse in 1982. By the time it was determined he was missing, ship's officials couldn't figure out for sure whether he'd disappeared while the ship was at sea, or immediately after arriving in San Juan, Puerto Rico, for liberty call. One crewman provided a sworn statement that he'd seen Seaman Lardner in a bar in San Juan, which was enough for the Navy brass to declare him a deserter. Jack Lardner's father, however, refused to accept the Navy's findings, and managed to keep up the political pressure. The elder Lardner, a successful building contractor, spent tens of thousands of dollars on private investigators over the years, none of whom could find any corroboration for his son's having ever been anywhere in Puerto Rico. And all of whom came to believe the boy's disappearance was far more likely related to his association with shipmates of dubious character. Mr. Lardner's relentless pursuit of the truth eventually led NCIS higher-ups to put Nick on the case.

It hadn't taken Nick long to realize the private investigators were right. Every law enforcement agent likes to believe they can sniff out deception. But he felt he had a genuine gift for spotting a lie. And as soon as he found Brett Antonolli, the crewman who'd claimed to have seen Lardner on liberty in San Juan, he knew the man was lying. And he was able to elicit the truth; that Antonolli was put up to the lie by the two men who'd thrown Seaman Lardner overboard for unpaid drug dealing debts, a hundred miles off the coast of Puerto Rico, the night before the ship pulled into port.

Once Antonolli began to cooperate, it was a relatively easy sell to induce one of the killers to testify for the government against his accomplice, in exchange for sentencing considerations. And just like that, another old cold case was put down.

The success of the investigation provided something for everyone. Mr. Lardner got to see some measure of justice for his son, albeit long delayed. NCIS got to toot its own horn in the press, something every government agency loves to do in order to demonstrate its worth for all those taxpayer millions. And Special Agent Nickalus Maynard was getting special consideration by the Secretary of the Navy on his request to remain in service beyond the mandatory retirement age of fifty-seven. If the Secretary approved his request, he could continue with NCIS for another three years. If not, he'd be forced to retire.

He knew that retirement would not be good for him. There was far too much solitude in his life already. But more troubling than losing his identity, his career, his purpose, retirement would mean he might never see her again. Might never have another chance to smell her perfume. Or small talk about her weekend. Or win her affections, as he'd been fantasizing about doing ever since that glorious weekend so long ago.

If he couldn't see her anymore, he wasn't sure what would happen. He wasn't anxious to find out.

All the more reason to focus on the task at hand. After all, closing another cold murder case could only strengthen his cause with the Secretary. He pulled out the Cooper file and began re-reading. He always liked to study all the material through thoroughly, usually several times over, before creating a prioritized list of actions for follow up.

A flat out whodunnit. Faith Cooper had been murdered sometime between late in the evening of June 10th, a Tuesday, and the early morning hours of June 11th, 1980. She'd been beaten and strangled, left in the dunes near the public beach Nick had just visited in the Oceanview section of Norfolk, a few miles from the Little Creek Naval Amphibious Base. Her body had been discovered by a young mother and her two children at approximately 0920 on the morning of June 11th. The Norfolk city coroner estimated her time of death as sometime in the previous six to twelve hours. It couldn't be determined whether she'd been killed elsewhere and dumped, or if the murder had taken place at the spot where the body was found.

The Norfolk city police department were first on the scene. The victim had no identification on her person, but a tattoo on her left hip, just above the line of her pink bikini bottoms, led police to believe she was likely a member of the U.S. Navy. The tattoo depicted a replica of a Navy enlisted member's white hat, with the phrase *USN Never Again*. NIS, as NCIS was known at the time, was immediately called in to assist. There was little physical evidence at the scene. No discernible footprints, other than those of the mother and children who discovered the body. No drag marks. No blood. No fresh litter or debris which could be linked to the crime.

There weren't many Navy duty assignments open for women at that time, only non-combatant ships and shore elements, so it hadn't taken long to get a preliminary ID on the victim. Local squadron, group, and unit commanders were contacted, and a list of female Unauthorized Absentees was generated, along with a brief physical description of each. By 1400, the Officer-in-Charge of the health clinic at Little Creek was able to make a positive identification at the coroner's office, verified later by the use of dental records and fingerprints. Faith Cooper had been one of his troops, a Hospital Corpsman Third Class, assigned to the general sick call division. NIS took primary control of the case at that point, and assigned Special Agent Keith Wilson -- now deceased -- of the Little Creek field office as lead investigator.

Wilson's investigation generated a basic profile of the victim. She'd been a good worker, easy going, well liked by colleagues and patients. She loved to party, and had lots of friends, but wasn't especially close with anyone. She had a room in the Little Creek "wave cage," as the female barracks was commonly referred, but regularly spent the night out with friends, or male acquaintances. She had no steady boyfriend, and no one knew of anyone who might have wanted to do her harm. She frequented several different nightclubs in the area, and was known to be promiscuous. She didn't own a car, and usually took taxis, the city bus, or bummed rides with friends when going out, which she did nightly.

Toxicology reports indicated a moderately heavy blood alcohol level of point-one-two at time of death, and a positive indication for marijuana, as well as barbiturates. Co-workers did not believe she was a heavy drug user, but probably used in moderation, as was common for many young military members in those days before mandatory random urinalysis screenings became policy.

There were thirty-seven unremarkable interview summaries in the file, including some local parolees and sex-offenders who were known to be living in the area, along with about four dozen pages of notes taken while questioning local residents in an effort to find anyone who might have seen or heard anything relevant to the case. One of the interviewees, Faith's barracks roommate, Susan Lamonica, indicated that Faith usually went to a local nightclub on Tuesday nights called *Flyin' Brian's,* in Oceanview. Long since out of business, they offered fifteen-cent drafts from 1800-2000 on Tuesdays at the time. None of the bar's employees recalled seeing Faith inside the club that night, but one of their regulars thought he saw her in the parking lot speaking with two unidentified males in an older model station wagon, at around 1900. Local taxi cab companies had records of several fares being dropped at the club before 1930 on the night in question, but none of the drivers could provide a positive identification of Faith as a passenger, nor could they recall seeing her in the parking lot. Same for the city bus drivers who serviced the Oceanview route.

The forensics report indicated the victim had sex within the twenty-four hour period prior to death, yet there were no signs of trauma normally associated with rape, which meant the sex had probably been consensual. A vaginal swab had been collected, but investigators had never been able to develop a viable suspect for comparison. A DNA profile had been developed from the swab in 1987, and had been compared with the profiles in every known DNA registry at the time, including CODIS, and the Armed Forces Repository. Then in 2003 it had again been submitted, each time without a match.

At the time of her murder, there was only one apartment building within a thousand feet of the location where her body was found. The Waterview Oasis apartments consisted of twenty-eight units. Sixteen one bedrooms on the second floor, and twelve two bedroom units on the first. Almost every resident was a junior enlisted military member, and there was a constant turnover of occupants, most of whom weren't even listed officially as residents. The off-site management team only required a four month lease, and weren't all that concerned about paperwork, as long as the rent got paid on time. Every known occupant had been contacted. No one reported seeing or hearing anything suspicious.

Maynard wasn't impressed with Special Agent Wilson's work - God rest his soul. It didn't appear he'd followed up on the station wagon, or much else. No wonder the case had never been solved.

While reading through the investigator's notes regarding the apartment resident's statements, all of whom denied having been acquainted with or knowing anything about the victim, one name fairly leapt off the page. Martin Stillwell, a young signalman stationed aboard the USS Fitzpatrick, was the sole lease-holder for unit seventeen, one of the two-bedrooms. Nick knew that name well. He could never forget it in a million years. Holy shit.

The hairs on the back of his neck suddenly stood on end. There was no such thing as a meaningless coincidence to a seasoned investigator. A name on the periphery of one murder investigation suddenly pops up in another apparently unrelated murder case? The odds that he must be involved somehow were extremely high.

What a fantastic break. A promising avenue of investigation right out of the starting blocks, before he'd even finished reading the file. The brass would surely let him stay on active service if he put this one to bed quickly, especially with congressional interest.

Martin Stillwell. C'mon down, son...looks like you're our next contestant on *The Price is Life.*

Chapter Four
April 13th, 1979

His division Leading Petty Officer, Signalman First Class Warren Wilhite, had just delivered some very bad news on that Good Friday morning. "Sorry Stillwell, but the XO has ordered me to pull your liberty card for the duration of the port call in Naples. So you'll just have to cool your jets on board until we hit Malaga."

"Damn, SM-One. That's pretty harsh for one harmless little bender, ain't it? Especially after forty-one days at sea."

"I know. It blows. But you were totally faced last night, you little chucklehead. The Chief Master-at-Arms said you didn't even know where you were when he found you in an alley in the off-limits area up past the New York Bar, hanging out with a bunch of Italian hookers and winos. I know MAC can be an asshole, but you could've been rolled, or worse...you mighta lost your virginity. And you could barely stand up by yourself coming across the quarterdeck. You probably don't even remember seeing me there on watch, do you?"

"That's horseshit. I was buzzed, sure, but I wasn't all that jacked up. Just having a little fun with some of the local gals. I didn't know that area was off-limits. I'm still a boot-camp...can't a new guy get a break? And besides, there wasn't any trouble brewin'. MAC just likes to throw his weight around and make a big deal out of everything. He had no reason to drag me back to the ship. And by the way, I got my cherry popped before we left Norfolk...just ask your sister."

Wilhite ignored the sister wisecrack. All his siblings were males. "You're right. MAC does tend to exaggerate. The XO knows that, too. But he still wants you to get a handle on your drinking issues before you really get yourself in trouble. And I agree. I told him you're the best signalman striker we have, and we can't afford to lose you. Especially since we'll probably be at EMCON this entire deployment, thanks to that damn Soviet AGI. Visual comms only. We're gonna be busier than hell. So square your young ass away, and be glad you aren't going to Captain's Mast for drunk and disorderly, or failure to obey a lawful order. You gotta check the maps on the quarterdeck before you go over, and stay away from those off-limits areas. Otherwise, you're gonna pay the piper if you get popped."

So that was that. What a drag. The Chief Master-at-Arms, Wilhite, and the Executive Officer had decided his fate. Stuck aboard the USS Fitzpatrick, pier-side in Naples for ten days, while his shipmates went out hoopin' and hollerin' and partyin' all over southern Italy. It was a pretty tough pill to swallow. But Wilhite was right. Marty had known from jump-street that the area he was in was officially off-limits. Hell, that's why him and Radar went there in the first place. They were looking to score some poontang, and some hash. Even boot-camps know that the off-limits areas are always the most fun. That's why they're off-limits.

Fortunately for Radar, he was tucked away with one of the working girls inside an upstairs room at Mama Rosa's house of ill-repute when MAC and his Shore Patrol flunkies happened by and busted Stillwell in the alley. Lucky bastard. Stillwell was usually the one with the good fortune when it came to evading authorities. Maybe Radar had the luck this time because he was a Catholic kid, and they were in Italy on Easter weekend.

Oh well. At least he'd had one night over to let off some steam. Better than nothing. And Malaga was supposed to be a much better liberty port than Naples, anyway. He could save some scratch, and use these nine days to practice his Spanish. He'd purchased a Spanish/English dictionary before leaving Norfolk, and had been practicing with one of the deck guys - Joe Cruz, a Cuban immigrant who moved to New York City as a kid. Whenever Cruz stood port or starboard lookout on the forward part of the signal bridge, he'd drill Marty on his vocabulary. He couldn't wait to get to Spain, and try his new skills with some pretty señoritas.

After supper that night, Marty went back up to the signal shack to study. As sunset approached, he began preparing for evening colors when Cruz showed up on the signal bridge. Cruz was standing Messenger of the Watch duty, and was accompanied by one of the brand new crewmen they'd picked up upon arrival in Naples the day before,

"Hey Marty. How's your Spanish practice going?"

"*Muy Bueno*, Jose. *Que Pasa*?"

"Duty-booty. It sucks, man. The OOD wants us to make sure someone has colors covered. You gonna take it?"

"Yeah, I told Smitty I'd handle it for him, since I'm stuck onboard anyway. The XO pulled my liberty card. Hey, how do you say asshole in Spanish?"

"*Pendejo*. But I don't know if they use it in Spain. *Estupido* might be better."

"Well, either way I'm stuck onboard until we hit Malaga."

"Bummer." Cruz motioned toward the new guy. "Hey, have you met Rick Patterson yet? He just checked aboard yesterday. He's standing U/I with me tonight."

Stillwell extended his hand. "Man, they dogged you already, huh? You'd think they might give a guy a couple days before they put you 'under-instruction' on the watchbill. Welcome aboard the fucked-up Fitz, Rick. Where you from?"

"Pittsburgh." The way he pronounced it sounded like 'Pixburgh.' "How bout you?"

"Kansas City."

"KC. You a Royals fan? That George Brett is one sweet swingin' mofo."

"Hell yeah. I can't wait to see them kick the Yankees ass this year." Stillwell looked at Cruz.

"Hey, don't look at me. I hate the fuckin' Yankees, too. I'm from Queens, man. Mets country."

"Hey," said Patterson. "Maybe the Pirates and Royals will match up in the series this year. That would kick-ass, huh? I'll put five-hundred on the Pirates if it happens."

"You're on, brother."

"Well, we better get back down to the quarterdeck before the OOD starts sweatin' the load," said Joe. "Take it easy, Very-Young Martin,"

"*Buenas Noches*, Havana-Joe," said Stillwell.

After taps that night, Stillwell was listening to music in the signal shack when Patterson showed up.

"Mind if I hang out?"

"Not at all. Wanna play some backgammon, or cards? We could play blackjack."

"Sounds good to me. I prefer cards."

Stillwell put a gray wool Navy-Issue blanket on top of a two drawer filing cabinet to serve as their table, and pulled two brand new decks of cards from the desk drawer. He shut the door to the shack, in case one of the khakis happened by.

"I'll deal first, since it's my home turf. We have two decks, so we can switch the deal and re-shuffle after every ten hands."

"Okay," said Patterson. "Dollar a hand to start?"

He nodded as he shuffled. After the first fifteen minutes, the deal had switched hands three times, and Stilwell was up twelve dollars. Patterson was obviously experienced, and lightning quick with decisions, but nobody he knew practiced more than he did, or was faster with calculations. Mister Pixburgh new guy was about to get some trainin' in Kansas City card playin'.

"This is kinda slow. Wanna go five a hand? Or are you chickenshit?"

Patterson looked at his competitor. Was that a wisp of a smile on his face? "I thought you'd never ask."

Things didn't quite work out the way Marty anticipated. For the next thirty minutes, Mister Kansas City card player learned a very valuable, but very expensive lesson: Never let your five-dollar mouth talk trash that can't be backed up by your one-dollar ass. And never gamble against anyone who's better at it than you are.

For several extended periods, it seemed like Patterson simply could not lose. Time after time, Stillwell was sure he had a winning hand, only to be crushed. Down two-hundred, he raised the stakes to ten dollars a hand, only to see his debt rise quickly to five-hundred.

The game finally ended on Stillwell's deal. He had a nine showing and a queen in the hole. Patterson took a hit on eighteen, and drew a three for the winner.

"That's bullshit, man. There's no way you're playing this straight. You have to be cheating somehow. Did you mark these cards?" Stillwell had been looking hard, but couldn't find any obvious marks. And he'd grown up playing cards his entire life against some pretty good cheaters - his brother Danny, and his sister Hollie.

"What are you whining about, man? They're your fuckin' cards. How am I gonna mark 'em?"

"Somethin' shady's going on. There's no way anyone can be that damn lucky. And when you're dealing, you keep hitting blackjacks almost every other hand. I think you were dealin' off the bottom."

"You sound like a sore loser to me, Stillwell. Maybe you're just not as good as you think you are."

"You're pretty mouthy for a brand new boot-camp, Patterson. Why don't you get the fuck off my signal bridge."

"No problem. Just pay up the five c-notes you owe, and I'll gladly be on my way."

"I ain't payin' you shit, asshole."

Just as the two gamblers got to their feet, there were three quick raps on the door of the shack, and a somewhat drunk Jimmy Petarsky opened it up and stepped inside.

"What the hell's going on, losers?" Petarsky said with an inebriated laugh. Then a look of puzzlement passed over his face. "Who the hell are you?"

"Rick Patterson. Just reported aboard yesterday."

The two shook hands.

"Jimmy fucking-Petarsky. But everyone calls me Radar, for some stupid-ass reason."

"Maybe it's because you look exactly like that guy on MASH, only uglier," said Stillwell. "And you wear the same round frame glasses."

"Screw you, Very-Young Martin. Hey, I heard you got your liberty card yanked after last night. Busted by that fat-ass Deputy Dawg, MAC. You need to work on your skills, man. I heard 'em haulin' your ass off the street, so I snuck out through a side door down into a different alley. That place is like a maze, man. Then that hooker took me to some friends of hers to score some of that other stuff we were talking about." Radar pointed his thumb toward Patterson. "Is he cool?"

"I know he's a card cheat, but I don't know if he's a narc."

"I get high. And if I was a card cheat, I'd never get caught by anyone as thickheaded as you."

"All right, all right. Calm down, ladies. Don't get your girdles in a bunch. I got somethin' I know you're both gonna like." Radar pulled a small lump wrapped in tinfoil from his pocket.

Stillwell moved to the door of the signal shack, dogged it all the way down, and secured it in place with chain. Then he taped a small piece of thin cardboard over the little round window in the door, so nobody could see inside.

"Boys, this is gonna totally blow your feeble freakin' minds. See, this little chunk of hash right here might look just like your run-of-the-mill, standard, kick-ass Lebanese blonde. But it is much, much more than that, my brothers. Cause this right here is some blessed, holy hash. And we are about to get righteously fucked up."

"What the hell are you talking about, Radar?"

"I took the train to Rome today, dipshit. Went to Saint Peter's Basilica for mass with the Pope. And after the mass, this little Polish-Catholic boy from Chicago here held up my hand, which held this here Saint Christopher's necklace, and this here little chunk of hash, and the only Polish Pope in history came by and blessed them for me. Can you believe that shit? My mom's gettin' the Saint Christopher. But this has got to be the rarest, most potent hash in the world, man. And I wanted my best pal to smoke it with me."

Stillwell and Radar slapped hands. Then Stillwell pulled an empty soda can out of the trash and fashioned a makeshift pipe by cutting a tiny hole in one crunched in side, with a smaller carburetor hole in the end, while Radar put a Led Zeppelin tape into the boom-box.

There was enough hash for about four good hits for each of them. It was more than sufficient. Radar had located a great supplier, in addition to securing sacred blessings from the Pope.

"How much more do you think you can get?" asked Stillwell.

"The guy had a decent sized brick. I'd guess we can probably cop a half pound chunk for around five-hundred, maybe six. That's enough to keep us all stoned the entire deployment, and make a nice little profit to boot."

"I'm in," said Patterson.

Radar and Stillwell looked at each other.

"I don't know about doing business with a card cheat," said Stillwell.

Stillwell saw a brief flash of pure rage in Patterson's eyes. It looked like his pupils rapidly dilated, and the cornea got cloudy for a second, then just like that, it was gone. He'd never noticed that reaction in anyone's eyes before. Was it just the hash?

"Tell you what, Stillwell. I'll flip you this quarter for the five-hundred you owe me, double or nothin', right now."

Marty didn't hesitate. "You're on. Radar can flip it. I call tails."

Radar took the quarter and flipped it, then missed it in the air. It fell on the deck between them, landing tails side up.

"I guess we're even now, Stillwell. And I'm in on the hash deal."

"It's probably best that way, Marty," said Radar. "You can't go over, and I could use some back up, anyway. I'm pretty sure it's cool, but you never know with these Italians."

"All right," Stillwell replied as he reached for his wallet. "Here's my two-hundred. Just let me know if you end up getting more. Get as much as you can. We can stash it up here on the signal bridge, if you want. There's plenty of hiding places Wilhite and MAC would never find. I'll be standing a lot of mids,too, and we can look out for each other when we stoke up."

"Sounds good to me, slug," said Radar. "So we're all in this thing together?"

The three of them put their right hands on top of each other in the middle between them, then slowly raised them up in the air at the same time, while yipping like coyotes.

"I just have one question," said Rick. "I know why they call you Radar, even though you're a lot bigger than that guy on MASH. But why do they call you Very-Young Martin?" said Patterson.

Radar laughed and slapped his thigh. "Let me tell you a little story, Rick," he said in a a gleeful and excited voice. "See, one night a few months ago back in Norfolk, ol' Marty here went out and really tied one on, shortly before we deployed to the Med. And it was a real world-class bender, too. He got so drunk, he lost his shoes somewhere, which didn't matter much since he couldn't walk anyway, and he had to be carried back to the ship, all the way down the pier. Someone asked him what he'd been drinkin', and he said 'Very Old Barton,' which is just about the cheapest rotgut liquor you can buy.

"So anyway, the next morning we had a big ceremony on the messdecks to commemorate the twenty-fifth birthday of the good ol' USS Fitzpatrick, the Fightin' Fitz. And there was a big-ass cake, and the Navy has this tradition where the oldest and youngest crewmen both hold the ceremonial sword and cut the cake together at those types of ceremonies. Well, Marty here was the youngest crewmember by a longshot. He probably still ain't even eighteen yet. And he went up there with Master Chief Billings, who was the oldest, and he looked like hammered shit, standing right up there in front of the whole crew. His boondockers looked like they'd been shined with a Hershey bar. And his dungaree shirt was so wrinkled, it looked like he'd tried to iron it with a fuckin' ball peen hammer. You never saw anyone look so hungover in your life. I mean, he was in some serious pain, man. A few guys started snickerin'. Then someone said 'I guess that Very Old Barton really did a number on Very-Young Martin,' and everybody just busted a gut laughing. Even the old man couldn't keep from crackin' a grin. And from there on it just stuck. Huh, Very-Young?"

"Unfortunately," said Stillwell. "But a lot of people just call me Barton, or Bart, too, which ain't so bad."

The next day, as Radar and Patterson walked down the pier towards the off-limits area to score the brick of hash, Radar Petarsky came up with an apt nickname for Patterson, too. It turned out that Rick had a ghetto pimp's cocky smooth strut, and was a real cool customer in a pinch. From that day forward, Rick Patterson would be known as "The Pittsburgh Pink Panther" - easily the best nickname on the ship.

Chapter Five
October 06th, 2010

Marty was reflecting on the current state of affairs as he made his way home from work. Of course, the Mildenhall deal had fallen through. It was all going to hell lately. The sellers refused to correct some minor discrepancies deemed "cosmetic" from the property inspection report -- a small dent in one of the garage doors, and some stains on the carpet in one of the spare bedrooms that needed to be re-carpeted -- but the Mildenhalls were insistent. No sale, no commission check. So he was back to square one with his clients, with whom he'd already spent a considerable amount of time searching for the "perfect" home.

A once enormously prosperous business, the real estate game was a tough slog in a tight economy. Buyers were in the driver's seat, and were refusing to compromise. His sales were off by 60% from peak, four years previous. He'd been forced to reduce his firm's staff from seven to three, including himself, and it would soon be just him, working from home, if things didn't turn around in a hurry.

On top of all that, he had two daughters in college, a wife who was a prolific shopper yet didn't seem to know the price of anything she purchased, and some blackmailing jackass from his misbegotten youth was probably about to try and shake him down over a dead girl he'd lied to the police about not knowing thirty years ago. It was enough to make a man want to drink. Even a man who'd been sober for more than twenty-five years.

He wondered what he should do about this meeting with the unknown writer of the note. It was set for tomorrow, Thursday evening. How should he handle the situation? He thought he knew who the person was. Radar Petarsky, a former associate from his days in the Navy. But he couldn't be sure. He'd always just assumed that Radar was long since either dead, or in a perpetual state of hiding, given the nature of his disappearance while in South America. And just because he couldn't think of who else it could possibly be, that didn't mean that it actually was Radar.

He also couldn't be sure what the person wanted. Money seemed the most obvious motivation, but it was entirely possible that whomever it was might have a different agenda in mind. Could it be someone from law enforcement, trying to trick him into an admission of lying, or guilt? But how would they have gotten that picture?

There were too many unknown variables to make any determinations right now. He would simply have to wait until the meeting. He could only think of one thing to do. He had an old microcassette recorder he occasionally used to create a record of certain types of business meetings, such as complex, multi-party transactions. It was small enough to easily conceal. He knew that the blackmailer had been watching. Otherwise, he wouldn't have known about his red cap and green bike. But since he already owned the recorder, he would not have to risk being spotted making a potentially damning purchase. Having a record of the meeting could be an asset, down the road. That idea was all he had. He couldn't go to the police, for obvious reasons. He'd never trusted them anyway. Nobody in his family did.

He pulled into his driveway and the garage door opened. Melissa's car was gone. He left the door up and walked back out to the street. He didn't see any cars, and didn't think he'd been followed. He pulled out his cell phone and called his wife as he walked back into the garage.

"Hey, what's up?" said Melissa.

"I just got home. What's up with you?"

"Kelly and I are at the Cherry Creek Mall. She needs some new shoes, and I want to pick up some cosmetics at Dillards. We should be home by eight or eight thirty. Want me to get some carry out on the way?"

"Sure. Anything's fine by me. You two have fun. And make sure you leave something on the shelves for the other shoppers."

"It's the least I can do for my fellow human beings. I'm a real humanitarian, that way. Oh, I almost forgot. Bob Ellis called, and he asked me to remind you about the Legion Post meeting tomorrow night at eight. I guess you're having another election or something?"

So why the hell is Bob Ellis calling her phone? "Okay. I'm surprised he called you, though. I'm pretty sure he has my number."

"Yeah, I wondered about that too. But he said he didn't want to interrupt you in case you were busy with a customer. Anyway, I'll see you in a bit."

He went into the house and changed into sweats. His mind was racing. He decided to go for a jog. They lived in a very nice subdivision near Daniels Park, close to the well known Castle Pines golf course. He hated running up and down hills, so he'd developed a route that allowed for several long horizontal stretches, and only a few gradual uphill grades.

He cranked up his ipod, and started down the cul-de-sac at a slow but steady pace, towards the main entrance to their subdivision. His mind began to clear as his breathing became more rhythmic and deliberate. His forty-nine year old joints began to loosen, and he broke a light sweat. It was a pleasant evening. The setting sun had disappeared behind the mountains to the west, but was still casting a beautiful glow. *Lightnin' Hopkins* was singing those "Penitentiary Blues," and Marty began to feel better as he focused on possible solutions to his most significant problems.

Second semester tuition was coming due. Kelly was a freshman at Metropolitan State University of Denver. She lived at home, and held a part time job at a local fitness club. Her expenses at an in-state public university were extremely low compared to her sister Katie, a junior at the very expensive Colorado College in Colorado Springs. Katie had managed to land a partial scholarship for creative writing, and another for public oratory from his own American Legion post, but the remaining fees and expenses were substantial. She'd rapidly depleted the college fund they'd set aside for her long ago.

Fortunately, he still had a little money tucked away, even though their stocks had taken a significant hit in the recent collapse. And they had a couple of properties to sell if things got really bad, but in this market they too had been seriously devalued. All in all, they had enough resources to weather the storm, but that situation could change rapidly, depending on the demands of the blackmailer. Or probable blackmailer. There was no sense worrying about it for now. He would meet whomever it was as instructed, and go from there.

As he jogged up the drive into Daniels Park, he noticed a young couple with two dogs playing fetch with a green tennis ball, and a lone man at a picnic table not far away, watching him jog. He tried to act as if he didn't notice the lone man at the table, but the guy kept staring as he ran on past. He decided to take a circuitous route through the eastern part of the park, and within ten minutes had circled back near the picnic table. The lone man was still there, and was still looking directly at him. Only now he was standing, hands in his blue windbreaker pockets.

Suddenly, Marty veered toward the man and returned his stare. He turned off his ipod, and stopped a few feet in front of the stranger. Then all of a sudden it clicked. He realized the man was not a stranger at all. He definitely knew him from somewhere, but where? When he noticed the gold *NCIS* stencil on the breast-area of the windbreaker, it dawned on him in an instant.

"Do I know you? Aren't you the NCIS agent who interviewed me aboard the USS Fitzpatrick?"

"Yes, I believe so. Nick Maynard. How are you, Mr. Stillwell? Or Mahoney, I guess I should say."

Neither man spoke for a moment. Marty was having trouble catching his breath. His heart pounded furiously. He held up his index finger. "I need a drink of water," he said as he jogged off towards a spigot some thirty feet away.

He was stunned. The situation had now turned from merely surreal to completely bewildering. Was Maynard the guy who sent the note, instead of Petarsky? But why? It wouldn't make much sense to create such a ruse using a fake name and cryptic note, only to present yourself the day before the proposed meeting. And Maynard wasn't dumb. That much he remembered for sure. But it would be too much of a coincidence for it not to be him, wouldn't it? He had no idea what was going on, but all he could think to do was act as nonchalant as possible, and play it by ear.

The spigot produced nothing. "Shit. They must've turned off the water before the first freeze." He walked back towards Maynard, wiping his forehead with the sleeve of his sweatshirt.

"I have an extra bottle of water, if you want it. They had two of these little free samples in my hotel room, and I brought them out here with me to get some fresh air. Just flew in from Virginia this afternoon."

Marty took the six-ounce bottle extended by Maynard, and gulped it down quickly.

"Thanks. That hit the spot. So...fancy seeing me here, hey?"

"Yeah. Small world. I'm just out here looking at some homes for sale. Hey, you're in the real estate business now, right? Got any advice?"

"My advice would be to look elsewhere. There's no way you can afford a place in this neighborhood, unless you're taking bribes."

Maynard chuckled. "Well, you're probably right about that. I'm definitely not in your income tax bracket. Kinda surprising, too, given your background. You're doing pretty well for a high school dropout with a BCD. I'll bet your buddies at the American Legion hall would be surprised to learn about that little tidbit."

A slight shiver went up Marty's spine. "So what do you want with me?"

"Just a little chat. I was planning on dropping by your office tomorrow to set up an appointment. I only came out here this evening to have a first-hand look at your digs. I had no idea you'd come jogging by like this. I was actually a little taken back by that, to be honest. Wasn't even sure it was you until you approached me."

"I guess we've all changed a lot since... what – thirty years? When and where do you want to meet?"

"Tomorrow afternoon, three PM at the FBI office in Denver. They've been kind enough to allow me use of their facility. Stout Street, I believe. Just tell the security guards you're there to see Special Agent Herrera. He'll come down and escort you up to the interview room."

"So what's this all about? Do I need a lawyer?"

"Only guilty men need lawyers, Mahoney. But it's your right to have an attorney present, if you so choose. Of course, I highly doubt that a lawyer would even let you meet with me in the first place. Which would be most unfortunate, as I might then feel compelled to inform the American Legion of your true military service status. And that could be really problematic for your daughter's scholarship. Not to mention what a scandal like that might do for your real estate business, especially if the story made its way to the newspapers. I mean, it's gotta be tough enough to earn a living as it is already, with the down market and all."

Mahoney held his hands up, palms out, in the universal sign of surrender. "Okay. No lawyer. But what do you want with me?"

"Just a few questions about an old case. I'd rather wait until tomorrow to get into detail."

"Fine. I'll see you tomorrow, then." He went over to the shelter and threw his empty water bottle into the trash. Then started jogging back home.

Special Agent Maynard waited until Mahoney was out of sight, then retrieved the discarded bottle and placed it into a Ziploc bag he pulled from his inside jacket pocket. Once again, he couldn't believe his good fortune. One of his goals for the interview had been to obtain a DNA sample, either voluntarily, or through deception. But now that he had one, he could afford to use more aggressive tactics during the interview. This investigation was shaping up nicely. That extension of service was practically in the bag.

Chapter Six
November 21st, 1979

Jesus Lives in Allegheny County.

A grimy, faded bumper sticker on a rusted out '71 Ford Pinto.

"Hallelujah, brother," shouted Radar Petarsky as they passed the Pinto, waving wildly and laughing. "Can I have an amen?"

The driver of the Pinto didn't seem to be feeling the spirit at that moment, however. He shot them a nasty look by way of reply as they drove past.

Radar Petarsky, Rick "The Pittsburgh Pink Panther" Patterson, and Very-Young Martin Stillwell were riding in Marty's '67 Chrysler Town and Country station wagon, on their way to Patterson's hometown - Braddock, Pennsylvania, for the holiday weekend. And they were feeling no pain.

"Are we there yet? Are we there yet? Are we there yet?"

"Shut up, Radar. Don't make me come back there," said Patterson. "Take a right on South Braddock, Marty. We're only a couple of miles away, now."

It had been a good trip up from Norfolk. The car was running nicely, not always the case, and the three friends were enjoying their freedom as only the young can. They had money, wheels, good pot, and liquor. And the prospect of willing women when they reached their destination. They had the world by the balls.

Marty was maintaining well, too, a relief to his passengers. Just a couple of beers, and a few tokes on each joint. He wanted to present fairly straight if pulled over, and when he met Patterson's sister, Colleen. He'd seen the pictures, and was keen to try his luck. Rick said she had no boyfriend at the moment, having recently broken up with some local loser. He figured that Radar would be his only competition, and he was confident he could win that battle.

Rick had also asked his sister to contact a couple of other girls he knew, one of whom he had long had a thing for, so all three of them figured to have a reasonable shot at getting laid - a Thanksgiving blessing that would be worthy of the term.

Patterson's family turned out to live in one of the first units near the main entrance in a large complex of shoddy townhomes. His Mom and his sister came rushing out their front door as the boys pulled into a parking space. As Rick and his family embraced, Marty was pleased to see that Colleen was even prettier in person.

They all went inside and talked for awhile. Rick's Mom was named Ellen. Tough on the outside, a softie within. She'd been cooking all day, and was ready to put on a feast for her guests. Marty turned on the charm, showing off his pearly whites at every opportunity. He knew he was scoring some points with the mom, if not with her daughter, who was a little harder to read.

The other girls, Tina and Carol, were expected at 7:00 PM, a couple of hours later. It was a nice afternoon, not yet dark, low fifties, and Rick suggested they go shoot some hoops at the neighborhood playground. At first, the three boys and Colleen had the court to themselves. Then several neighborhood kids showed up, and a three on three game ensued between the Fitzpatrick sailors and the neighborhood boys. Rick obviously knew them, black kids of about fifteen or sixteen, one of whom he referred to as "Little Bean."

The game quickly turned heavy, with lots of pushing and shoving under the basket, and the black kids soon had the upper hand. They were slightly younger and lighter, but possessed far superior ball skills and quickness, and were enjoying the smackdown, and talking trash about it. Rick became agitated, and began playing with a fierce determination, better than Marty had ever seen him play before. He was throwing up rainbows from all over the court, sinking many of them, and driving hard to the hoop, elbows flying. But Marty was marginal at best, and Radar -- a hard-nosed player on the gridiron -- was hopeless at basketball. They had no chance, which seemed to make Rick only madder.

After twenty minutes or so, a gaggle of five more black kids showed up, and began jawing with Rick, too. Marty and Radar soon had enough, and asked a couple of the others to take their places. Rick kept on playing. As Marty watched the game from the sidelines, he could see that although Rick was a barely average baller by this groups' standards, his smack-talk skills were world class by anyone's measure. Marty had seen those skills in action many times during card games, often playing the role of a secret accomplice for a split of the proceeds. Rick could unnerve most of his opponents at will. But these boys didn't get rattled. They loved every minute of it, and gave as good as they got.

"I'm thirsty. Wanna go back and get a beer?"

"Sure, Marty," said Colleen. "He'll probably be out here for awhile, anyway."

"I'm thirsty, too," said Radar. "I hate fuckin' roundball, anyway. Can't even tackle anybody."

"I might go shoot some dice with Little Bean," Rick hollered as the three of them walked away from the playground. " But I'll be home by seven or seven thirty. Tell Tina to wait up for me."

As they walked back to the townhouse, it dawned on Marty that every resident they saw in the complex was black, except for the Pattersons. The Pittsburgh Pink Panther, with his ghetto strut and brash style, suddenly made sense. Rick came by his style honestly. He wasn't some poser. It was who he was.

"How long have you guys lived in this neighborhood?" Asked Marty.

"A long time. Twelve years, I think. We moved here a few years after Dad took off. The rent's based on your income."

"Are there any other white families living here?"

"Used to be. But they all moved out. Mom says they couldn't drag her out with a bulldozer. She hates moving."

"How about you?" Asked Radar. "You like it here?"

"Not really. I hate Braddock. But there aren't any jobs around, and I can't seem to get anything going so I can afford to get out of here. That's why we're so happy for Ricky, in the Navy and all. I tried to get in too, but they wouldn't accept me with a GED. They took Ricky, but the recruiter said girls have to be high school graduates to get in, and score higher on the ASVAB test, too. That doesn't seem fair, you know?"

"That sucks," said Radar. "But you're not missing much, anyway."

"You got that right," said Marty. "USN, never again. That's my motto,"

"You're so full of shit, Stillwell. You're a lifer-dog and you know it. Don't buy his BS, Colleen. He loves the Nav."

"Well, they did give me my first pair of shoes. And introduced me to indoor plumbing."

Colleen laughed. Marty looked pleased, and shot a sideways glance at Radar: *Score one for Very-Young.*

"And fortunately, the Navy took me without a diploma, too. See, the Kansas City school district forced me to drop out after the fifth grade."

"Really?", Colleen asked incredulously. "Why did they do that?"

"Cause my Dad was in the sixth, and they didn't want me to pass him up."

The quizzical look on her face showed that Colleen didn't understand Marty's feeble attempt at humor. Radar snickered, and gave Marty a smirk: *Subtract one for Very-Young.*

"It's just a joke, Colleen. As if to imply that my father was still in grade school in his forties. You know, like Jethro Bodine on the Beverly Hillbillies."

Colleen smiled, and said "Oh. I get it now."

So much for humor as a weapon in the battle for female companionship. Marty would have to rely on his charm and good looks. Failing that, he could always ply her with alcohol and drugs - a sure-fire fall-back strategy if there ever was one.

While taking turns showering and changing, Radar and Marty had fun chatting up their hosts. Neither Colleen nor her mom had ever been more than a hundred miles from the Pittsburgh area, and they enjoyed hearing the boy's stories of adventures overseas, and of life aboard ship. The drinks flowed, along with the good-natured banter. At 7:15, the phone rang. Colleen's friends, Tina and Carol, were at a house party nearby. It was rockin', and the girls didn't want to leave, so Colleen suggested they go there and meet them. She told her Mom to let Rick know where they'd gone, so he could come too, whenever his dice game ended.

The party turned out to be a kegger, at a house less than five miles away. It was a good one. Parents out of town. Plenty of beer, and girls, for everyone. Radar broke out his stash and began twisting some up, and the boys were immediately accepted into the group. Colleen introduced them to Tina and Carol. Everyone was in good spirits. Stillwell was careful to nurse his beers slowly. He didn't want to get too drunk, and ruin his chances with the ladies.

Suddenly, shouting and screaming rose up from the backyard. Everyone rushed out of the house to check out the commotion. It was Colleen and her recently estranged boyfriend, a guy named Randy Mueller. Randy had Colleen by her arms, and was shouting for her to calm down, but she kept jerking away from his grip, screaming for him to leave her alone.

Radar and Stillwell and several of the other guys separated the two, attempting to play the role of peacemakers. Tina and Carol took Colleen, who was now crying, back into the house. Randy asked for a beer, and chugged it straight down.

"Fuckin' women," he said, as he lit up a smoke. "She's so damn hard-headed. She drives me fuckin' crazy."

Not a long trip, Stillwell thought. Randy was six-foot-two, with wild and bushy blonde hair, and a thick bushy beard. His eyes were kind of wild, too, like a horse that's just seen a rattlesnake on the trail. But he didn't seem dangerous, at least at the moment. Instead he looked beaten. Like a man in love.

A few minutes later, Tina came out and announced that Colleen wanted to speak with Randy upstairs, in private. He bolted into the house like a man on a mission, seeking reprieve.

So much for fun with Colleen, Stillwell thought.

"So what do you think about all this drama?" Tina asked as she walked up to Stillwell. "Do you fight like this in Kansas City?"

"Way worse than this. We usually break out the pitchforks and torches, and commence to burnin' up barns and such. Then we all meet at the hoedown for some victuals and square dancin'."

"Well, there aren't any barns around here, cowboy. Is that all Kansas City boys know how to burn down?"

She hooked an index finger into his belt loop, and gently tugged. Stillwell hesitated for a split second. Was he hearing what he thought he was hearing? Tina's impish grin told him he was. He knew that Patterson was hot for her, but Rick wasn't here. And it wasn't like they were married or anything, not that he was sure even that would have mattered at that moment. He'd never met a girl who was this forward, this quickly, before. He liked it.

"Care for a demonstration?"

"I thought you'd never ask."

They left in his car and drove to her house. Her parents were divorced, and she lived with her Mom. They went down to the basement, where there was a couch and an eight-track stereo. She put in a *Steve Miller Band* tape, then they practically tore each other's clothes off. No wonder Patterson had a thing for her. She was pretty, and very sexy. Tall and trim, with an athlete's firm body. Her shiny brown hair, and soft, smooth skin, were driving him wild. He couldn't believe his good fortune. Pittsburgh was quickly becoming his favorite city in America.

After awhile, they were relaxing in the afterglow, smoking and laughing.

"So I guess this is turning out to be a pretty good liberty port for you, huh sailor? Did you think you'd be getting laid on Thanksgiving?"

"Well, I was *really* hoping for some homemade cobbler. But this is okay, too, I guess."

She slugged him in the arm, and he threw her back down on the couch, and kissed her, and they were at it again.

The next morning, her Mom fixed them breakfast. Eggs, sausage, and toast. He was really beginning to like these people. They were going to Grandma's for dinner with the family. So Tina wrote down directions to the Patterson house, and made sure he had her telephone number.

They said their goodbyes in the driveway.

"When are you going back to Virginia?"

"Tomorrow morning. I have duty on Sunday. Radar's going back with me. Rick's staying here for two more weeks, on Hometown Recruiter Assistance duty. So you might be seeing him around."

"Rick's okay. But I'd rather see you around. I hope you come back here sometime," she said.

"Hmmm. That sounds like it could be fun for you. But what's in it for me?"

"Asshole." She punched him in the arm again. She had a pretty good right cross for a chick.

"You could always come down to Virginia, too, ya' know. I'm almost certain the highway runs in both directions."

"I might just surprise you and do that some time. You'd probably shit your pants if I showed up at your ship some day, unannounced."

"Are you kidding? I'd love it."

"Well...see ya' sailor boy. Take care of yourself."

He felt like a million bucks as he drove away. What a girl. Sometimes, life was just so damn good. That feeling of euphoria changed quickly, however, when he pulled up in front of the Patterson townhome. Rick was sitting on the front step, fire in his eyes. Marty parked and got out slowly, not knowing what was about to happen. He looked Rick in the eye, and began walking towards him.

"Rick…"

Patterson jumped to his feet and extended his hand, palm out. "Stop right there, motherfucker. Don't say another fucking word. If you do, something is going to happen that I don't want to happen. And believe me, you don't want it to happen either."

The two boys stood where they were for a minute, a few feet apart, in silence. Neither of them moved. Rick stared down at the ground for awhile, then looked up and flicked his cigarette hard at Marty, bouncing it off his chest. "Fuck it, " he said as he stormed off towards the basketball court.

Marty stood where he was a moment longer, thinking. Well, that wasn't so bad. He'll probably calm down, and come around. It wasn't like he had a ring on her or anything, after all. He walked into the townhome.

"Hi Marty," said Colleen. "Is everything okay?"

"I think so. Rick's a little pissed, I guess."

With a grimace, she replied "You and Tina left about twenty minutes before he showed up at the party last night. He was really upset. I'm just glad he didn't go looking for you two."

"Well, let's not let it ruin Thanksgiving," said Mrs. Patterson. "There are plenty of fish in the sea. No need for you boys to fight over one of them."

"Where's Radar?" Nick asked.

"He spent the night at Carol's", said Colleen. "I guess all the Fitzpatrick sailors were getting lucky last night, except for Rick."

"No wonder he's so mad."

"By the way, we need to go and pick Radar up at Carol's place. He's called twice already. Mom's car is on the fritz. I'll show you the way."

It turned out Radar hadn't gotten so lucky after all. Carol had too much to drink at the party, and had thrown up all over him when they got to her house. He'd slept on the couch by himself. And to top it all off, she'd been mortified to find him still there the next morning, embarrassed from the night before, and was anxious for him to leave. He was just as keen to oblige, having been made to feel unwelcome after getting puked on. It'd been a memorable evening for everyone. Even though some would rather forget it.

"Me and Randy are back together," Colleen said as they drove back home after picking up Radar. "He promised to stop doing downers, and he got a job at an auto upholstery shop. Starts next week. It's the first job he's had since he got kicked out of the Army almost a year ago."

"Wow, that's great, Colleen," said Radar. "I hope it works out for you guys. Randy seems like a good dude. Is he coming over for dinner today?"

"Yeah. Mom's making macaroni and cheese especially for him. He loves that stuff."

When they got back to the Patterson house, Rick was sitting in the living room, drinking a beer. He had a cooler beside the recliner, and he reached in and offered one up to Stillwell, who accepted it, relieved.

It turned out to be a good dinner and a nice Thanksgiving, even though Radar was bummed when his beloved Chicago

Bears got blown out by Detroit. The second game was better, a shootout between Houston and Dallas. Rick won forty bucks on the games, a twenty from each of his two shipmates. He was a gifted gambler all right, and always seemed to have good luck as well as great skill. But he wasn't so lucky in other endeavors.

Chapter Seven
October 07th, 2010

"I really appreciate you guys letting me use your facility, Miguel," said Nick Maynard.

"No problem, Nick," said FBI special agent Herrera. "We're always happy to help our law enforcement colleagues at lesser organizations like NCIS. Working closely like this gives us more opportunities to lord it over you people who weren't quite good enough to make it in the big leagues."

"Well, that is what you guys do best. That and humility, of course."

"You can use interview room three. It has a terminal I'll log you into for access to the web, and a phone. Help yourself to coffee, but leave a buck or two in the can. And let me know if you need anything."

"Thanks. The subject will ask for you at the front desk. His name is Martin Mahoney. He's supposed to be here at three."

"Okay. I'll let you know when he arrives."

It was just after 9:00 AM. Plenty of time to get some work done, and prepare for the interview. He'd been working the Faith Cooper murder case for almost two months now. After Martin Stillwell's name had surfaced on day one, he'd spent a lot of time finding out everything he could about the man who was now known as Marty Mahoney.

First he'd dug up all the old files from the Roy Bantam murder and robbery case aboard USS Fitzpatrick, which had taken place while docked in Brazil during deployment to South America. That was the case Nick had been working when he first ran into Martin Mahoney, Martin Stillwell at the time, in 1980. Stillwell had been best friends with the two prime suspects in the robbery-murder, Jimmy Petarsky and Rick Patterson, though there was no evidence he'd been directly involved. The Bantam case was still officially open, too, since nobody had ever been prosecuted for the crimes. But the investigation had left no doubt that Petarsky and Patterson were the perpetrators. Their fingerprints were all over the crime scene. And they'd disappeared immediately afterwards. The robbery of the disbursing office had netted over $400,000.

Patterson's dead body had been found in the Brazilian country-side a few days after the crime, but Petarsky had never been located, and was still an international fugitive with an open warrant at INTERPOL. Authorities had never gotten so much as a whiff of activity from him since the crime, which led most at NCIS to believe he was probably dead, too. Brazil was a dangerous place, especially for a rank amateur like Petarsky, walking around with $400,000 in a duffel bag. Nick figured he'd probably been murdered and robbed soon after Patterson, or perhaps at the same time as Patterson, but had his body dumped elsewhere. Still, Petarsky's body had never surfaced. And there'd been no reports of local thugs suddenly flashing big American bucks around the time he vanished, so he couldn't really be sure.

Nick decided to write down every detail he could remember about that 1980 trip to Brazil, and all the events that transpired until his abrupt and shocking return to the States. He needed to focus on that first encounter with Mahoney. Maybe he could recall some item that could help him form a successful interview strategy. He wanted today's interrogation to be successful, and result in a confession.

He remembered thinking that Mahoney had been lying when he swore no prior knowledge of the Fitzpatrick disbursing office robbery plans. After all, he'd been very close with both of the prime suspects. But the kid had stuck to his guns pretty good for a nineteen year old. He didn't get rattled. He was a good liar. That was probably useful in his current profession. Nick new it was a skill that helped him in his own.

One tidbit that might be useful - the barbiturates he'd possessed. Nick could try and tie that into the Faith Cooper murder, given that her autopsy had revealed traces of Valium in her system at the time of her death.

Mahoney had pled guilty at a special court-martial to two relatively minor charges in return for sentencing considerations. He was awarded four months confinement and a Bad Conduct Discharge - a slap on the wrist compared to what he would have received had Maynard been able to connect him in any way to the robbery or murder.

In addition to the link with the Valium and the toxicology report, there was also the fact that he'd lived in the apartment building that was closest to the location where Faith's body was discovered.

Nick had also managed to make contact with many of Stillwell's former shipmates. One of them, a corpsman named Dan Moroni, said he could vaguely recall that Stillwell had once owned an old station wagon. And one of the last people who claimed to have seen Faith alive on the night she was killed had reported seeing her speaking with two guys in a station wagon in the parking lot of a bar on Oceanview Avenue.

But he hadn't been able to officially confirm that Stillwell owned a station wagon, because Virginia DMV records from 1980 were spotty. If the car had been scrapped, or taken out of state and titled elsewhere, the DMV clerks weren't confident they could find anything in the old files just using one owner's name. Still, he might make Stillwell think he had been able to verify ownership, just to see how he responded.

In total, it wasn't a lot. He had a link with the barbiturates, the apartment's proximity to the body, and the car. But cold cases had been cracked with a lot less. And it was definitely enough to get Mahoney spooked if he had anything to hide, or if he knows anything at all about the case.

Nick also had his DNA sample, and he could use the fraudulent DD-214 Mahoney had used to gain membership in the American Legion, which ultimately led to his daughter's scholarship, as leverage. That was the beautiful thing about working with a federal agency. Any U.S. Attorney worth their salt could probably come up with at least half a dozen federal crimes on someone like Mahoney. The head of a small real estate firm, who'd forged a military document just to help his daughter get a scholarship, had probably broken all sorts of regulations in his business. There's no telling how many shady transactions the guy has done over the years. There were thousands of federal regulations governing land usage and transactions, and there's a good chance that any long-term real estate professional had done *something* counter to the rules, whether they realized it or not.

Nick looked at his watch - 1100. 1300 in Norfolk. She'd probably be back from lunch by now. But there was another call he wanted to make first. The phone was answered on the third ring.

"Hello," said Joy Barry.

"Mrs. Barry, this is special agent Nick Maynard from NCIS. How are you today?"

"Fine, thanks. And you?"

"Very good, thank you. Listen, the reason I'm calling is to give you an update on Faith's case. I don't want to get your hopes up too high, but we're working a fresh angle, and we're hopeful that it could possibly lead us closer to a resolution. I know how concerned you've been about the lack of progress."

"Well, that's encouraging news. I have to admit I'd pretty much given up hope of ever finding out who killed Faith, after all these years."

"Perfectly understandable. It has been a long time. But we haven't forgotten, and we're working very hard."

"Well I appreciate it, Mr. Maynard."

"Hey, did Faith ever mention anybody named Martin or Marty Stillwell to you before she died? Or Marty Mahoney?"

"Stillwell? I don't think so. Mahoney doesn't ring any bells either. She never really talked that much about the people she ran around with...not by name, anyway. She bragged about all the cute guys she was meeting, but I don't remember any specifics. Is he a suspect?"

"He's more a person of interest at this point. Nothing concrete linking him to Faith, yet. But I'm looking at him as a possibility."

"I do know the name of one of her Navy friends. Peter Phoenix, I think it is. He called here a couple of months ago asking about Faith's case. As a matter of fact, he was very encouraging when I mentioned that I was thinking of contacting you guys. He was a good friend of hers, apparently. He said they worked together at the clinic on base. If he wouldn't have called, I may not have written that letter to my congressman, which is what I assume got your cold case unit involved."

Nick's antennae immediately went up. A call out of the blue after almost thirty years? The investigator in Nick knew this was no innocent coincidence.

"Did Mr. Phoenix mention what prompted him to call after all this time?"

"As a matter of fact, he said he was in the process of moving, and was going through an old photo album from his Navy days, and came across a picture of Faith. I guess he'd lost a sister himself to cancer recently, and the photo reminded him of how much he'd missed Faith after she was killed. Anyway, he did some internet sleuthing and located me here in Iowa. He was hoping that her killer had been caught, and he was very disheartened to find out her case was still unsolved."

"Did he mention where he was calling from, or where he was moving to?"

"Not that I recall. It was such a shock to hear from one of old friends, I didn't think to ask. Is that important?"

Nick didn't want to alarm her. "Not really. I just want to make sure my notes are as complete as possible. It might be better if I was able to speak with him myself, though. He might have knowledge of some small tidbit that could prove helpful. Is there anything else you can remember about Mister Phoenix, or the call? An accent, or any distinct background sounds...anything like that?"

"No. Nothing stands out that I can think of. We didn't talk long. We both became pretty emotional. He said he'd send me copies of some of the photos once he settled in to his new place. I gave him our address. It was really nice to know that at least one of her old friends cared enough to go through all the trouble to track me down. Sometimes over the years, it felt like I was the only person that missed her, and that made me really sad."

Nick knew exactly what she meant. "I understand completely." He gave her his cell phone number and asked her to call him if she remembered anything else, or got any more calls about Faith.

Nick checked his watch again as he ended the call to Mrs. Barry. She would definitely be back at her desk by now. He could feel his palms begin to sweat, and his heart rate quicken, as he dialed her direct line. She answered on the third ring: "NCIS, Deanna Sherman speaking."

"Hi Deanna. It's Nick, checking in from Denver. How's everything going?"

"Same old shit, Nick. Claire has her panties in a wad over the budget review. All the division chiefs have to submit revised figures by Friday. There was a lot of blood on the floor after the status meeting yesterday. I thought we were going to have to break out the weapons and settle things the old fashioned way for awhile. It was very entertaining, though. I think there were even a few tears. How are you?"

Claire Tottel was the Norfolk NCIS station chief, a little blonde spitfire whose engines were constantly stuck on all-ahead-full, hence one of her primary nicknames - "Full throttle Tottel." The others were somewhat less flattering.

Deanna Sherman was the station's senior administrative assistant. She was married to Steve Sherman, a former NCIS agent who'd retired a few years prior. She was also the woman Nick Maynard had been hopelessly in love with for the past thirty years.

"Pretty good. I might actually get somewhere on the Faith Cooper case soon. Not that I don't wish I was back there to participate in all the budget battles and turf-war squabbles. I love a great sideshow."

"Steve always gets a big kick out my stories about the office antics, too. I guess now that he doesn't have to wallow around in the muck with the rest of us anymore, he can enjoy it a lot more. Lucky bastard."

Lucky bastard, indeed. Nick knew that to be true, as well as anyone.

"So how's Steve doing, anyway? Is he bored with retirement yet?"

"He's not really retired. He's actually working almost as many hours now as he did for NCIS, doing home remodeling work. He loves it, working with his hands, after all those years in a jacket and tie."

So the guy was fit, healthy, handy, and married to the best girl Nick had ever known. Nick hated him even more.

"Wow. Sounds great. I'm jealous."

"So what's the latest with your retirement? Any word on your request for continuation of service?"

"Nothing yet. I'm hoping I can put this case down and influence the Secretary's decision in my favor. By the way, speaking of law enforcement work, can you run a full background check on a Peter Phoenix for me? I don't have any other details, but he may have served in the Navy as a corpsman in the early eighties at Little Creek. It's probably just a phony alias, but someone using that name has attempted to interject themselves into the investigation, and we need to follow up just in case it's actually legit."

"No problem. I'll call you if anything interesting turns up. Otherwise I'll just email a summary of the results."

"Thanks Deanna. Talk to you later. And give my best to Steve."

Miguel poked his head in at noon and invited Nick to eat lunch at a small café near the building. He was glad for the distraction. He needed it.

....

Martin Mahoney was in a foul mood as he left his office in Englewood for the twenty-five minute drive to the FBI building in downtown Denver. His day had begun in a heated argument with his wife, and would probably go downhill from there as he met first with NCIS, then with a blackmailer whose identity and motives were also unclear, but whose sinister intentions were anything but.

After a restless and fitful night's sleep, he'd been awakened by the sounds of men delivering furniture. He quietly seethed as he dressed, and went downstairs just as the workmen were taking out the last few pieces of their perfectly fine, very expensive three year old living room set, which had just been replaced by a brand new set of even finer, and obviously more expensive quality.

"What the fuck, Melissa," he exploded with rage as he picked a glass up off the kitchen counter and flung it against the wall with a crash.

"Oh my God. What's wrong? What did I do?"

"What the fuck are you thinking? You know how lousy business has been lately, yet you go out and spend thousands of dollars on new furniture we don't even need? Are you fucking crazy, or just stupid?"

Melissa was stunned by the ferocity of his sudden attack. Her mouth was agape in astonishment as she looked at the broken glass spread all over the kitchen's hardwood floor. Marty was an easy-going man by nature, which made the few times she'd seen him lose control of his temper that much more shocking. They rarely had cross words, and he'd never lashed out this vehemently in twenty-six years of marriage.

"I don't understand. We talked about getting the new furniture three months ago, after you sold the Bartlett house. You gave me the okay, and I placed the order. It takes awhile to get this stuff in from Italy. But I'd never make a big purchase like this without your approval. Don't you remember?"

The instant she began speaking, he remembered the previous conversation about the furniture, and all the anger rushed out of him, like air out of a punctured inner-tube. In its place was an overwhelming sense of shame and regret.

"You know I've had a lot on my mind lately, with the business and all. Why didn't you ever mention it again?"

"Because once you gave the OK, there wasn't anything else to talk about. I simply placed the order, and waited for delivery. Honestly, Marty, where did all that just come from? You owe me an apology."

"You're right," he said as he reached to put his hands around her waist in an attempt to pull her in close, a gesture she rebuffed by turning away from him toward the kitchen sink, where she busied herself by rinsing out an empty coffee cup.

"I'm sorry for blowing my stack like that, honey. I was wrong. I guess the downturn is beginning to take a toll on me. Our stocks are in the toilet, savings is taking a huge hit, and business seems like it might never come back. That's no excuse for the way I lashed out. It's not your fault. But we have to really tighten up our spending for awhile, okay?"

"I don't have a problem with tightening things up, Marty. I know business is bad. But I'm not gonna be a punching bag for you or anyone else. I don't deserve to be cursed at like that, and I don't want to be around someone who thinks it's okay to throw childish temper tantrums and break our things."

They didn't speak further as he cleaned up the glass. She was gone by the time he showered and left for work. He knew he'd crossed way over a line, and it would be some time before Melissa would forgive. But he couldn't do anything about it now. And he had more pressing concerns at the moment. Nothing like the threat of a little blackmail, and a possible murder beef to provide a sense of priority.

He found parking and made his way to the entrance of the FBI building, then waited while the guard notified Miguel Herrera of his arrival. It was 3:01 PM. Funny how much of a habit punctuality had become. Must be an old age thing. He could remember a time when he'd always been late, for everything.

Maynard closed a binder he was reviewing, stood up and shook Marty's hand as Estrada escorted him into the interview room where he was waiting.

"Thanks for coming, Mahoney. Can I get you something to drink?"

"Coffee would be great. Black."

"Read and sign these rights waivers while I'm out."

As Maynard went out to fetch him a cup, Marty initialed and signed the waivers, and was sorely tempted to peek at the contents of the binder. But he could see that the place was outfitted with video. His dad had often wistfully remarked "You can't outrun a radio." Harry Mahoney would have loathed today's sophisticated law enforcement technologies.

"Quite a surprise running into you like that yesterday. I know it must've been a shock to you, too. But I honestly had no idea I'd see you there. As I said, I just wanted to see where you live for myself. I must say, I'm very impressed. Congratulations on all your success."

"Thanks."

"I must admit I'm intrigued, too. I've never personally known a criminal fuck-up like you who ever managed to turn things around so completely. How did you do it?"

"Well, I wasn't exactly John Dillinger. A fuck-up, maybe. But criminal? More like a stupid, immature jerk-off of a kid who finally wised up."

"Well...impressive, anyway. Was there a single experience that finally shocked you into going straight? A woman? Jesus?"

"Being locked up in the brig was a serious wake-up call. But I honestly believe it was just a matter of normal maturation. I finally decided to stop doing things that led to misery, start acting like a grown man, and make something of my life. I haven't had a drink in over twenty-five years now."

"That makes sense, I guess. 'Bought learnt is the best learnt,' my dad used to always say. But how does forging a DD-214, and obtaining scholarship monies under false pretenses fit into your 'grown man, upright sober citizen' narrative? Maybe you really haven't changed at all. Maybe you've just gotten better at hiding...though not good enough, apparently."

Marty sat silently for a few moments. He knew that acknowledgment of any criminal act would not be in his best interest. On the other hand, he also knew that Maynard probably already had copies of the fraudulent document. He couldn't have known, otherwise. In the end, he decided to remain silent. He took a sip of coffee, then looked straight into Maynard's eyes without saying a word.

"What's the matter, Mahoney? No ready-made excuse to justify your actions? I guess there's nobody else to pin the blame on this time, huh? Well...no matter. I really couldn't give a shit less about your little scholarship scam. It isn't worth my time, although I can't pretend to speak for the federal prosecutor for Denver. I hear she's a real ball-buster, too. A regular pit bull. I sure wouldn't wanna be in your shoes if she decides to sink her teeth into your ass. But I might be able to help you out on that front, if you're willing to help me on another matter, which is why we're really here in the first place. I want to talk about a girl who was murdered thirty years ago. Faith Cooper...Ring any bells?"

Marty's heart began pounding furiously in his chest as he heard the name he'd been dreading to hear. At least now he knew the stakes. He only hoped he could keep from vomiting as he contemplated his play. He reached for his coffee again, took a sip and replied, "Yeah, I remember Faith."

Maynard feigned shock as he replied, "You do?" He opened the notebook and paged through the old case notes until he found the entry he was looking for, which he tapped several times soundly with the tip of his index finger.

"Says right here in Special Agent Wilson's notes that one Martin Stillwell, a resident of the Waterview Oasis apartments, denies ever knowing or having ever met or seen the victim. Are you not that same former Martin Stillwell?"

"Yes, but I don't remember talking with any agent. That was during my heavy drinking phase. Did I sign a statement? If I had, I certainly wouldn't have denied knowing Faith. She was a casual acquaintance, although we always called her by her nickname - 'Turtle.' Anyway, I remember when she was killed. I think that's when I first realized her real name, when I saw her picture in the newspaper. But I didn't know a thing about what happened to her then, or now."

Maynard leaned back in his chair and stared at Mahoney for awhile, thinking. The man was clever. He knew full well he'd never signed an official statement regarding his denial of knowing the victim. And he'd also created the illusion of an alibi by claiming he only knew her as 'Turtle' in case his false denial had been recorded over the telephone thirty years ago.

"Okay, Mahoney. You seem sincere. Maybe you didn't lie to a federal official during the course of a murder investigation. Are you willing to make an official statement now?"

"About what?"

"About your activities and whereabouts on the night of June 11th, 1980."

"That's crazy. How the hell can I remember what I did on a given night thirty years ago? I can barely remember what I did last week. Besides, like I said, I was drinking and doing a lot of drugs back then. You know my record."

"Well, that particular night was the one when your so-called 'casual acquaintance' got herself brutally murdered and dumped like so much garbage on the beach, not more than a couple hundred feet from your apartment building, to be picked over by sand crabs until some poor woman with a young child in tow found her discarded body the next morning. I would think that kind of night might be more memorable than most, even for a drunken drug fiend."

"Look, Special Agent Maynard. If I knew anything at all that could in any way help you find out who killed Faith Cooper, I'd be glad to tell you. I liked her. She seemed like a nice person.

She didn't deserve what happened to her. I'd love to be able to help. But I just don't know anything."

"Okay. How about you at least make a statement to correct the record, saying that you knew the victim casually. Describe your relationship, details about the last time you saw and spoke with her, and deny all knowledge of her murder – if that's all true. That way at least I can show my bosses I didn't totally waste all the taxpayer's money by flying out here and running up my expense tab for nothing."

"Okay."

Marty took his time and wrote out a vaguely worded statement with a few strategically placed double-negatives. He'd seen many a poorly worded legal document in his business, all intended to afford wiggle-room for different interpretations in case a deal ever went sour. Politicians were masters at that style of obfuscation. But they had nothing on a real estate pro.

"Your statement is bullshit, Mahoney. It sounds like you're trying to be evasive."

"I'm hesitant to make definitive statements about incidents from thirty years ago for reasons I've already explained. I don't want to get myself jacked up any more than I already am by making inadvertent mistakes in a meaningless statement."

"Meaningless?"

"Meaningless in the sense that you obviously don't believe me, anyway. Besides, I emphatically deny any knowledge of her murder. That much is clear in the statement. It's just the minor details I can't speak to with as much certitude."

"Minor details like whether or not you saw her, or spent any time with her on the night she was killed?"

"I certainly don't remember seeing her or spending time with her that night. But I was a blackout drinker. And it was so long ago."

"Well, then maybe you killed her but you just don't remember that, either. That would certainly explain your sudden conversion to a life of sobriety. I'd quit drinking too if I came to from a wicked bender, only to discover I'd done something horrible like that. Is that what happened, Mahoney? You lost your temper while drunk out of your mind? Maybe you were on a bad trip, and imagined she was some kind of demon from hell or something. Or maybe she did something to really piss you off. Who knows...maybe she even deserved it."

Marty sat silently for a several moments. "I didn't kill her. You're looking at the wrong guy."

Maynard sat silently for several more moments. "This is getting us nowhere. Would you be willing to take a polygraph test to help us clear you as a suspect?"

"Clear me as a suspect? That's horseshit, and you know it. Even if I passed, you'd just think I beat the machine with trickery, or that the polygrapher screwed up, and keep pressing me anyway. A lie-detector test is a no-win proposition for me. There's a reason those tests are inadmissible in court."

"So you refuse to take a polygraph?"

"I didn't say that. I'll just have to think about it first. Maybe I should consult with an attorney, after all. It seems like this whole thing is headed in that direction, anyway."

"Your call. We can stop this little farce right now as far as I'm concerned. I'm just waiting for the lab tests to come back, anyway. Shouldn't be more than a week or two, at most."

"Lab tests?"

No Faith in Justice

Maynard smiled broadly. "I swabbed your water bottle from yesterday and sent it in for comparison to the post-mortem vaginal swab we have in evidence. If your DNA matches, I'd say you're in some pretty deep kimchee, partner. A whole big boatload full of rotten cabbage."

Marty could feel the color drain from his face, as tiny beads of sweat started to form on his forehead. It had suddenly become very warm in interview room three. In all these years, he'd never even considered that they might have collected his DNA from Faith's body. He'd tried so hard for so long to forget all about Faith Cooper. He didn't know with 100% certainty that he and Faith had intercourse the night she was killed, but he knew it was highly likely. He could remember bits and pieces of that night, and he knew they'd been in bed together at some point.

"I think it's about time for me to go now, special agent Maynard."

"Just two more questions. One - did you ever own a station wagon during the time you served aboard the Fitzpatrick?"

"Yeah, I had an old Chrysler wagon back then. Why?"

Maynard smiled broadly, and said "Two - do you know anyone named Peter Phoenix?"

Another curveball. Peter Phoenix was the fake name on the return address listed on the envelope that contained the blackmail note. Was Maynard playing some kind of game?

"Sorry. Doesn't sound familiar. Why do you ask? Is he a suspect, too?""

"Not really. Not the number one suspect, at least," Maynard replied with another broad grin.

"Well, I'm outta here. I think I'll go ride my bicycle on the Waterton Canyon trail to clear my head a bit."

Marty could detect no reaction on Maynard's part at the mention of the designated meeting location with the blackmailer. But how did he know the blackmailer's alias? Had he received a letter from him as well? Maybe that's how this whole thing got started after all this time.

"I'm sure we'll be talking again real soon," Maynard said with another broad grin while shaking Marty's hand as they both rose from their seats.

Marty started to leave and then stopped, as if suddenly remembering something else he wanted to say.

"I'm sorry about what happened to your wife, by the way. Back when you were on the Fitzpatrick with us in Brazil, I mean. I'm sure that must've been terrible for you."

Maynard was floored. It'd never occurred to him that the crew of the Fitzpatrick would have known and gossiped about Carla's death. But he shouldn't have been surprised. Every juicy tidbit that happens on small ships during deployments becomes so much grist for the gossip mill. Given the circumstances surrounding his brief time there -- a brazen robbery, two murders, the disappearance of the prime suspect in both cases, and the sudden death of the wife of one of the NIS agents sent to investigate -- there had probably been little talk of anything else for months, if not years, aboard the ship.

Still, the nerve of this arrogant prick, going out of his way to dredge up an obviously painful episode from so long ago. The only conceivable reason Mahoney would have to mention it now is because he wanted to take a parting shot. Payback for some of Maynard's unflattering remarks about his character. He seethed with rage as he stared Mahoney down for several tense moments.

"Agent Herrera will escort you out."

Chapter Eight
June 11th, 1980

"Hey, I think I know that chick," Marty Stillwell said as he and Rick Patterson pulled into the parking lot of Flyin' Brian's, a 3.2 beer joint located on Oceanview Avenue in Norfolk, Virginia. "Her name's Faith, but they call her...Crawdad, or...Froggy...or somethin' like that. I met her at the club on Little Creek when I was in Advanced Signaling School last week. We played some pool and did a bunch of shots. She's a lot of fun."

"No shit?" Patterson replied, checking out the girl who was headed to the entrance as they drove to the back end of the parking lot and pulled into a spot. "I'd love to jump those bones, man. I dig the skinny babes. Think I might have a shot? Let's see if she wants to smoke a joint."

"Okay," Stillwell said as he leaned out of the window and hollered "Hey *Faith*...c'mere for a minute."

Faith Cooper looked up and grinned, and said "Hey Marty" as she turned away from the door of the bar and walked over to the driver's side of the station wagon and leaned in the window."What the fuck's goin' on, man?"

"Not much. Me and my buddy Rick here were just wondering if you might wanna stoke up a number. We got some kick-ass redbud, straight off the boat from Colombia."

"Hell yeah," she said as she opened the back door and slid into the back seat. "I've been jonesin' for some good bo'. All I've been able to find around here lately is a bunch o' skunkweed, sprayed with paraquat or something, probably."

"Yeah, you gotta be careful," Stillwell replied. "I heard that shit can wreck your lungs. Thanks for everything, Jimmy Carter – you peanut farmin' douchebag."

The three of them laughed hardily as Patterson lit a joint and took a big toke. He began waving the lit match back and forth. "Guess what this is," he said as he held the smoke in his lungs. Stillwell shrugged his shoulders and Faith just smiled as she took the joint from Patterson. "Richard Pryor runnin' down the street."

"Oh, man, that shit ain't right," Stillwell said through his laughter.

The mood quickly turned mellow as the potent reefer began to take effect. Stillwell popped a cassette tape into the player he'd mounted to the bottom of the dashboard – Pink Floyd's "The Wall."

When the joint was finished, nobody made a move to exit the car. "It's still early," said Stillwell. "Why don't we go to our place and do some shots? We got a fifth of Jack and two cases of Milwaukee's Best."

"Milwaukee's Best? God, that's some rank shit."

Rick and Marty looked at each other and smiled. "That's the exact same thing I said when this chucklehead brought it home this afternoon," Rick replied.

"Hey, what can I say? It was on sale at the package store for three dollars and forty-nine cents a case. I couldn't pass that up. Too much of a cheapskate, I guess. But after a couple shots of Jack, you'll never know the difference anyway."

The apartment was less than a five minute drive. They each did a couple of shots, then a game of quarters ensued. It quickly became apparent that Faith could more than hold her own. She was easily the best player, almost never missing the glass on her turn to bounce, and the two boys were drinking twice as much or more than she did. Patterson broke out the Minolta 35MM camera he'd won in a poker game the previous week. It had a delay timer feature, and the three of them were able to get into several photos together.

After about thirty minutes of the game and picture taking, Faith looked at Marty, and out of the blue said "Hey...are you a 'True Turtle'?"

Stillwell broke into a huge grin and replied "You bet your sweet ass I am!" And with that they slapped five, then Marty filled up the shot glasses which they clinked together before downing the whisky.

"Now I remember...'Turtle' is your nickname. That explains that. Where did you become a True Turtle at?" asked Marty.

"In Des Moines, about a year before I joined the Nav. I loved it so much, they gave me the nickname."

"What the hell is a True Turtle?" asked Patterson.

Faith looked at Marty and said "Whaddaya think...is he worthy of induction into the club?"

"Hell yeah. He's got a killer memory. You oughta see him play cards. Why don't you do the honors?"

Faith looked at Rick, "You game, hotshot?"

With a leer on his face, Patterson replied "I'm game for anything, baby. Bring it on!"

"Okay. The first thing we gotta do is test those killer memory skills of yours, to see if you're sufficiently intelligent to join the exclusive ranks of the elite True Turtles. You will repeat after me a series of phrases, and every time you make a mistake, you will take a drink of beer. Got it? Okay...let's begin. One red hen."

"One red hen."

"One red hen, two cute ducks."

"One red hen, two cute ducks."

"One red hen, two cute ducks, three brown bears."

"One red hen, two cute ducks, three brown bears. This is too easy, man. Give me a challenge."

"One red hen, two cute ducks, three brown bears, four running hares."

"One red hen, two cute ducks, three black bears…"

Faith shook her head as Marty howled with laughter and Rick took a big swallow of his beer.

"Okay," Faith said. "Ready? One red hen, two cute ducks, three brown bears, four running hares."

"One red hen, two cute ducks, three brown bears, four running hares."

"One red hen, two cute ducks, three brown bears, four running hares, five fat females, sitting, sipping scotch, and smoking cigarettes."

"What the hell?"

Marty howled again as Patterson finished off his beer and popped open a fresh one so the game could continue. Over the course of the next ninety minutes, Rick downed at least a twelve pack before he finally got through the ten phrases and successfully entered the ranks of the True Turtles. He struggled most with "eight egotistical Eagletons, echoing egomaniacal ecstasy."

Within minutes of completing the game, Patterson was passed out cold in one of the bedrooms in their two bedroom apartment.

Marty and Faith sat on the couch listening to "Led Zeppelin II," smoking a joint. It was only 9:00 PM. The night was still young.

"This really is some good shit," Faith said, enjoying the fine buzz. "Hey…you wanna trade for some ten milligram Valiums? I got a full script from one of the new PA's at the clinic. He's got a little thing for me. All I had to do was casually mention that my back was hurting one day, and he was all over that script pad."

"Okay," said Marty. "How 'bout a quarter o.z. for twenty blues?"

"A quarter? How 'bout a half ounce for twenty-five?"

"Deal."

Faith took five pills out of the prescription bottle she was carrying and laid them out on the coffee table, then handed the bottle containing the remainder of the pills over to Marty, who fetched a baggie from the kitchen and cut out a half ounce of pot from their stash under the couch. He didn't need scales. He'd been dealing pot since junior high. He knew what fourteen grams felt like.

"Wanna do one now?" Faith asked, as she used her finger to twirl one of the pills in a little circle on the table.

Marty hesitated for a few seconds, then said "I'm down if you are. But I'm only gonna take one, cause the booze is hitting me pretty hard already, and I gotta be at the ship by 0700."

"Yeah, one is good. Just enough to mellow you out, without any hard crash. Besides, I gotta be at the clinic by 0630 myself." They each took one of the pills, then Marty suggested they go for a walk on the beach. He filled a small Styrofoam cooler with a few beers and some ice cubes, and they strolled through the dunes outside the apartment building and onto the beach. It was a beautiful evening. A cool breeze and a clear night sky, with a three quarter moon. There was nobody else out on a Wednesday, so they picked out a spot and sat down in the sand to watch the ocean.

They drank some more beer, and talked for awhile. Faith told him about growing up in Iowa. She loved her mom and her sister, but couldn't wait to get out of the Midwest and do some traveling. She'd enlisted after dropping out of community college in the second semester of her freshman year. She'd wanted to work in the medical field in some capacity anyway, so she figured why wait? Besides, she liked to party a little too much to make it as a full-time student for any length of time. She enjoyed being a corpsman, and was having a good time in the Tidewater area. She was even thinking of making the Navy a career, though she'd never admit that to her friends at work. She didn't want them to start calling her a lifer.

Marty was three sheets to the wind, and very talkative. He told her about his hometown of Kansas City, and how much he enjoyed his job, too. Even though it wasn't a skill worth anything in the civilian world, being a signalman was fun, especially when they were underway. He told her all about the Mediterranean cruise of the previous year, and how much he was looking forward to going to South America soon. He was enjoying his time in Virginia as well, and felt like he and his two running mates -- Jimmy Petarsky, who was standing overnight duty that night aboard ship, and Rick Patterson -- had a great thing going with their own apartment, and various money making enterprises through gambling, drug deals, and miscellaneous other activities.

They killed off the cooler and went back to the apartment, arm in arm, and flopped down on the couch. Another shot of Jack, and the conversation began to turn raunchy.

"Holy shit, I'm fucking wasted," Marty said after downing the last shot.

"You're such a lightweight, Stillwell."

"Lightweight? Well, sticks and stones might break my bones...but whips and chains excite me."

No Faith in Justice

Faith moved in closer, and smiled seductively. "Oooh. Whips and chains, huh? Sounds interesting. Tell me more."

Marty picked up the camera and his beer, and said "Follow me and I'll show you."

They went back into his bedroom, shut the door, and began making out on the bed. He slid off her jeans, and went to his closet and pulled out two neckties, one Navy issue dress black, and one blue. He playfully tied Faith's hands to the posts of the wooden bed he'd bought second-hand at a local thrift store. Then he placed the camera, still set up on the thirty second delay timer, on the dresser across from the bed and took a picture, him leering down on her all tied up.

After several more minutes of playful kissing and teasing, Marty untied Faith's hands and they began making love in earnest. They were good together, and the booze and the downers seemed to enhance and prolong their ecstasy. At some point they nodded out for an hour, but awoke and picked up right where they'd left off, before nodding out again.

In the bedroom next door, Rick Patterson awoke from his drunken stupor to the sounds of the headboard banging into the wall, along with their moans and exclamations of pleasure. He lay there listening for a few minutes, getting his bearings in the process. He looked at the clock - 1:07 AM. The last thing he remembered was playing that stupid drinking game about four or five hours earlier. His stomach began to churn. And he could feel the heat rising in his neck and face.

He went into the bathroom and splashed some cold water in his face, then went to the living room and flipped on the TV. He'd never lived in a place that had cable before. All these channels. And it never went off the air. He flipped it on HBO, "Superman" was about a third of the way through. He'd seen it twice before, but it didn't really matter. He just wanted some background noise to help drown out the sounds coming from the other bedroom.

That fucking bastard. This was the Tina Mayes situation all over again. Rick had made it clear that he had a thing for Tina. But Stillwell couldn't wait to dog him out, and snake off with her by himself. And tonight was just more of the same. As soon as Stillwell knew Rick was interested in Faith, he schemed up a plan to get him out of the way by getting him drunk. Should've seen it coming. But he couldn't quit the game once they started, or Faith would've thought he was a pussy.

He sat in the recliner, seething, chain-smoking Newports. He'd had about enough of Stillwell's bullshit. He'd let him slide too many times, and now it was completely out of hand. He never should've let him off the hook for that $500, the first night they met. That was just the beginning. It was Rick who'd made the reefer connection they'd been using to rake in cash for the last six months. It was Rick's card skills and brains they capitalized on to bleed out the losers on the ship. It was Rick who came up with the DD-214 scam idea, and identified their customers. Stillwell could barely keep up most of the time, half-shitfaced every night. A real lump of dead weight. And how does he repay the kindness? Shits all over you, of course. Just goes to show you, being nice is a sucker's play. Weakness just gives assholes like Stillwell a license to take advantage.

Well, no more. That shit is gonna quit right here and now. No more free rides. From now on, Rick would decide the split for proceeds, and it would be based on talent and contribution to the enterprise. And if Stillwell didn't like it, he could find himself a new gig, and some new partners.

No Faith in Justice

As Superman was about to end, the bedroom door opened up and Faith walked into the living room, wearing only pink bikini bottoms and a t-shirt. Her hair was disheveled and she appeared very tired, but she smiled at Rick and said "You a True Turtle?"

Rick just looked at her with disgust in reply.

"You're supposed to say 'you bet your sweet ass I am,' Rick. Don't you remember?"

"Sorry," Rick said, his voice dripping with sarcasm. "Guess I forgot."

"Who put a bug up your ass?"

Rick ignored the remark.

Faith lit up a cigarette and looked at the clock. "Shit. Two fifteen? I gotta be at work by zero-six-thirty. I need at least a couple hours of sleep. Can you take me to the barracks at Little Creek, or at least drop me off at Gate Five? I can walk from there."

"What do I look like, a fuckin' taxi cab driver? Wake your boyfriend up. He's got a car."

"I tried for like ten minutes, but he's out like a rock. Won't budge. C'mon, Rick, I'll pay you for gas."

Patterson gave her a wicked leer, and said "It's gonna cost you a lot more than gas money, baby."

Faith could feel herself getting angry. "Oh yeah? Tell me Rick, what's it gonna cost? Huh?"

"A blowjob."

Faith was livid. "You motherfucker." She stood up and stared at him for several seconds, her fists balled at her side. Then she walked over to the kitchen counter and picked up the telephone handset.

"Fine, I'll call a taxi."

"It's outta service, Faith. Our idiot roommate Petarsky ran up a huge bill talking to his mommy and four skanky sisters in Chicago and doesn't wanna pay it so they cut us off last week. Guess you'll just have to walk back to Little Creek. Or..."

Faith placed the handset back in its receiver, then lifted the whole unit up and hurled it as hard as she could at Patterson's head. He raised his arm up to protect his face just in time to deflect the phone off his forearm, but it left a big welt and a nasty bruise when it hit clean bone, down near his wrist. It hurt like a son-of-a-bitch.

"You bitch!" he screamed as he leapt up from the recliner. His first punch was a right roundhouse to her jaw, and he knew immediately that it was broken. There was no turning back now. He felt a rush of adrenaline course through his body as he jumped on top of Faith, who'd gone down in a heap, stunned by the force of the powerful blow. He punched her six more times in quick succession in the face, breaking her left cheekbone and eye socket, and her nose, which began spewing blood down into her mouth and neck.

He began choking her with his bare hands, using his thumbs to exert as much pressure as possible directly on her larynx. Faith tried to pull his hands off her throat, but she was totally unprepared for the ferocity and speed of the vicious attack, and she quickly began to feel herself blacking out as she struggled in vain.

He felt her go limp while staring into her eyes. He could detect no fear, only shock, surprise, and rage. He kept up the pressure for over a minute after he felt her take her last breath, just to be sure. Once he knew she was dead, he rolled off of her and reached for a cigarette. His hands were shaking, but he felt a strange sense of exhilaration. How was he going to get himself clean of this jam? He didn't know yet, but he was confident in his ability to formulate and execute a bold and successful plan of action. He thrived on taking risks, outsmarting opponents, and escaping from peril. This would be the ultimate challenge: Getting away with murder.

He went into his bedroom and emerged with an empty seabag. Fortunately, Faith was a petite girl, and the seabag he owned was unusually large. He'd traded his standard U.S. Navy issue model for it, along with a zippo lighter, to an Italian Marine during their Med-Cruise the previous year. He put Faith into the bag head first, but he still couldn't totally conceal her inside, even by bending her knees up to her chest. Her legs from about mid-calf to her feet were sticking out the top of the bag, so he tucked an old bedspread around them to cover them up.

He went into Stillwell's bedroom and dug the station wagon keys out of his blue jeans, that were lying on the floor. He also put on Marty's blue KC Royals ball cap. If anyone was awake in the apartment building, if he saw any lights on or curtains moving, he'd put Faith into Stillwell's car and drive out of the parking lot. Just a guy with an overstuffed seabag departing very early in the morning. Not such an unusual sight in an area chocked full with sailors and marines. And if anyone did see, they would assume it was Stillwell at the wheel.

But if no one were up or about, he'd head straight for the dunes on the beach. Luckily, they lived in an end unit on the bottom floor of the building, which was positioned perpendicular to the road that ran parallel with the beach, so no one in the other apartments would be able to see him once he cleared the corner of the building. He just had to hope there were no passing cars on the road, and no one on the beach or in the dunes nearby. If he did see someone on the beach, he would take Faith back to Stillwell's car and figure out a new dumping place for her body. There was a very good chance that at this time of night, there would be nothing to worry about. But either way, he was mentally prepared.

He struggled mightily to get the seabag situated on his shoulders, and staggered a little on his first few steps. Faith might have been small, but this was not going to be a picnic. He hesitated just long enough outside the front door to look at all the apartment windows, and around the parking lot. Not a movement or a sound anywhere. He turned the corner, crossed the road, and began making his way through the sand dunes north of the building. He went several hundred feet before coming to a good spot, not visible from either the road or the beach. After dragging Faith out of the seabag, he noticed she was wearing a silver necklace with a sea turtle medallion around her neck. Funny, he hadn't even been aware of it when he strangled her. He yanked it off her neck and stuck it in his pocket.

He retraced his steps through the dunes, using the empty seabag to carefully brush away his tracks as he went. When he reached the road, he folded the seabag under his arm and walked straight back to the apartment. He'd seen or heard no one. He went back into Stillwell's room and collected all of Faith's belongings: Cigarettes, jeans that contained her ID card and twelve dollars in cash which he pocketed, socks, and shoes, and placed them into the seabag. He set Stillwell's alarm clock for 0545, and he also retrieved his camera, and put it back into his own bedroom, after rewinding and removing the roll of film.

It would be awhile before he knew for sure, but he felt pretty good about his chances. His best bet was to play dumb with Stillwell from here on out. He'd pretend to wake up when the alarm went off, with no knowledge whatsoever of Faith's whereabouts or any comings and goings of the previous night. All the alcohol he'd consumed during the True Turtle initiation was good cover as an alibi.

The next few days were going to be interesting. But he was ready for anything. He wouldn't rattle. He'd been facing down trouble since grade school. He looked forward to this test.

He dozed off, but was awakened an hour and a half later by the sound of Stillwell's alarm, followed quickly by some barely audible mumbled profanities, the clink of a cigarette lighter being flipped open, and an ensuing coughing fit. *Good morning, sunshine*, he thought as he began to get dressed.

The two roommates barely spoke as they drove to the ship for work.

"I was pretty wasted last night," Stillwell said shortly after the guard waved them through Gate Four.

Patterson just shrugged and nodded his head.

Ten minutes later they began the daily hassle of finding an open, unreserved parking spot within a half mile of Pier Five

"So what time did Faith leave?" Marty asked.

"I have no idea. That stupid turtle game did me in, man. I was out cold until your alarm went off this morning...next row over. Hurry up before that Buick spots it."

The work day was uneventful. The Fitzpatrick was in predeployment work-up mode. Lots of working parties, loading of supplies, with liberal leave and liberty in effect to the maximum extent feasible. The signal gang was well ahead of the game in preparation for the UNITAS cruise. SM1 Wilhite ran a tight bridge. By early afternoon, Marty was on his own as duty-sigs for duty section two. He had a couple of hours to nap in the signal shack before the evening fire drill.

After the drill secured, he ate evening chow, then went to the COMMS Division berthing compartment to relax until sweepers would be called away at 1830. He flipped on the TV to catch the early local news broadcast. The lead report knocked him flat: Faith Cooper's body had been discovered on the beach near his apartment in Oceanview. Police suspect foul play. Anyone with information is asked to call.

It was a good thing he was already sitting down when the report was broadcast, because he nearly passed out. His face went white, and the voices from the TV suddenly sounded more distant, and harder to hear over the sound of his pulse pounding in his eardrums. Luckily, the only other person in the berthing compartment at that moment was RM2 Stinchcomb, who was already in his rack with the curtains drawn, resting up for the mid-watch on the Quarterdeck.

When his light-headedness began to subside, Marty went into the head and doused his face with cold water. His color began to return. He looked at himself in the mirror. What the fuck? What the hell happened to her? Could I...? He looked at himself good and long. No...No way...Gotta be someone else.

He went up to the signal bridge and turned on the radio. "Fire Lake" again, for the hundredth time in the last couple of weeks. He'd begun to despise Bob Seger. He switched off the radio and popped in a cassette - "London Calling" by *The Clash*. He sat and smoked, cigarette after cigarette, mind racing, until "Sweepers" was called away. After a quick clampdown of the berthing area, he went forward to the chain locker. He found Patterson engaged in a game of blackjack with Jose Cruz and a brand new deck seaman, straight out of Apprenticeship Training, named Jeffries. The new hand was being indoctrinated into the large and growing club of Fitzpatrick sailors who'd been taken to school by Rick Patterson.

"Rick, I need to talk to you."

"Now? Can't it wait? I'm kinda busy here." Patterson was already up a hundred-fifty, but he figured the kid was flush with travel pay, good for at least two-hundred more. Jeffries seemed to be one of those guys you could goad along for awhile, before realizing he was hopelessly over-matched.

"It's urgent."

"It can't be more urgent than what I've got going on here. Why don't you sit in?"

"Can't. Come see me up at the shack as soon as you're finished. It's really important."

Patterson showed up on the signal bridge an hour later, a huge grin on his face.

"You shoulda stuck around. Easiest three bills I ever made. Havana Joe got a nice little taste, too. What's so urgent?"

'We got a big problem. Let's go inside. And dog the door behind you."

"Okay," Rick replied as he followed Marty into the shack. "What the hell's going on? You look scared."

"Have you seen the news tonight?"

"No. Why?"

"Faith Cooper's dead. They found her on the beach near our apartment this morning."

"No shit? Holy fuck, man...Maybe she went for a swim and drowned, or something."

"No. The news said the police suspect 'foul play,' which means she was murdered."

"Damn. That's hard to believe. I wonder what happened to her? How much do you remember from last night?"

"Not much. You know me. I was wasted. I kinda remember snippets of me and her being on the beach together, but then I remember coming back to the apartment, and I think we ended up in bed together. But I'm not sure."

"You don't think you got mad at her...maybe lost your temper and killed her for some reason, do you?"

"C'mon, man. That's crazy! You know I'm not violent like that. I've never hit a chick in my *life*! Much less killed one. And what possible reason could I have to get mad at Faith Cooper? I barely even knew her."

"Okay. Calm down. I'm not accusing you of anything. I know you're not violent. But then again...you never really know what someone is capable of doing. Mixing booze and drugs can make people do some crazy shit. All I know for sure is it wasn't me. I was passed out cold after that True Turtle initiation."

Neither of them spoke as they pondered the situation in silence for a few moments.

"Maybe she tried to walk or hitchhike back to Little Creek, late at night or early in the morning, and got picked up by some psycho," said Marty. "Wasn't there another girl killed recently in Hampton, or somewhere?"

"Yeah. I think so. You're probably right. I bet some psycho bastard got her. Poor Faith. I feel bad for her. But there's nothing we can do about it now. If she would've just stayed with us, we could've given her a ride this morning and she would've been fine."

"Yeah. You're right, Rick. There's no point in getting ourselves involved. The cops might get the wrong idea. You know how they are. They'll try to pin this thing on the first dupe they can find. And we can't really tell them anything that would help their investigation, anyway. Neither of us knows anything worth telling, right?"

Patterson nodded. "Did you mention anything about last night to anybody else today?"

"No. I didn't talk much to anybody, all day. I was pretty hungover this morning. You?"

"Nope. Not a word. Let's keep it that way. And don't tell Radar anything about it, either. Did you see him before he split today?

"No."

"Good. I didn't either. I know he'd never talk outta school, but the fewer people who know, the easier it'll be to keep a lid on the situation."

"Agreed. So if anyone ever asks either of us, we don't know Faith Cooper, never heard of Faith Cooper, and we were with each other -- and nobody else -- last night, all night long."

And so began Martin Stillwell's life-long mission to suppress all thoughts and memories of Faith Cooper. He would not be successful.

Chapter Nine
September 18th, 1980

"How long do you think you'll be gone?" Carla Maynard asked as he finished packing his bags, and carried them to the front door.

"No telling," Nick replied. "Could be weeks. We may have to do some traveling in Brazil and some of the neighboring countries, and meet the ship at different ports. Plus we'll have to interview a huge chunk of the crew. Depends where the leads take us."

She could sense his excitement. She wondered whether it was the case, or the prospect of being away from her for awhile that was making him so giddy.

Nick and Carla had been married just under three years, and were living in Jacksonville, Florida. Carla was a nurse. She worked a standard day schedule at a local cosmetic surgery clinic. It was a pretty good gig as nursing jobs go. But there were severe problems in the marriage. Everything seemed great between them the first year or so, but once the intense heat of their initial physical attraction began to cool, and he realized they had almost nothing in common, and didn't even seem to really like each other very much, Nick had wanted to throw in the towel. He began to move out on two separate occasions during their last year together, only to see Carla break down into an emotional mess to such a degree that he caved in to her pleas for another chance at making it work, even though he knew in his heart it was hopeless.

So when his supervisor assigned him to travel to Rio de Janeiro and investigate the murder of the USS Fitzpatrick's disbursing officer, and the robbery of hundreds of thousands of dollars, he jumped at the chance, and hoped that a substantial period apart might make Carla more accepting of the inevitable permanent break up to come.

"I hear there are a lot of beautiful women down there."

"This isn't a pleasure trip, Carla. It's a murder case. I have to focus on the investigation, and do everything necessary to bring the killers to justice. But I don't want you sitting around brooding while I'm gone. Go out with your friends and have some fun. You're only twenty-seven, for Pete's sake. No kids. Get out and live a little, already. Don't sit here alone, waiting around for me."

She knew what he really meant. She stood and looked at him for a long moment, hurt and sadness in her eyes, then walked into the bedroom and shut the door. He thought about going after her, but he knew whatever he would say would either be a lie, or would only make matters worse, or both. So he didn't say anything, just left.

Special Agent Bob Friedberg had been assigned as the lead, his partner on the case. The brass arranged for an immediate flight to Rio aboard a small personnel transport plane for the two of them, along with a military lawyer, Lieutenant Commander George Moles, who would represent the interests of any accused, and Navy Supply Corps Lieutenant Mike Weir, who would replace the deceased Roy Bantam as the Fitzpatrick's disbursing officer.

They were met upon landing in Rio by the American Embassy's naval attaché, and a small contingency of U.S. Marine guards, working temporarily out of the consulate's office in Rio. That was when Nick realized Lieutenant Weir was also accompanying a small wooden crate filled with cash, which was meant to plus up the Fitzpatrick's coffers after the robbery had left them short. Nick didn't know how much money was in the crate, but he was somewhat relieved when they arrived on the pier and it was whisked up the brow by two of the ship's disbursing clerks, accompanied by their new boss.

Maynard and Friedberg were met by the ship's Executive Officer, Lieutenant Commander Josh Langer, the Legal Officer, Lieutenant Steve Rodriguez, whose full-time position was Ship's Navigator, and the Chief Master-at-Arms, Chief Curt Souter. They were taken to a vacant two-man stateroom in "O-country," where they dropped off their bags, then headed immediately to the wardroom for an in-brief.

"We're glad you guys are here," said the XO. "We really need you." He glanced at Chief Souter, who was looking down at his clenched hands on the table, and quickly added "MAC has done a great job so far, but murder and robbery are not the types of offenses he's accustomed to investigating."

"Well, we're glad to be here, Commander Langer," said Friedberg. "Nick and I have both handled homicides in the past, and we'll give our best to get this thing right. You want to catch us up on everything to date, Chief?"

Chief Souter, the Chief Master-at-Arms referred to as MAC by the crew of the Fitzpatrick, was a six-foot-five giant, with a girth to match. He slid copies of an investigative summary to the two agents. His eyes were bloodshot, and he had the look of a man too tired for small talk.

"I typed these outlines up a couple of hours ago. The XO and Lieutenant Rodriguez already have one. I'll give you the entire case file once I have a chance to make copies, immediately after the in-brief. As you can imagine, I haven't slept much in the forty-eight hours since it happened.

"I'll start with the basic outline, along the timeline we currently know. Wednesday morning at approximately 0710, DK2 Jason Belknott discovered the body of Lieutenant JG Roy Bantam in the disbursing office. After finding no pulse and getting no response, he immediately called the quarterdeck, who paged our senior corpsman - Chief Jackson, the CDO, and me to report to the scene. Chief Jackson verified Bantam was deceased, and I secured the area around the disbursing office and the ship's office with some masking tape, and posted Petty Officer Belknott to keep everyone clear. I also notified the quarterdeck to close the brow until further notice.

"The CDO went to notify the Captain, XO, and Command Master Chief, who all arrived on the scene soon thereafter. After a brief discussion, the Captain decided to call all hands to muster immediately topside so we could begin an unimpeded search of all the ship's interior spaces. At the time, we had no idea what we were dealing with, or who we were looking for. We just wanted to get everyone where we could keep an eye on them, and figure out who might be missing."

"Did you take any pictures of the scene?" Maynard asked.

Chief Souter slid a stack of Polaroid snapshots across the table. Roy Bantam was bound chest to ankle to a chair with what appeared to be half inch nylon line, and duct tape. His mouth was also covered with duct tape. His head lolled to the left, and there was dried blood from a nasty looking gash near his right temple. He also appeared to have some bruising and cuts on other areas of his face. He'd been beaten, but not so badly as to have caused his death, at least from a cursory look at the pictures.

"Where's the body now?" asked Friedberg.

"*Lieutenant Bantam* has already been flown to Portsmouth for an autopsy," said Commander Langer, with an emphasis on the Lieutenant Bantam part of the sentence. It was his way of letting the investigators know they were referring to a departed shipmate, not an inanimate object.

"Anyway," continued Chief Souter, "my first priority was to take control of the crime scene and begin processing the evidence. The safe was open, and Petty Officer Belknott, our senior disbursing clerk, confirmed that a significant amount of cash was missing - at least four-hundred thousand."

Maynard let out a little whistle and said "So robbery was obviously the motive. And the perpetrators probably had to cuff Bantam around a little to get the safe combo. Any suspects?"

Souter glanced at Commander Langer, and the Legal Officer, and then said "We think it's two guys: James Petarsky, and Richard Patterson. Petarsky's a Storekeeper Third Class, from Chicago. Patterson's a First Division seaman, from Pittsburgh. They were off the ship on a Welfare & Rec organized tour to the city of Petropolis when we discovered Lieutenant Bantam. The tour group had departed the ship at 0630, about forty-five minutes before we secured the brow and mustered the crew. The two of them disappeared from the group during the tour, and haven't been seen since. Patterson was carrying a large knapsack that he claimed was full of laundry he intended to have done during the tour. Petarsky also had a bag, supposedly for the same reason. We figure they had the money in those bags."

"What evidence is there, besides the fact that they're unaccounted for?" asked Maynard.

"I got a bunch of good fingerprint lifts at the scene, from the duct tape, especially. We're still waiting on official word about matches from the Bureau. We tried to telefax copes of the lifted prints from the consulate, but they didn't transmit clearly enough. But the embassy has a courier enroute to DC with 'em right now, so we should have confirmation within twenty-four hours. I'd bet my next paycheck we'll get a match with Petarsky or Patterson, probably both."

"Excellent. But we know the defense will try to claim that those fingerprints got there from some sort of benign contact. Sailors borrow rolls of duct tape all the time. And for all we know, there might be lots of prints from other people on the duct tape roll, too, and all over the disbursing office as well. We'll need more. But don't fret...we'll get it. What else should we know about?"

Mac shifted uncomfortably in his seat, and glanced nervously at the XO.

"There are more reasons to suspect Petarsky and Patterson," said Langer. "They're part of a small group of...characters we have onboard, They're rumored to be prolific gamblers, something we may have let go on a little more than perhaps we should have. Like most Navy ships, we figure the crew needs a few outlets to let off some steam, given the amount of time we spend at sea. Besides, as long as they don't flash any cash at the table, they always claim to just be playing for fun, and we can't really prove otherwise."

"Perfectly understandable," said Friedberg. "Nick and I were both in the military ourselves at one time. We know how it is."

Commander Langer continued. "Anyway, they've both had a few minor scrapes with the law in Norfolk. Underage drinking, possession of less than an ounce of marijuana. Nothing big. But they were investigated by some of your NIS colleagues in

Norfolk for selling falsified DD Form 214 Discharge Certificates before we deployed. MAC can elaborate."

Souter flipped through his "wheelbook," a pocket-sized green notepad carried by virtually every senior enlisted member in the Navy. "It was some guy named Mueller, who'd been BCD'd out of the Army for dealing dope a few years ago. He passed off a forged 214 to an employer in the Pittsburgh area, an auto upholstery shop I believe, when he was hired for a job. The boss was a veteran, and he noticed some kind of inconsistency on the form. So he contacted Army CID, and Petarsky and Patterson's names came up during their interrogation of Mueller, but then he clammed up and lawyered before the CID guys could nail down any details.

"CID notified NIS about the situation, who tried to squeeze Petarsky and Patterson a little bit, but didn't get anywhere. I sat in on the NIS interviews. Petarsky and Patterson both adamantly denied any involvement, and implied that Mueller was just trying to get the heat off himself by dragging their names into it, without any justification. We searched their shipboard lockers and didn't find anything. There was nothing left to go on, so it basically just got dropped."

"Let's get back to the night of the murder," said Maynard. "Have you been able to establish Bantam's activities? Did anyone see him with Petarsky or Patterson?"

Souter and Commander Langer exchanged glances, then Langer took a deep breath before he replied to Maynard's question.

"There's reason to believe that Lieutenant Bantam may have been playing cards with Petarsky, and perhaps Patterson as well, in the disbursing office, when he was killed," said Langer.

No Faith in Justice

There was a moment of uncomfortable silence as all assembled contemplated the implications. A commissioned officer, the ship's disbursing officer no less, gambling with two junior enlisted sailors inside what should have been one of the most secure areas aboard the ship. No wonder the Fitzpatrick leadership was squirming. A murder was bad enough. But a scandal like this could lead to some ancillary career wreckage as well, though that was far from a foregone conclusion.

"Petty Officer Belknott was standing the mid-watch on the quarterdeck Wednesday morning, when Bantam and Petarsky came across the brow together at about 0100. Bantam appeared mildly inebriated, and told Belknott he was going to cash a money order for Petarsky, and they went towards disbursing. Belknott thought it was odd that Bantam would volunteer to cash a money order that late at night for anyone, much less for a junior enlisted man. He had never done so before, to Belknott's knowledge. So we can't be sure, but given the cards and other evidence in the disbursing office, and the fact that Bantam was known to like card games as well, it's possible that Petarsky and Patterson were invited in by Bantam to gamble, then executed the robbery and murder together. But we don't know that for sure."

Friedberg sat silently for a moment, thinking carefully about what he would say next. "Look, XO...it's very early in the investigation. At this stage, it's not crucial to know the pretext for the suspects' entry into disbursing. For all we know, Bantam very well could have intended only to cash a money order to help out a shipmate in need of funds, just as he told Belknott, but was overpowered by the assailants as he opened the safe to get the cash box. Just because there were cards and a makeshift playing surface in the office doesn't necessarily mean they were gambling together. Let's just keep the focus on what we know for sure, and on gathering more evidence and statements. We need to build a solid case against the bastards that murdered Lieutenant Bantam and stole all the Fitz's money first, then we'll worry about the secondary details."

A look of relief flashed across Commander Langer's face. The Captain would also be relieved to learn they'd drawn a senior NIS agent who appeared to be level-headed, discreet, and not unsympathetic to all the potential career ramifications of this case.

"XO, you said Petarsky and Patterson were part of a small group of...'characters" onboard," Maynard said to Commander Langer. "Have you questioned any of their associates yet?"

"Yes, and there's one kid in particular we think might know something. A young signalman named Martin Stillwell. He and Petarsky and Patterson have been running mates for quite some time. Some of the crew have told us that the three of them shared an apartment in Oceanview for awhile in between deployments. But the deckplate scuttlebutt is they apparently had some kind of falling out recently. Otherwise, he probably would have been in on this caper, too.

"MAC interviewed him and he denied any knowledge or involvement, of course. But when we searched his locker, we found something you might be able to use as leverage. He had a valise full of blank DD 214's, and one that was partially filled out in a fake name. He's definitely not authorized to have those forms. He probably stole 'em from the supply storeroom, got 'em from Petarsky, or picked 'em up during a SERVMART run. We can check all the supply records and find out for sure. Anyway, it ties him to the previous case we mentioned, and demonstrates a probable attempt at conspiracy to commit fraud, at the very least. Not to mention misappropriation of government property."

"And that's not all we found," Chief Souter added. "He also had half a bottle of Valium, about sixteen pills. He tried to claim they were prescribed by a doctor for back spasms when he was on temporary assignment for advanced signaling school in Little Creek, but there's nothing in his health record about it, and no prescription label on the bottle."

"Do you think he was involved?" asked Maynard.

"Don't know," said Souter. "Maybe he knew the plan, and that's why they fell out. He coulda got scared, maybe. But it's also possible he knew nothing. If he did know something, he's a pretty good liar about it, I'll tell you that."

"He'll be our first interview," said Friedberg as he looked around the table. "Anything else?" After a brief pause, he arose, "Then let's get to it. MAC, we'll need copies of that case file ASAP. And please arrange to have Stillwell sent to our stateroom in one hour. Lieutenant Rodriguez, please have your yeoman type up a charge sheet on Stillwell for illegal possession of narcotics, misappropriation of government property, and conspiracy to commit fraud, for now. Nick will conduct the initial interview while I walk through the crime scene with MAC, and sort through the suspects' belongings for additional clues. If Stillwell wants an attorney, we'll bring Lieutenant Commander Moles into the interview."

"Let's also set up an in-brief with the Captain," said Langer, as he glanced at the chronometer on the bulkhead in the wardroom. "1700 gives you guys three hours to get started. Meet us in the Captain's cabin, then we'll eat supper back here afterwards."

Nick stowed his gear away in the two-man stateroom, and washed up in the sink. Nice digs, compared to the Deck Department berthing compartment he'd called home for three years during his enlisted days. There were some things he missed from his time as a sailor -- the camaraderie, the travel, the sense of teamwork -- but sleeping in one big room with thirty or forty other smelly snoring hard legs wasn't one of them. It was a different story for officers, or zeros as he and his buddies used to call them. This O-country living wasn't half bad. There was a small desk and chair in one corner of the room, and a fold down table with chair between the two racks.

He placed his notes from the in-brief, writing materials, and a microcassette recorder out on the table. He rarely used the recorder during an initial interview, but he liked to see how suspects reacted to its presence. The art of the interrogation was an inexact science, but one in which he believed himself to excel. He never knew what direction the process would take. Sometimes he found the empathetic nice guy approach most effective. His easy-going Oklahoma accent could be disarming when he wanted. Other times a more brusque and intimidating manner would serve best. The most important thing for him to be successful was to create at least an illusion that the Law of Psychological Reciprocity was at play: Give the other person credit for their beliefs, and they would feel obliged to do likewise. The direct approach was his preferred method. But he had no qualms about altering that philosophy as the situation dictated.

Lieutenant Rodriguez dropped off the charge sheet, along with Stillwell's service record and a pre-typed waiver of rights statement, about twenty minutes prior to the start of the interview. Nick noticed that Stillwell was from the Kansas City area of Missouri, was nineteen, and had scored extremely high on the ASVAB test at the time of enlistment. He'd also received decent marks on his performance evaluations with regards to job performance, but with some minor disciplinary infractions noted. Probably would have made a pretty good sailor if not for a few bad decisions. What a waste of potential. But we make our own choices, and we all have to live with the consequences. No exceptions. His mind wandered to Carla for a moment. He wondered how she was doing.

There were three quick knocks on the stateroom door, then it was quickly opened by a young second class petty officer who stood in the doorway.

"Petty Officer Smith here, sir. I have Seaman Stillwell standing by in the passageway whenever you're ready for him. And I'll escort him back to the Master-At-Arms shack when you're finished."

"You can send him on in, Smitty."

Maynard introduced himself to Stillwell, advised him of the charges for which he was being investigated, and of his right to refuse to answer any questions and retain counsel.

"I've got nothing to hide," said Stillwell as he signed the waiver of his rights. "I'll be glad to cooperate."

Maynard paged through Stillwell's service record again for a couple of minutes, pretending to read entries he'd already seen, as the two of them sat silently. It was Maynard's experience that although most of these nineteen-year-old perpetrators were cocky and full of bravado, it was often just a defense mechanism. They were mostly frightened kids, down deep. This one had probably been too afraid to pull off the heist with his buddies. Or maybe too smart, based on the ASVAB scores. He briefly wondered about the test scores of the two missing suspects in the case. He closed the record and smiled warmly at young Martin Stillwell.

"I see you're from Kansas City."

"Yes sir. Born and raised."

"I always liked KC. My Dad took me up there a few times in the late sixties to watch the Chiefs play. I played high school ball at the time, and the Chiefs had some great teams back then. Len Dawson. Otis Taylor. Mike Garret. And that dominating defense...man, those guys were fun to watch."

"Where you from?"

"Small town called Blackwell, in North-central Oklahoma. Dad used to drive us up on Saturday and we'd spend the night at a Howard Johnson's right off I-35. We'd always eat some Arthur Bryant's barbecue brisket, or Stroud's pan-fried chicken. Dad loved that chicken. Then we'd go to the game on Sunday and I'd drive us back Sunday evening while Dad slept off the beer in the back seat. It was the most fun we ever had together."

"It wouldn't be worth the drive to watch them play now. They've sucked ever since Hank Stram left for New Orleans."

"Yeah, but they sure were somethin' back in the day. Oh well...life moves on, I guess. So tell me about the bottle of Valium Chief Souter found in your locker."

"Well, it's like I told MAC. I had some back spasms while I was TAD to Advanced Signaling school in Little Creek, a couple months before we deployed on this UNITAS cruise. The doctor I saw at the clinic there gave me a script for Valium. I didn't have my health record with me cause I was only assigned there for five days, so they just filled out a sheet and told me to have our corpsmen put it in my record when I got back to the ship. I dropped that sheet off at sickbay when I came back. Maybe Doc Moroni just misplaced it or something,"

Nick hesitated a moment as if contemplating something. "Hmmm. Okay. Sounds plausible. It should be easy enough to verify. I'll have radio send a message to the Little Creek health unit and ask them to check their pharmacy records. In the meantime, I'll need you to write out an official statement summarizing everything you just told me. I'll witness your signature to the statement when I get back." He detected no sign of anxiety as he handed Stillwell a notepad and a pen, picked up his files, and walked out of the stateroom. He sent Petty Officer Smith to radio to initiate the message to the Little Creek pharmacy, then went to the wardroom and poured himself a cup of coffee, and one for Stillwell, who was finishing up his statement as Nick re-entered the stateroom with the cups and the files balanced on a small serving tray.

"Thanks," said Stillwell as he handed over his statement and took a sip of the coffee.

Nick immediately noticed the statement was well-worded, with correct spelling and grammar - somewhat unusual for such a junior sailor in trouble with the law.

"Okay. Sounds good to me. Now, before I have you sign it and make it official, it's important to make sure you understand that this is an official statement. And lying in a statement to an NIS Agent during the course of an official investigation is a court-martial offense." Nick couldn't detect any sense of hesitation as Stillwell replied "I understand" and signed and dated the statement he had just made.

MAC was right. This kid is an awfully good liar.

"It'll probably take a day or so to get a response back from Little Creek. In the meantime, I just have one more question about those Valiums. Why do you suppose there wasn't any prescription label on the bottle?"

"Maybe it was on the box the bottle came in. Or maybe the corpsman at the pharmacy didn't have time to type one up. She was pretty busy, and it seemed like maybe she was new at it or something."

"Do you recall her name?"

"Not really."

Smart. The kid was attempting to set up his alibi. They both knew that there would be no record of his prescription on file at the Little Creek pharmacy. And they both also knew that the Navy's health care system was notorious for its lackadaisical approach to record keeping, especially given the chronic personnel shortages experienced by every branch of the military in the post-Vietnam era. The reduced performance standards were a burden to the chain of command, but a boon for NIS and other military law enforcement organizations. There was plenty of work to go around for law enforcement.

"Well, enough about the pills. Let's talk about those DD-214's in your locker."

"I didn't even know what those things were until MAC told me. What would I know about discharge papers? I was just holding that bag for a shipmate who said he needed to make some more room in his locker for all the souvenirs he was buying in liberty ports on this cruise. I haven't been buying much of that crap, so I agreed to hold on to it for him."

"Holding it for a friend, huh? Wow, Stillwell. I would have figured you for a better alibi than that lame-ass story. That's right up there with 'my little brother ate my homework.' C'mon, you can do better than that."

No Faith in Justice

With a straight face, Stillwell replied "That's the God's truth, sir. That bag isn't mine. It belongs to Jimmy Petarsky."

"Interesting you should mention Petarsky. I understand you were pretty tight with him and Patterson. What can you tell me about this latest caper of theirs?"

"You mean Lieutenant Bantam? I don't know anything about that. Nothing whatsoever."

For the first time, Nick could detect some anxiety. Nobody likes being mentioned anywhere near a murder rap.

"The way I hear it, you three were practically inseparable. Even roomed together back in Norfolk. What happened? Did you chicken out after getting briefed on the big robbery scheme?"

"No sir. I stopped hanging out with those guys a few weeks before we left Norfolk. Me and Patterson had a falling out over a couple of chicks. I beat his time and he got a major case of the red-ass over it. Plus, we had a disagreement over some minor damage he did at my apartment. I had to pay for some drywall repair because of him, and he refused to make good on it. Him and Petarsky were real tight, so I just quit hanging out with both of them. Life is too short for those kind of hassles. I mean, there's plenty of women to go around. If one of them wants to be with someone else, who cares? Just go find another one, ya' know?"

"If you had a falling out, then why did you agree to hold Petarsky's valise?"

"We stopped hanging out together, but we didn't stop being friends. Besides, it wasn't that big of a deal, just holding a bag for awhile. I would've done the same for any shipmate."

Nick sat silent for a moment, staring at Stillwell, who held his gaze for a moment before looking away.

"Well it sounds like everybody had you figured all wrong, huh Stillwell? You're not really a doped-up, two-bit little shitbird who was too much of a pussy to step up into the big time with his buddies whose balls are bigger. Or a pathetic little coward who puts the blame for his own feeble attempts at forgery on one of his pals who isn't here to defend himself. You're really just a kind, considerate shipmate. Sort of a Mahatma Ghandi in dungarees. Is that about right?"

"Look, special agent Maynard. I can't help how it sounds. All I can do is tell it to you straight, the way it happened. Petarsky asked me to hold that bag. I saw it had some papers in it, I had no idea what they were and didn't figure it was any of my business anyway, and I didn't think anything else about it. I got those Valiums from a legitimate doctor's prescription. And Petarsky and Patterson neither one said a single word to me about the disbursing robbery plans, or the murder. I was just as shocked as everyone else when I heard about it. I mean, a lot of people thought Bantam was a swaggerin' little asshole, but he didn't deserve killin' over it."

Maynard sat and stared at the young sailor for a few moments. "Ya' know, for a real smart guy, you sure are thick-headed. Has it occurred to you yet what's going to happen if Petarsky and Patterson never show up? Don't you think the old man, and the rest of Bantam's wardroom buddies will be screaming for someone else's blood? And just who do you think all that lust for vengeance will be focused on then?

"So you better start coming clean with me now, so I can help you figure a way out of this mess. Cause nobody else on the Fitzpatrick is gonna lift a finger to save your sorry ass, that's for sure. Now tell me where we should start looking for Patterson and Petarsky, and everything else you know about this case, *right now.* "

The two sat silent for what seemed like a very long time. Maynard had employed the 'impending doom' style tactic, where you attempt to convince the subject that he is in a very tough predicament from which you and only you can help him recover, with great success in the past. The key to closing this type of sale was patience. Whoever speaks first, loses. Unless you know the magic phrase. As it turned out, Stillwell did. He took in a long deep breath, and said "I want a lawyer."

And just like that, Nick's heart sank as he realized he'd over-played his hand, and blown any chance of getting meaningful information from the best source they had at their disposal. He was trying to decide what his next move should be, and was considering just acting as if he hadn't heard the kid's request for legal representation, even though he knew that wasn't exactly "According to Hoyle."

Suddenly, the growler on the bulkhead began chirping. Nick was relieved for the well-timed intrusion. "Special Agent Maynard," he said as he picked up the handset.

"Sorry to interrupt, Nick," Friedberg was on the other end of the line. "But we've just had a huge break in the case. You need to meet me on the quarterdeck in twenty minutes. Some Brazilian police in a town about three hours from here have found a burnt body and a charred piece of a money bag with a USS Fitzpatrick stencil on it nearby. It may be one of our suspects.

"The consulate is sending a van and a translator over. They're also sending one of their Diplomatic Security Service guys, Tim Graves, to help us run interference if need be with the local cops. We'll take the Fitz's senior corpsman, Chief

Jackson, to help identify and retrieve the body, if it is one of those two numbskulls."

"Wow. That is huge. I can pick this back up when we get back."

"We might end up staying there a few days if we can generate any leads in the area, so please grab my duffel bag, and bring yours, too. I suspect we might be able to get some traction if we drop a few greenbacks on some of the locals. We might have to dig into some of our per diem money, but it probably won't take much given the state of their currency and economy."

"I'm willing to drink a few less rum-colas to help the cause."

"You're a regular Ghandi, Nick. The wardroom has taken up a collection, too, and we'll be able to offer a thousand dollar reward for information leading to their arrest. See you in twenty."

Maynard wondered briefly whether Friedberg had been listening in on his interview, somehow. But that was absurd. Friedberg hadn't even been in the stateroom but for a few seconds since their arrival. Must be just a coincidence.

"I'm going to have to cut this short for now, Stillwell," Nick said as he opened the door and saw Petty Officer Smith standing by in the passageway.

"The COMMO released that message to the Little Creek health clinic for you, sir."

"Great. Thanks, Smitty. You can take Stillwell back into custody. Our interview is over for now."

"For the record, I'm asserting my right to an attorney before answering any more questions," Stillwell said loudly enough that anyone in the vicinity could hear.

"Our interview's over, Stillwell. I have to leave the ship now. We're finished for the moment, and we'll talk about it when I get back," Nick said in an even, yet authoritative tone. He was hoping he could still salvage the situation somehow. He knew that the involvement of the JAG as a representative for the accused would effectively end any opportunity for leads in the murder case, which was his primary concern. Valiums and fake DD 214's were very small potatoes.

As the four Americans and their Brazilian driver and interpreter rode through the beautiful countryside on their way to the city of Juiz de Fora, Nick chatted with Hospital Corpsman Chief Jackson.

"I was interviewing Stillwell earlier today, and he mentioned a Doc Moroni. I assume he's one of your guys?"

"He's my assistant," Doc Jackson said. "There's only the two of us in sickbay. He's a second class. Decent troop, but a little scatterbrained." Jackson was curious about the context in which Moroni's name had come up, but was too much of a professional to pry.

Sensing concern, Nick eased his mind. "It's no big deal, by the way. Stillwell was just trying to justify having some Valiums in his locker, and claimed that he dropped the paperwork off for his medical record at sickbay. Claims it may have been mis-filed."

"Yeah, I've heard that story already. It's possible, I suppose. As in 'anything is possible.' But I highly doubt it. Moroni is competent. And the idea that somebody at Little Creek would dispense Valium for back spasms without making sure it got entered in the health record...remotely possible, but highly unlikely. The sailors around here like to joke that if they got shot, I'd give 'em three Tylenol and send 'em on their way.

There's a reason Tylenol is called the 'Navy's Cure-All.' I wouldn't put much stock in anything Stillwell has to say."

"I figured as much. What else do you know about that little group of slugs?"

"The three of them, Stillwell, Patterson and Petarsky, used to hang out with Moroni in sickbay and play cards occasionally, whenever we were underway. I never thought too much about it. They were always respectful around me. And I trust Moroni not to let anything get out of hand. Patterson claimed he wanted to strike for corpsman, and used to help us out with paperwork and shots and simple crap like that. But after what happened to the DISBO, I put sickbay completely off limits to everyone except designated corpsmen and sick people from now on. Official business only. It sucks to have to be that way, but you can't even trust your own shipmates nowadays." Jackson paused for a moment, then added "Rotten motherfuckers."

It was dark by the time they arrived at Juiz de Fora, a bustling city of about 300,000 people. They met up with the local Chief of Police, Gustavo Silva, who took them to a grubby looking little restaurant that served up heaping mounds of some of the most delicious food the Americans had ever tasted.

After dinner, they all went to the morgue. Doc Jackson had brought the dental records of both Petarsky and Patterson. They all looked at the burnt body, but Jackson wasn't able to make a positive identification. It was too badly charred and disfigured to make a visual ID. They would have to employ the services of the local pathologist to compare the dental x-rays with the remains. The translator convinced Silva to call the coroner in from home, who arrived in less than twenty minutes. He was curious about the Americans, and a little excited to be part of such an unusual incident, with international implications. This was definitely not a run of the mill case.

It took about fifteen minutes for him to conclude that the body was that of Richard A. Patterson, with 99% percent certainty. Which left Jimmy Petarsky as the primary suspect in two murders, now. The coroner offered to conduct a more thorough autopsy in order to determine the full cause and manner of death. He said it appeared the victim had been shot twice in the head, but that he'd have to cut the cadaver open and examine the lungs to determine whether the fire was pre or post-mortem. The translator explained that regulations compelled the American Navy to conduct its own autopsy. He thanked him for the excellent service, and gave him a business card with the Embassy address, to where he could forward his bill.

"Me and Nick and Graves will go to police headquarters with Chief Silva and take possession of the evidence they collected from the scene where the body was discovered," Friedberg said to the group. "We'll drop you off at the hotel on the way, Doc Jackson, so you can call the ship and give them the news. Tell 'em to make arrangements to fly Patterson's body back to Portsmouth for official identification and autopsy."

At police headquarters, Friedberg took possession of what little physical evidence there was; a partially burnt canvas bag with a USS Fitzpatrick stencil that was picked up near the body, a badly burned wallet, and a set of keys.

Through the translator, Chief Silva told the investigators he would take them to the location where Patterson was found in the morning, and arrange for them to meet the farmers who'd first reported the body, which they'd found on an isolated dirt road some twenty-five kilometers outside town. In the meantime, he said he would call the national police headquarters in Brasilia and advise them to send a teletype to INTERPOL in order to update the international fugitive status and last known location for Petarsky, and change Patterson's official status to deceased.

The local newspaper was planning a front page story about the murder in its morning issue. And that evening's television news broadcasts would be running the story as well. Chief Silva contacted the stations and provided physical descriptions of Petarsky and Patterson, and asked that anyone who'd seen the two men, or had any information at all, to contact police. Friedberg cursed softly when they realized that no one had thought to bring recent photos of the two suspects, so he telephoned the ship and sheepishly asked Commander Langer to obtain one of Petarsky.

"I was so keyed up when we got the call about the body, I didn't even think about pictures. I knew Doc could identify them, and we had the dental and medical records, so..."

"Don't sweat it," said Langer. "Just tell 'em he looks exactly like Radar O'Reilly, only bigger."

"Thanks, XO, but I doubt if there are a lot of *MASH* fans out here."

Graves contacted the consulate staff in Rio and asked them to pick up the photo at the ship, and courier it up to Juiz de Fora first thing in the morning. That meant there would be at least a two-day lapse between the last time Petarsky was known to have been in the area, and the initial public release of his photograph.

Juiz de Fora was a surprisingly cosmopolitan city, it turned out. There were a large number of Europeans -- Dutch, Germans, Brits, Italians -- in the area, including many younger tourists and students on extended stays. Petarsky wouldn't stick out by appearance alone, but there weren't a lot of Americans in the area. If he was still around, there was a pretty good chance they could nab him.

Silva convinced Friedberg not to advertise a reward just yet. He feared they would be overwhelmed with false leads.

Ready to call it a night, Silva dropped the Americans and their translator off at their hotel, the *Paraibuna*, with a promise to pick them up the next morning at 0830.

After a quick shower, Nick went to the lobby to place an international call to his wife Carla, but there was no answer, so he met up with the rest of the group in the small bar. There was a postage stamp sized dance floor, and the bartender was cranking up the salsa music. Soon, Maynard and Graves were shimmering for all they were worth with a couple of the local lovelies. Graves knew a fair bit of Portuguese, but was hardly fluent. Nick couldn't even order a drink, but it didn't matter. Everybody had a good time laughing and drinking and dancing until well past 1:00 AM. They all knew they were there on business, and the job always came first, but only a fool would pass up a good time in Brazil when the opportunity presented itself.

One particularly pretty young lady, a classic bronze-skinned amazon beauty named Luiza, appeared more than a bit smitten with Nick. They ended up making out a few times on the dance floor during some of the slower songs, and she seemed keen to take it a step further. He'd stopped wearing his wedding band months before, and hadn't gotten around to mentioning his wife at any point during the evening. But none of the other guys seemed to look down on him for it. Or if they did, they kept it to themselves Everybody understood: What happens in Brazil, stays in Brazil. She spent the night in his room. It was the most fun Nick had had in quite some time.

The next morning, Doc Jackson left with the van to escort Patterson's remains back to Rio, for further transport to Portsmouth, while the NIS agents, Graves, and the translator drove with Chief Silva out to the location where Patterson's body was found. It was well off the beaten path, miles from the nearest paved highway. There was nothing nearby, and the road received almost no traffic. An ideal place for a murder, or a body dump and burn. When questioned by Friedberg, Silva said they hadn't discovered any castable tire tracks the previous day when the body had been discovered and picked up. The Americans doubted it would have done much good anyway, but it made them feel a little less foolish for not having had any photos of their suspects on hand. Misery loves company. So does incompetence.

"I don't see how Petarsky could have known about this place, given the likely assumption that he's never been in this part of the world before," Friedberg commented. "Makes me wonder if some local boys might not be involved."

"I agree," said Nick. "We're as likely to find Petarsky dead and crispy-fried somewhere as alive. Two young Americans flashing fistfuls of cash could have attracted all kinds of attention from local badasses."

"Or maybe Petarsky enlisted some help from a local or two, and paid them off for assisting in the elimination of his partner in crime," Graves interjected. "No doubt four-hundred thousand sounds a helluva lot better than two-hundred thousand, especially to a desperate fugitive trying to stay one step ahead of the hangman."

They drove another five kilometers up the road to speak with the farmer who'd discovered the body. He hadn't seen anyone else on the road for days, and wasn't able to provide any useful information, so they headed back to the city to see how many leads had been generated by the previous evening's television broadcasts, and the morning newspaper story.

It turned out that over three dozen people had phoned or walked in to police headquarters claiming to have seen one or both of the fugitives, at conflicting times and locations scattered all over the city, and Silva's men were busy compiling the statements and reports and following up on the most promising leads. Unfortunately, nothing panned out by late afternoon, so Friedberg had their translator transcribe the pertinent details from the statements into one consolidated report in English, and then the three Americans sat with the report and created a prioritized list for follow-up of their own.

A driver from the U.S. consulate in Rio showed up at 1300 with a decent photograph of Petarsky.

"Holy shit, he is a dead ringer for Radar O'Reilly," Friedberg said as he passed the picture around to his colleagues, before handing it to Silva for dissemination to the local media outlets. The consular's office had already telefaxed a copy to INTERPOL before the driver left Rio.

Just as the men were about to leave headquarters for a mid-day meal, Silva advised Friedberg that he was wanted on the phone by his boss at NIS in Jacksonville.

"Uh oh, this can't be good," quipped Friedberg as he went to take the call. "They can't be firing me already, can they?"

He was gone for what seemed like a long time, at least twenty minutes, and when he came back he was visibly upset. Everyone was immediately on edge.

125

"Well?" said Maynard, after a moment of silence.

"Uh, Nick, I need to speak with you for a moment in private."

"In private? What about?"

"Let's go back into Silva's office."

Nick's heart did a quick two-step as he followed Friedberg down the hall. His mind began racing through all the possibilities. Was he in trouble, somehow? It couldn't be the botched Stillwell interview. There's no way HQ could have heard about that so rapidly. He quickly started thinking back through his recent cases, but he couldn't think of anything that would have warranted a dressing down from 4000 miles away. As they got to the empty office, Friedberg closed its door and motioned for Nick to sit down while he sat on the corner of Silva's desk.

"It's Carla, Nick. I'm so sorry, but I'm afraid she's dead."

Nick was stunned. "Dead..Are you sure?"

"She didn't show up for work yesterday, and her co-workers couldn't raise her on the telephone. So when she didn't show up again this morning, one of her friends went to your apartment and saw her lying in the kitchen through the window and called the police. The police got the manager to let them in, and while they were investigating they saw some of your NIS paraphernalia around the house and notified HQ."

"What the hell happened?"

"I hate to have to tell you this, Nick, but they believe it was suicide. It looks like she shot herself in the head with a thirty-eight revolver."

A spasm of nausea hit Nick as he choked out "Oh my God, it was probably my pistol...I brought the nine with me." He buried his face in his hands and let out a tortured kind of sob, a primal sound that alarmed everyone within earshot, especially

Friedberg. He'd heard that sound before. It was 100% raw emotion, and it was always unsettling. His friend was in dire distress, and there was nothing to be done for it.

Nick leapt to his feet, "I can't breathe…I gotta get some air," and he bolted out of the office and down the hall, and burst out into the afternoon sun on the bustling street outside police headquarters. He began walking furiously, tears streaming down his face, mind racing, oblivious to the curious looks of passersby.

About six blocks down the street, he came upon a small but beautiful old Catholic church. He entered without hesitation. His family were Baptists, but hardly devout. They would occasionally attend services on Easter, but very seldom at any other time of year. He'd never been religious-minded himself, although he did believe in God. But when he sat down in a pew in the back of that nearly deserted church, he began to pray for forgiveness in earnest, with every fiber of his being.

He was bewildered as to why Carla had decided to end her own life so abruptly. But he was pretty sure that as her husband, the man who'd willingly pledged before God and man to love and cherish her forever, forsaking all others, only to try and bail out on her less than three years later, that he featured prominently in her reasons for despair.

He sat with his forehead resting on his arms on the back of the pew in front of his and wept for his wife. And for himself. And for her mother and sisters, who he knew loved her dearly. The pain was crushing. Unbearable. He didn't want to move, but he couldn't sit still.

After a time, he left the church and trudged slowly back to the station. Friedberg was waiting for him in the main lobby. Graves and the translator were nowhere to be seen.

"Has anyone contacted her mother?"

"I don't know, Nick. I don't think so. I'll sit with you when you place the call, if you want."

Nick nodded as they walked back to Silva's office.

"Did you get any other details?"

"The coroner estimated she'd been dead for ten to twelve hours, which places the TOD as roughly eleven PM Jacksonville time."

"Which is what...0100 our time?" asked Nick.

Friedberg nodded his head, as they both thought about where Nick ha'd been the previous night at 1:00 AM. Nick wanted to die.

"You'll be going back to Rio with the courier who brought the photo up this morning. He'll be waiting for you in the lobby of the hotel, as soon as you're ready. By the time you get there, a small military transport plane should be at the airport ready to take you back to Jacksonville. Patterson's body will be on the same plane, along with an escort from the Fitzpatrick, on the way for autopsy at Portsmouth."

Nick didn't know his mother-in-law's number, so he called directory assistance in Corpus Christi Texas only to find that she was unlisted. So Friedberg called the NIS personnel office, and had them pull the number from Nick's file. The conversation with her mother was brief, and excruciatingly painful. His penance had begun. Nick knew it would not be paid up for a long, long time. If ever.

On the long and silent ride back to Rio, it occurred to Nick that he was leaving Friedberg in quite a lurch. This case was way too much for one guy to handle. But then again, Graves would be a big help. And one of his colleagues from Jacksonville was probably already on the way. He wondered who it would be. Parker maybe? Sherman? Both? No matter. They were all good hands.

Nick had wanted another crack at that cocky little prick, Stillwell. He was sure he could convince him to rescind his request for a lawyer, and give them something to help with the investigation. But that was somebody else's problem now. Nick had bigger issues. A living hell.

Chapter Ten
October 07th, 2010

It was almost 5:30 PM by the time Marty made his way home through Denver's rush-hour traffic, after the interview with Nick Maynard. Not much time to prepare for his next unpleasant rendezvous. Fortunately, Melissa wasn't home. He was glad not to have to answer any questions as he loaded his bicycle into the car, and changed into jeans and a t-shirt underneath a baggy hooded sweatshirt. He wondered if she'd cooled down any from that morning. He'd call her later, while making the drive to Waterton Canyon.

He put new batteries into the voice-activated microcassette recorder he'd brought from work, and placed it inside the small tool pouch he always carried while riding, velcroed to the bicycle frame. A quick test with the pouch half-unzipped indicated it would work okay. Although the clarity wasn't ideal, it could still pick up normal-toned conversation from up to ten feet away. He considered duct-taping the recorder to his body instead, as he'd seen in countless movies and TV shows, but decided it was too risky. The blackmailer might pat him down, but wasn't likely to take much interest in a bicycle tool pouch. And even if he did find it...so what? He was already being blackmailed. How much worse could it get? He had to try to do *something* to protect himself.

He dialed Melissa as he drove to the Canyon, but she didn't pick up. He left a voicemail message apologizing again for his behavior that morning. She was as sweet as they come under normal circumstances, but could hold a grudge with the best of them when she felt slighted or disrespected. He'd nicknamed her "The Sicilian" only half-jokingly, because she would always figure out a way to even the score. He had a lot of work to do on that front. And he knew things between them would only get more difficult soon, since he would eventually be forced to tell her about the troubles brewing with NCIS. That confrontation was not going to be pleasant. But he would put off telling her anything as long as he could. There was nothing to be gained by fessing up before he there was no other choice.

The parking lot was empty when he arrived at the trail-head. Waterton Canyon Trail officially closed every evening thirty minutes past sunset, but there was no gate, and police didn't usually check the lot until well after dark. He should be back to his car and gone in plenty of time.

He pondered his earlier meeting with Nick Maynard as he pedaled toward the designated rendezvous point. It probably wasn't wise to have broached the subject of his wife's suicide like that, but he just couldn't help himself. He knew that Maynard held all the cards. But he also knew that Maynard had no inclination to give him the benefit of the doubt, and wouldn't help him in any way, even though he'd pretended he would in return for "cooperation." A man like Maynard was truly interested only in convictions, and seeing people like Marty fry. Bringing up what his wife had done was his only chance to inflict a little pain in return, and he'd taken it – even if he might live to regret having done so.

As he neared the Mill Gulch Bridge, his sense of anticipation grew. It had to be Radar, didn't it? It didn't seem like Maynard knew anything about it, given his lack of reaction when Marty had mentioned the bike trail. And it wouldn't have made any sense, anyway. If he was going to blackmail Marty, he wouldn't have conducted an official interview in FBI headquarters.

No, it had to be Petarsky. He'd probably sent a letter to the NCIS to get the Faith Cooper investigation back in play, before sending the note to Marty. But why put NCIS on Marty's trail before extorting any money? That approach would run the risk of backfiring, especially if your target ended up under arrest. It'd be a lot tougher to get money out of a man who's already been caught. Maybe Petarsky only intended to turn up the heat a little. Maybe he didn't know there was DNA evidence in the mix. And he surely didn't know that Marty had used a fraudulent 214 to get a scholarship for Katie, and that the cops would be using that fact as an excuse to jack him up but good.

Or maybe it wasn't Petarsky.

His odometer indicated he'd gone nine-tenths of a mile past the bridge when he saw a bench and trashcan on the side of the trail just ahead. He stopped and dismounted, leaned his bike against the trash can, made sure the zipper was still half open, and took a few gulps of cool water as he checked his watch – 6:29 PM. Punctual, even when meeting his extortionist. He suddenly wished he'd been purposely late, instead.

It was darkening and quiet in the canyon at this hour. The steady flow of the South Platte River babbling over boulders and submerged logs generated the only sounds. Marty had enjoyed many a quiet evening on this trail, where bighorn sheep were routinely encountered, but he wasn't very receptive to its tranquility and beauty at the moment.

Suddenly, he heard the sound of gravel shifting over rock from a hundred-fifty feet or so further up the trail. He could just make out a large boulder on the side of the gravel road, a few feet from the steep canyon wall. From behind the boulder a horse and rider emerged. Marty knew there were many well-concealed game trails that led up and out of the canyon. He and Melissa had hiked a few and picnicked up in some beautiful and secluded mountain meadows. You could hike or ride trails from the canyon and connect to many other trails that led to various points throughout the Colorado Rockies. The rider had probably been waiting from a higher vantage point, watching him arrive, to make sure he was alone.

The horse trotted up to the bench, and its rider dismounted, uttering not a word, but grinning from ear to ear. Marty was astonished as the true identity of his tormentor dawned on him. It wasn't whom he'd expected at all. The hair was no longer jet black, mostly gray now. But there was no mistaking the cocky manner, the coal-black eyes, and the devilish smile of the rider.

"Well, if it isn't Very-Young Martin Stillwell," Rick Patterson said to a stunned and speechless Marty. "Or Martin Mahoney, I guess I should say. Although I have to tell you, I don't really think Mahoney is right for you. Stillwell suits you better, in my opinion. But I guess it doesn't matter much. An asshole by any other name still smells the same, and all that. What's the matter, Marty? You look like you've just seen a ghost."

"How the hell did you pull it off?"

"You mean how did I convince the authorities that I was dead, so they'd spend all their time looking for someone who actually was dead instead of looking for me? C'mon now, Marty. You know me better than that. Since when did I ever reveal any of my secrets?"

Suddenly, the realization struck Marty, like a bolt of lightning. "Dental records! They said Radar's body was burned beyond recognition. Somehow you must've switched his dental x-rays for yours. I remember now. You told Doc you wanted to strike for corpsman, and he used to let you work in sickbay sometimes. That means you must've had the whole thing planned out in advance.

"You killed Radar in cold blood, just so you could keep all the money for yourself, and have an escape cover based on the mis-identification. That's some cold-blooded, evil shit, Patterson. Even for someone as fucked up as you."

Patterson kept grinning as he replied. "That's one possibility, I guess. But I don't know...sounds a little far-fetched to me. Can anyone really be that clever, or heartless? I mean, to kill one of your best friends just for a couple hundred grand, and an alibi? You're right...that does sound evil."

"And now you're trying to fuck me over, too. After all these years...Why?"

"I don't know. Mostly for the money, I guess. But also for the fun. Man's gotta make a living, ya' know? But they say it's always best if you can support yourself doing the things you love. By the way, how did you like that old picture I sent of you and Faith together? I've got some more with me, if you'd like to see."

"So what's your angle, Rick? How much to make the pictures disappear?"

"I was thinking fifty-K down, then a small monthly stipend to help offset some of my living expenses. Nothing you can't afford. We'll price it well within your reach. Just put me on the company payroll. I must say, you've done far better for yourself than I ever would've imagined. I pretty-much figured you'd have been dead long ago, as a matter of fact. I was mildly surprised to find you were even alive."

"So fifty thousand dollars is only a start? Then I spend the rest of my life bending over for your monthly shake-down? I don't know, Rick...doesn't sound like a viable option to me.

Maybe I should just let you go ahead and send whatever pictures you have to NCIS. I mean, they're already on my ass anyway, thanks to you. You might've jumped too soon, this time. They probably already have my DNA from Faith. And they've got me jacked up on a fraudulent DD-214 beef to use as leverage. I'm pretty-much screwed already. So you may have prematurely killed the golden-goose, before getting any eggs."

Rick thought for a moment before he replied. "I should've known you'd still be into somethin' shady. And here I thought you were all squeaky-clean, now. Still doin' the 214 hustle, huh?

"That's the biggest problem in this type of deal. You have to motivate your client to cooperate, yet still make sure he can survive and earn enough to pay for your services. Very tricky proposition. But I had to get your attention and motivate you somehow, and what better way than to put NCIS on your tail? Maybe I should've just threatened to tell your wife everything I know about you, instead. By the way...wow. Congratulations for landing that piece of top-shelf action. And two beautiful young daughters to boot. The world can be such a cruel place, but you've done a great job protecting them so far. You wouldn't want to blow it all now, would you?"

Marty decided to ignore the thinly-veiled threat against his family, and quickly changed the course of the conversation. "I can't believe we were actually friends at one time. It's obvious to me now that you're the one who killed Faith, in addition to Radar and Bantam. I knew you were ruthless, but I never had you figured for a cold-blooded serial murderer. And Radar loved you like a brother, too."

"You're right. Radar was a good friend. What happened to him was unfortunate. But you, on the other hand. You were never a friend to anyone. You're no different than me in a lot of ways, really. You just don't have the balls I do."

"So what about Faith? Why did you kill her? Was it jealousy, because she slept with me instead of you?"

Patterson smiled. "Don't try to pin that one on me. You killed Faith Cooper, Stillwell. You can pull your 'but I was in a drunken blackout' routine with everybody else if you want, but I know better. You killed her, and you probably liked it, too."

Marty couldn't be sure of anything from that night. "I wasn't in any condition to kill anyone, and you know it. You probably woke up in the middle of the night, killed her, dumped her body on the beach, then pretended you'd been passed out all along."

"Sorry, pal. That one's all on you. Pictures don't lie. You had her all tied up, and you just got carried away. Too bad, too, cause I hear they don't treat lady-killers well in prison."

Neither man spoke for a moment.

"So how the hell have you survived all this time? I'm sure the heist money ran out long ago."

"Actually, it lasted for a quite a while. The economy in South America was so bad in the eighties, those hard greenbacks went a long way. And once I made it out of Brazil, that Spanish we picked up from Havanna-Joe helped me make some good business connections in Colombia and Panama. The livin' was pretty good down there, for a long time. I intended to stay permanently, but then I had a sudden change in plans, and decided to come back home."

"And now you're broke, and I'm your new meal-ticket. But like I said, it may already be over for me, Patterson. If my DNA matches the sample they have on file in the Cooper case, they're going to railroad me anyway."

Patterson's eyes narrowed as he replied. "I don't care. That's not my problem. For right now, you're a free man with plenty of assets, from what I can see. I'll give you a week to put fifty grand in cash together, or suffer the consequences. The pictures of you with Faith tied to the bed is are only a start. It will get much worse for you, and for your family, if you force me to get ugly. Unlike you, I've got nothin' to lose."

Suddenly, a set of headlights appeared from around the bend about three-quarters of a mile down the gravel road from the direction of the trailhead parking lot and began a slow approach towards their position. It was most likely either local police or park rangers, enforcing the curfew. Patterson hastily mounted his horse.

"One week. Don't test me, Marty. I'll be in touch." And with that, the Pittsburgh Pink Panther and his horse trotted back to the boulder, and disappeared up the same steep canyon trail he'd come down on.

After a friendly admonishment from a courteous young park ranger about over-staying the trail curfew, Marty's head was spinning as he pedaled back to his car. How long had Patterson been watching him? How had he managed to find him, living under a different last name? And where the hell did he ever learn to ride a horse like that?

Two things beyond question were his ruthlessness and cunning. He'd killed Lieutenant Bantam, his best friend Radar, perhaps Faith Cooper, and probably others – and gotten away with it all.

Marty was now being simultaneously targeted by both the U.S. government, and a murderous blackmailer who'd been officially declared dead three decades earlier. That morning's ugly episode with Melissa was now the unequivocal highlight of his day.

That thought caused him to consider a quote he'd once read, attributed to the manager of the absolute worst team in Major League Baseball. During a press conference conducted while his team was in the midst of yet another of the many long losing streaks they would experience that miserable season, where they were routinely blown out and hopelessly over-matched by every opponent they faced, he was asked if things had gotten so bad that they couldn't possibly get any worse. His reply: "I never say it can't get worse." A prescient response, as their season did indeed get worse from that point forward. Marty now understood exactly how that manager had felt.

Chapter Eleven
September 17th, 1980

"Instead of staying the night in Petropolis like we planned, we've decided we want to see Juiz de Fora instead," Rick Patterson said to one of the two Brazilian girls who were standing with him and Radar Petarsky in front of the Hotel Itaipava. "Can you negotiate a fare with one of the taxi drivers, in American dollars?"

"Juiz de Fora?" The girl whose name was Renata asked. "*Si*, a taxi can take us there. But it will be very expensive. It would be better if we take the bus. It is only a few hours...maybe half of one day."

"We'd prefer not to wait for a bus, and have to deal with all those stops and passengers. We can afford a taxi, I think. Me and Radar, er, I mean me and Teddy have been saving for this trip. We want to get going as soon as possible."

"OK," she replied with a big smile. "*Não fez mal.* No problem."

A taxi driver pulled up to the door a few moments later and dropped two elderly ladies with several large suitcases. Renata and her friend, Daisy, spoke with the driver for several minutes, gesturing towards the two Americans on several occasions. It seemed that the girls were negotiating in earnest, and after checking his watch several times, the taxi driver appeared to give in reluctantly and nodded his head.

"He say he can do it for one-hundred dollars. I think it is too much, but he say gas is very expensive right now, and it will take much of the day to go there and return here. He say first one-hundred-fifty dollars, but one-hundred is the best I can convince him to agree."

"No problem. One-hundred is fine. Let's go."

"One of us stays with the car at all times," Rick said to Radar in a hushed tone as he reluctantly allowed the driver to load their bags, along with the girls' single small knapsack, into the trunk.

The two young couples talked non-stop, enjoying the scenic ride to Juiz de Fora. Renata told Rick that one of her favorite teachers from college in Fortaleza was now teaching at a school in Juiz de Fora, and she would like to look him up while there. Radar's date, Daisy, didn't speak English quite as well as Renata, who was fluent. But she was passable, and seemed to improve and gain confidence in a fairly short time. Both boys knew some Spanish and enjoyed using it as often as possible in the many Spanish-language countries they'd visited, but that wasn't much help in Brazil. Neither knew Portuguese.

They'd met Renata and Daisy in a disco in an upscale suburban area near Recife, the liberty port the Fitzpatrick had visited immediately prior to Rio. The four of them had hit it off immediately. The girls were a perfect match for the boy's scheme, the final component needed to complete their plan. They told the girls they were merchant marines from a freighter which was also docked in Recife at the time. Once they'd agreed to meet the boys in Petropolis, the itinerary for the tour they'd already signed up for in Rio, Rick and Radar knew they could unwittingly assist in making a clean getaway after the robbery of the disbursing office. And once they were safely away from Rio with hundreds of thousands of dollars, they could make plans for more permanent arrangements. One thing they knew for sure: American money talks, especially in South America, where hyper-inflation made local currencies virtually worthless by comparison.

No Faith in Justice

By mid-afternoon, they were checked into a comfortable, mid-range "hotel" in Juiz de Fora. It seemed more like an apartment building than a hotel to the boys. Their flat, in a separate building from the reception desk, had two bedrooms, and some kitchenware, so the girls went off to buy food and supplies while the the boys settled in.

"Man...that was some fucked-up shit back there, Rick. You really lost it on Bantam, man. I think he was gagging on something. Maybe it was blood, or his own vomit or something, but I think he's dead for sure."

"Probably. But the motherfucker deserved it anyway for making us work so hard getting the combo to the safe."

"Yeah, but you went off on him after we already had the safe open, when he called you a pathetic moron and a loser."

"I had to tape his mouth shut. He was making so much fuckin' noise. I warned him. You heard me. Guy's gotta learn to keep his mouth shut...little jerk like that. I guess he knows better now."

"Bantam was a prick, yeah. But it's still fucked-up, Rick. The stakes are a lot higher for us now. There's no going back now...ever."

"True. But we weren't ever planning to go back anyway, even before what happened to Bantam. Nothing's changed. We've got enough money to live like kings down here for quite awhile. When it starts running low, we'll figure something else out. We always do."

"I know. But before, we were looking at ten or fifteen years if we got pinched - max. Now we're facing life...or worse. I just wish you would've held your shit a little better, that's all. We're in this thing together. Everything you do affects me, too. That's all I'm sayin'."

"That's right. Everything each of us does affects the other guy. So we gotta stick with the plan. No contact with family, and no going back to the states - ever."

Radar stared down at his shoes for a few moments. "I need to call my mom. Just one time. Her and my sisters will be worried sick when the Navy contacts them. I want her to know that I'm all right. And we aren't gonna stay in this city long anyway, right? So what does it matter? Just one call before we leave town, and that'll be it."

That was the moment when Patterson knew, without a doubt, he would have to go through with his original plan in its entirety. Otherwise, Radar would get them both caught, eventually. He'd make phone calls home. He'd been the only male growing up in a house full of women, and he was crazy about his mom and his sisters, even though he wouldn't admit it. There was only one way to prevent that from happening. And besides, if he did it right, the law would officially declare Rick Patterson dead, and would be looking forever for a fugitive named Jimmy Petarsky. That was just too good a caper to pass on, friendship or no friendship. Rick Patterson would rank right up there with D.B. Cooper as a mastermind, even if nobody else could ever know the truth about it.

"No calls, Radar. We agreed. They're too easily traced, and the law could be on us in a matter of minutes. Send 'em a postcard, instead. By the time they get it, we'll be long gone from this burg."

Radar stared down at his shoes again, without replying. Then he stood up, walked in to Rick and Renata's bedroom closet, pulled out the duffel-bag that contained the stolen loot, and dumped the bundles of bills on the bed with a huge grin and a laugh.

"Well, what's done is done, I guess. And this should make it a little easier to take."

Rick grinned too, and the two boys slapped high fives while they began to count. The twenties were separated into bundles of 100 each, totaling $2000.00 And the bundles were bound together in stacks of ten, equaling $20,000.00 each. There were also some stacks of fifties and hundreds, though the vast majority of the bills were twenties. They hadn't bothered taking any of the smaller denominations from the safe. The final count on their haul was $411,240.00.

They looked at each other, awestruck. They'd known there was a lot of cash in the disbursing office safe. The clerks had hinted about having several hundred thousand dollars on board. But they were totally unprepared to actually have this much cash in their possession. It didn't seem real somehow, yet there it was in huge stacks on the bed.

"We'd better put this away before the girls get back," Rick said as he pulled aside a small stack of twenties for each of them, then began re-packing the money back into his backpack, stuffing a few items of clothing around the money to keep it from being too obvious.

Renata and Daisy returned by early evening with two bags of groceries, and got busy cooking up a delicious meal of black bean stew with pork and beef and rice, while the boys sipped cold Skol brand pilsner beers and played Tonk, a card game Patterson had learned while growing up. He excelled at Tonk - as he did in every game of chance. Petarsky, knowing full well he was over-matched, insisted on small stakes, but the boys were enjoying themselves nonetheless. The distance they'd placed between themselves and the ship, along with the sense of anonymity that comes from being a complete stranger in a completely foreign land, gave them a momentary sense of security.

"Do you think they notified the Brazilian cops to start looking for us yet, Rick?"

"Maybe. But I doubt it. Too early for that, probably. That fat-ass deputy dog MAC couldn't find his dick with both hands. It'll take him awhile to figure out what happened. And the last thing the old man wants is bad publicity. They'll probably call some NIS investigators down from Norfolk. Or maybe have the embassy ride herd on the investigation. Anyway, they probably won't involve the Brazilians until they know what happened for sure. That should give us a few days, at least. And I don't think there's any way they could ever figure out we have the passports."

"I know," Petarsky chuckled and shook his head admiringly as he replied. "That was a stroke of fuckin' genius. Dutch and Bell have no idea we have official passports issued in their names, but with our pictures. Everybody thought I was just bein' a kiss-ass when I volunteered for all those collateral duties, but bein' the mail P.O. and PQS coordinator definitely had its advantages. The government is so stupid. I wonder how many times they get duped like that every year?"

Teddy "Dutch" Van Deusel and Mark Bell were storekeepers who worked with Petarsky aboard the Fitzpatrick. Jimmy had used information gleaned from their service records, which he'd accessed under the auspices of verifying Personnel Qualifications Standard entries, and had ordered original raised-seal copies of their birth certificates from Vital Statistics. He'd also swiped Van Deusel's ID card from his desk drawer after a messdecks payday. Patterson had convinced Bell to sell him his ID card, ostensibly because Bell's ID would allow him to purchase hard liquor since he was twenty-two and Patterson was only twenty.

Then he and Petarsky had submitted passport applications at the Norfolk post office using their own photos, along with the birth certificates. Rick and Jimmy had kept the postal clerk engaged with a steady stream of chatter about all the exotic places they were going to visit after getting their passports, and she'd barely glanced at the photos on the ID cards, which had been issued to Dutch and Bell when both had buzzcuts in boot camp. The clerk seemed satisfied merely that the names on the birth certificates matched the ID's. Nobody looked much like their boot camp picture, anyway. From there it was simply a matter of intercepting the passports when they arrived in the mail, easily accomplished in Petarsky's role as the S-1 division Mail P.O.

After their meal, the couples retired to their bedrooms for an early-evening siesta, then arose about 10:30 PM, and went out for a night on the town. Juiz de Fora was a small city, but it had lots of nightclubs. By midnight, the group was ensconced in a corner booth at a loud disco filled with boisterous revelers, a roughly equal mixture of Brazilians and Europeans. Rick and Jimmy were in generous spirits, buying drinks for many of their fellow patrons throughout the evening, endearing themselves to their new friends in the process.

"It's unusual for me to run across Americans I don't already know here in the city," a young man who had introduced himself as Jason Metter said to Rick. "There are only a few dozen or so of us here that I know of, and not many tourists make it this far from Rio."

"Really? That's kinda surprising. I've seen quite a few people around town who look like they could be American."

"Most of them are probably Germans, or Spaniards. There are lots of both. So what brings you guys here?"

"Just doing the tourist thing. We like to get a little bit off the beaten path, and we plan to see more of Brazil before we're finished. We've been working as deckhands on a freighter, and saved up for this trip for a long time. Now we wanna make the most of it."

"So how long are you planning on staying in Juiz de Fora?"

"We haven't decided yet. Hey, you wouldn't happen to know where we can get a decent deal on a used motorcycle, would you? That looks like a pretty popular way to get around here."

"How big?"

"I don't know. Big enough to take the two of us on a road trip. Six-fifty, maybe?"

"I know a German guy who has an old Yamaha four-fifty for sale. It's a little banged up, but it runs OK. If you're just looking for something to buzz around on a little while, it wouldn't be bad. He's going back to Germany soon, and wants to get rid of it. So you could probably pick it up pretty cheap."

"Can you arrange a meeting for us, tomorrow?"

Jason wrote down his address, and suggested he could have the motorcycle owner meet them there at noon the next day.

The next morning, Radar suggested that Rick go and check the motorcycle out on his own. "Me and the girls wanna walk around town a little bit, and grab some lunch." Rick knew exactly what Radar had planned. A trip to the local telephone exchange, and a call back home to Chicago - risks be damned.

Rick and Jason had time to get acquainted while waiting for the German and his motorcycle to arrive at Jason's apartment, a spacious third-floor one-bedroom with a balcony.

"Wilhelm is always late. Very un-German like. He would've made a terrible Nazi."

Rick learned that Jason was originally from Orange County California, and had been in Juiz de Fora for almost three years. He'd come there after graduation from college, to work for a family friend's agricultural export business. Unfortunately, not even friendship could prevent him from losing his job when chronic absences fueled by rum, late nights out with the ladies, and cocaine rendered his contributions to the enterprise minimal, at best. He'd been unemployed almost four months now, and his severely disappointed parents had made it clear when they wired the latest batch of funds that he was about to be dumped from the gravy train for good. He didn't want to go back to LA, where he'd be just another ordinary looking guy with no money and no pull, in a town brimming with better. In Brazil, the girls found him novel, exotic, and rich. Back home, he was just another loser.

"That's Wilhelm now," Jason said as they looked off the balcony at the rider pulling up in front of the building below.

Rick test-rode the motorcycle around the block. It was a little loud, but it didn't appear to be burning or leaking oil, and it ran okay. The seat had a small rip, and it was missing the cover for the battery compartment, but it was more than suitable for Rick's purposes. He didn't plan on needing it beyond the day.

"I'll take it," he said as he pulled six hundred dollars from his pocket and handed it to the smiling German, who gave him an envelope with the title and registration.

"I never been stopped here in two years riding, but..," said Wilhelm with a shrug of his shoulders. "The tank is almost full. And I always carry that extra gas can tied on the back. It is full, too. Many times I go out of gas in the back country. Petrol stations are not plentiful here. So be careful. Good Luck."

Rick shook hands with both men and rode the mile and a half back to the hotel, waiting for Radar and the girls to return. He double-checked his revolver, a cheap Colt .25 caliber with a wooden grip and a filled down hammer for no-snag removal from your front pants pocket, to make sure it was loaded and ready. He'd threatened and pistol-whipped Lieutenant Bantam with the gun the day before, but he'd only fired it once, back in Norfolk

"Did you miss me?" Renata said as they kissed when she entered the room.

"You know it. Did you guys have fun?"

"Yes. Teddy is very entertaining. He was telling us all about the snow and wind in Chicago, and his mother and his sisters, and all the places you have traveled to on your ship."

"Sounds more fun than Carnival."

"Fuck you," Radar said as they all laughed. "Did you buy the bike?"

"Yeah. We'll have to go for a spin later today."

"Well, Renata and Daisy said they want to go to the university this afternoon," Radar replied. "Why don't we go for a ride when they leave?"

The girls left at 2:00 PM, Jimmy and Rick soon thereafter. Rick drove while Radar kept up a steady stream of chatter, commenting on almost every person and car they passed. They headed out of town on a main road going East for about ten miles, then turned North on a dirt road leading further into the country, then East on an even rougher dirt road. Both the weather and the scenery were beautiful, and the homes and people were getting more scarce with each passing mile. Soon they saw no one, just an occasional small home in the distance.

"Wanna drive?" Rick asked as he pulled to the side of the road.

"Hell yeah. I'll show you how it's done."

Despite his brash talk, Radar was a careful rider, taking care to avoid the deep ruts that were becoming more prevalent the further into the backwoods they went. After several more milles along a lengthy straight stretch of road with no buildings, people, or livestock in sight, Rick told Radar to pull over so they could stretch their legs for a minute.

Radar kneeled down to pull the pack of Marlboro out of his sock, a habit many military men develop since regulations forbid the carrying of cigarettes in shirt pockets, when Patterson stuck the pistol to the back of his head and pulled the trigger. The shot seemed much louder than Rick had recalled from the time he'd test-fired the weapon. Radar immediately fell in a heap, seemingly dead before he hit the ground. Rick fired another round into his head from point blank range, to make sure, then removed everything from his dead friend's pockets. He placed his own wallet in Radar's jeans pocket, along with a few of his own keys on a ring. When the body was discovered, the keys – if still intact – would open all of Rick Patterson's personal lockers aboard the Fitz. He drug Radar's body into the brush in a culvert on the side of the road, and also placed a partial piece of canvas, which he singed around its edges, torn from one of the Fitz's stenciled cash bags, near the body. Then he poured most of the two-gallon can of gas onto Jimmy Petarsky's lifeless body, and watched it explode into flames as he lit it on fire.

The ride back to town was uneventful. He saw not a soul until reaching the paved highway, and nobody there seemed to give him a second glance. The girls hadn't returned from their outing by the time Rick finished packing. He wrote them a note, explaining that he and Radar had been called back to their merchant ship, and left them five-hundred dollars for the trip back home.

Jason Metter was surprised when Rick turned up at his door.

"Looks like my buddy and the girls decided to ditch me. Wanna split somewhere else for a few days...North of here, maybe? I'm anxious to see a little bit more of Brazil, anyway."

"I'd love to, but I'm dead broke. Remember?"

"No problem. You've got the car and the Portuguese language skills, and I've got the cash and the charm. Between us, we'll be knockin' 'em dead. Whaddaya say?"

Jason smiled as he replied, "I say let me pack a bag and let's blow this popsicle stand. I know where there's a bitchin' horse ranch community up in the mountains, about a day's drive North. The babes are everywhere. You'll love it."

Chapter Twelve
October 9th, 2010

It'd been a long time since Janine Estrada had last been on a date. And to this point in the evening, it hadn't disappointed. She didn't usually go for older men -- he was fifteen years her senior -- but he was also charming and worldly, very attentive, and a great dancer.

"Where did you learn to salsa like that?"

"I used to live in South America. Brazil for a little while, then Panama for quite a long time. I guess the natives rubbed-off on me. Not bad, huh?"

"So that's where you learned to speak Spanish so well. I guess I owe those South American ladies a debt of gratitude. I haven't had this much fun in quite a while."

"*Nos acaba de empezar, mi amor!*"

Janine felt goosebumps run up her spine as her date lightly brushed his hand on her thigh while nipping at her earlobe. They were on their third round of drinks, and she was feeling that giddy buzz that comes when you've consumed just the right amount of alcohol in the company of an attractive and willing potential partner. She hadn't been intimate with a man in more than five years, and the notion was making her tingle.

"I'm glad you were so persistent about asking me out, Mark. I wasn't so sure when we first met at Bally's. I always thought that guys who come on to women at the gym are kinda creepy, you know? But you're not like that at all. You're a real gentleman. And you were so good with Cece this evening. She loved that card trick you showed her."

"Well, I do love kids. As a matter of fact, one of my few regrets is that I never had any myself."

Janine excused herself and went to the ladies room. *Michael's* was little more than a dive, but it had a decent-sized dance floor, and the weekend DJ was known to sprinkle a liberal assortment of Latin-themed songs into his play-list for a friendly, mature crowd of mixed ethnicity.

She freshened her lipstick then stood back and smoothed out the wrinkles in her dress, with a sigh. She'd been working her ass off the past few months at the gym, and had lost twenty-five pounds since May. But she knew there was still a long way to go. Size sixteen was an improvement, but her long term goal was to be a size eight again, as she'd been before Celia was born six years earlier. It was just so damn hard getting there. After Benny had left them for good while Celia was still just a baby, Janine ate more junk food and sweets than was good for her. She knew she should watch it. Her mom and a sister had struggled with obesity most of their lives. But it seemed like the weight just snuck up on her so quick. One day she was tipping the scales at just under one-forty, well-distributed on her five-foot-six inch frame, and the next thing she knew she was a couple of Krispy Kreme crullers shy of two-hundred, wondering what'd hit her. Why was it so ridiculously easy to get fat, but a brutal struggle to get skinny? Such an unjust world. God had a cruel sense of humor sometimes.

While Janine was freshening up in the ladies room, the man she knew as Mark Bell -- whose real name was Rick Patterson -- was likewise busy back at their table. He'd ordered another round, and discretely mixed a small amount of fine white powder from a skinny vial into Janine's rum and coke. He smiled as he spotted her approaching the table, sliding the drink over to her part of their table.

"I took the liberty of getting us another round. What should we drink to?"

"How about to a wonderful evening?" Janine said as she hoisted her glass, clinked with her date's, and took a big sip. "I know I'm having a good time."

"Me too," Rick said as he slid his arm around her shoulders and began tenderly running his fingers through her thick dark hair.

"Let's dance," she said excitedly as Eric Clapton's "Wonderful Tonight" began playing while every couple in the place rushed onto the floor.

By the end of the song, the two were locked in a tight embrace, slowly and firmly grinding their hips together, kissing, completely oblivious to everyone else in the bar. Janine giggled like a schoolgirl as Patterson led her back to their table while many of their fellow bar patrons smiled as they shuffled past.

"Let's finish our drinks and get out of here," Patterson suggested as they sat back down at their table.

"Some privacy does sound good right about now," Janine replied as she took a another big sip. Within minutes, they were headed out the door. And as soon as they'd shut the doors on Rick's five year old Ford Ranger pick-up, they practically devoured each other in passion.

"Where are we going?" Janine asked as Rick started the truck and began driving out of the parking lot. She was beginning to feel a bit woozy, and her voice sounded kind of strange in her own ears all of a sudden.

"Well, we can't go to my place. My roommate is at home tonight, and I really don't feel all that comfortable there yet. But there's gotta be a motel around here somewhere."

The Blue Star Motel was less than a mile. By closing time that night, the place would be full, as would most every motel on Saturday night in America. But for now, there were still plenty of vacancies. They parked six feet in front of the door to their ground-floor room, and Janine leaned heavily on her date's shoulder as she wobbled into the room unsteadily.

"I'm not feelin' so great," she slurred as she belly-flopped down on the bed, just before rolling over on her back and going out cold, a dollop of spittle already starting to form in a corner of her mouth.

Rick didn't care much for fat chicks. He preferred skinny. But the combination of alcohol and the kissing had him a little revved up in spite of his tastes. He debated while gazing down at her ample form. It was one thing to do a fat girl. But doing one that was comatose seemed an especially unappealing prospect. Besides, he had work to do.

He went through Janine's purse and pulled out her keyring and a small bottle of Scope brand mouthwash. Then he washed his face, rinsed out his mouth, and drove the five miles to the Prime Choice Properties office building. It was located only half a block from a significant thoroughfare, but sat off by itself about fifty yards from a small suite of professional offices, with a small thicket of woods to its rear. Rick parked in the back, put on a pair of surgical gloves, and entered through a side door. He'd previously cased the building, picking up some flyers in the lobby during a time when he knew that Janine was at lunch and Marty was out of the office. He'd seen that there was no alarm system to worry about. It only took him two tries to select the right key from the dozen she carried on her ring, and he felt the familiar jolt of adrenaline as he opened the door.

Once inside, he closed all the blinds, and used a small penlight as he searched through the file cabinets and desk drawers in Marty's personal office. He found the letter he'd sent, along with the picture of Faith tied-up on the bed, tucked away behind the last folder in a desk drawer that was three-quarters filled with files containing bank statements and financial records. Rick pulled the picture aside and placed the envelope and letter he'd sent into his jacket pocket. Then he placed the picture of Marty and Faith into a fresh blank envelope, along with the turtle necklace he'd snatched from Faith's lifeless body so long ago, and placed the new envelope in one of the thick folders amongst some old bank statements.

Continuing his search of Marty's desk drawers, he came across the microcassette recorder. He listened to the cassette it contained, and chuckled as he realized it was a poor-quality recording of the conversation they'd had in Waterton Canyon two days before. Their words were barely audible. Marty had probably had the device taped to his body or something. Rick put the cassette in his pocket, and pulled a blank tape from a package of six that were in the same drawer, and placed it into the machine. It really didn't matter much if Marty discovered the missing tape, or even the switched envelopes. Rick had additional copies of the photograph. And even if Stillwell had duplicate copies of the recording he'd made -- which was doubtful -- it would likely be seen by law enforcement as a feeble attempt to deflect blame. It wouldn't be taken seriously. Rick Patterson was long ago confirmed officially dead, after all.

After completing the search, Rick pondered his next move as he drove back to the Blue Star Motel. He'd had to leave Panama in a hurry, fleeing for his life from some very bad men, with little more than the clothes on his back and a few thousand greenbacks in his pocket. He'd been living hand-to-mouth for the five months since his return to the U.S., surviving on the occasional back-room card game and petty thievery, mostly. Pickings were slim when you had to work on your own, without back-up, and had to maintain a low profile to boot. The Panamanians had reach, and more than a few connections in the U.S. Plus he didn't want to risk being recognized for his true identity from some chance encounter with a former shipmate, as remote as that possibility had become after all these years. He needed money, and Stillwell had some. It'd been pure dumb luck to see Marty's face on a Home For Sale sign in Denver while casing a neighborhood for potential burglary targets. Like many vain real estate agents, Stillwell was using a picture from his younger days. Otherwise, Rick may have never recognized him in the first place, especially given the different last name.

In an ideal scenario, he'd take at least fifty K -- hopefully more -- from Stillwell, then watch from the sidelines as his old buddy went off to prison for a murder he didn't commit. That would be perfecto. Stillwell had always thought he was smarter than everyone else. And he *had* done well for himself, Rick had to admit. But he probably wouldn't feel so high and mighty, locked up in the penitentiary with all the other scumbags.

The trick now was to make sure he got his money before Stillwell was completely wiped out by the government and the lawyers. But Rick wasn't too worried. He could apply pressure in ways the government wouldn't. Nothing like the threat of physical violence to a man's family to heighten his sense of priority. That was the thing about people who cared about others. Stillwell would have to cough up. He was smart enough to understand the dynamics.

No Faith in Justice

Loading Janine into the truck was a letdown after the elation he'd felt while rummaging through Stillwell's private belongings. He threw some cold water in her face and finally managed to shake her awake enough to get her up and walking unsteadily, leaning heavily against his shoulder, and strapped into the passenger's seat. When he got her home, he paid off the sitter -- a geeky-looking high school-aged girl with thick glasses and stringy brown hair who lived a couple doors down from Janine's apartment -- then got his date into her bed before falling out himself, exhausted, on the couch.

Cece woke him up four hours later by turning on the TV. Rick hadn't watched any cartoons in English for many years, and he rather enjoyed the Sunday morning Nickelodeon line-up that was mesmerizing Janine's six-year old daughter.

By the time Janine crawled out of bed at noon, befuddled and mortified at her total lack of memory about a huge portion of the previous night, Rick had already taken Cece to Denny's for a big breakfast, and had a duplicate office key made at True Value in case he wanted to return to Stillwell's place of business in the future.

"I can't believe I got so drunk last night. I've never had a blackout like that in my entire life. I've always been able to handle my liquor better than almost anyone I know. I just don't understand it."

"Don't worry. It happens to the best of us now and then. You didn't do anything to be ashamed of or embarrassed about. Maybe you had a touch of a twenty-four hour flu-bug or something that was triggered by the booze. Or maybe they poured one of your drinks from a bad batch of rum. Or it could be that you're just not a kid anymore. You were mixing some

157

really stout drinks from that bottle I had in the truck, after we left the club...remember?"

"You know, I was feeling a little nauseous earlier in the day yesterday. Maybe I do have some kind of bug working its way through my system. Are you sure I didn't do anything to be embarrassed about?"

"Trust me. You were a real lady. A little wobbly at the end, maybe, but overall it was a great first date."

"Thank you so much for looking after Cece this morning, Mark. I was out like a log. I'm still feeling a little groggy. But I hope we can see each other again soon. Next time I'll stay away from the rum."

Rick smiled broadly as he replied, "I can't wait to do it again."

Chapter Thirteen
October 02nd, 1980

It began when Deanna Sherman walked into his office not long after he returned to work, and found him with his head on the desk, trying to hide the tears in his eyes. Nick never knew when it would start. It sometimes came out of the blue. Other times, a random mention of a spouse by one of his colleagues, a sappy greeting card card displayed on someone's desk, or a framed photograph of a happy family would serve as a trigger. Even though he was looking for the exits before her suicide, he'd cared deeply for Carla, and had hoped to remain friends for the rest of their lives. He missed her.

He also bore the added burden of shame as a disloyal spouse. He'd failed her as a husband, as a friend, and as a protector. On a rational level, he knew it was impossible to stop someone intent on harming themselves. It was Carla's decision alone to do what she did. The ultimate selfish choice. But in a much deeper part of his psyche, he understood that her act of desperation had wounded him in a way from which he would never fully recover.

"I swore an oath of loyalty to her for life," he'd said to Deanna. "Then when the going got tough, I wanted to quit on her. What kind of a chickenshit asshole tries to back out of a sworn covenant with someone he claims to love?"

Being in a similar age group, and younger than most of the people associated with NIS, Deanna and her husband Steve had naturally socialized with Nick and Carla on a couple occasions. They weren't close, but they liked each other. After witnessing the depth of the pain and distress in her friend first-hand, Deanna grew concerned. She wanted to help. So that

Saturday, she dropped in on Nick unannounced, intending to try and get him out of the apartment for awhile, back into the world of the living. Steve had been assigned to take over for Nick on the Bantam investigation, and was still in Brazil attempting to track down Jimmy Petarsky. When she arrived at Nick's place, she realized he was in the process of moving out. Her timing was good. She helped him pack up boxes and haul them to his new place, a townhouse near the beach. She also helped him go through Carla's things, separating items that her mother and sister might want in the way of remembrance from a box intended for donation to Goodwill. By the end of the day, they were tired and hungry, and decided to pick up a twelve pack and a large pizza. They sat on the floor of the new townhouse and talked and ate and drank.

"So how is everything going for you, work-wise?", asked Nick. "We haven't talked in awhile."

Deanna had begun as a secretary at NIS shortly after marrying Steve, who was almost ten years her senior, six months before. She was twenty-one, and her previous work experience was mostly menial customer service work. She'd finished a course of study in Business Administration at Jacksonville Community College just the previous December.

"Dealing with asshole co-workers beats hassles with asshole customers. There wasn't much I could do at the restaurant, other than accidentally sneeze on the food, or finger the drinks. But I can always figure out a way to get back at a jerk I work with. And I don't just get even...I get ahead. So don't forget that, buster."

"Remind me to be nicer to my waitresses from now on, too."

"If you only knew. But seriously, I finally feel like a grown-up. Married. Career in civil service. Am I too young for all this?"

"You're smart. Civil service is the way to go. It nearly takes an act of congress to fire us. And with NIS, there's never any shortage of dumb sailors who break the law. That's what I call job security."

They gossiped about co-workers, and argued over movies. She loved "On Golden Pond," but he thought "Stripes" was the better film by far. Deanna was irreverent, funny, opinionated, and very attractive. Her eyes were a deep sparkling blue, and her fair skin made for a lovely contrast. Her father, whom she adored, had been a career enlisted man. A salty old seadog who loved to tell tall tales and racy stories. She'd inherited his wicked sense of humor.

As the night wore on, and the beer and the conversation continued to flow, they both began to sense where the evening was headed. Their eyes held steady. Their legs gently touched. The pressure went up as they firmly pressed them against each other. A few moments later, they embraced the inevitable with an overwhelming passion and intensity, and threw themselves head-long into the pleasures of the moment with a reckless abandon.

The next morning, Deanna arose and went home early in anticipation of the usual Sunday morning phone call from her husband. International telephone rates were exorbitant, and they'd decided to limit their personal conversations to once per week, each Sunday during Steve's time in Brazil. The call wasn't one of their most pleasant. Steve seemed distracted, anxious to get off the phone and start on his work for the day. Deanna could sense his lack of interest in conversation. Or was it projection? Either way, she went back to help Nick finish his move, knowing full well how the day would end, again. She didn't try to resist the temptation. She didn't even consider it. She wanted it to happen again. They made love all afternoon.

Later that night, after she'd left Nick's place and gone home to sleep in her own bed so she could get up and get ready for work the next morning, Deanna was surprised when Steve called again.

"I didn't feel right after we talked earlier," Steve said. "I was distracted, I guess. Anyway, I want to make sure you know how much I love you. You're the most important person in the world to me, Deanna. And I can't wait to be with you again."

She was delighted. And wracked with guilt over her betrayal. She confronted Nick in his office Monday morning, her face distraught, eyes red and moist.

"I'm sorry, Nick. But I feel terrible about what we did."

"Terrible?"

"Even though I didn't do a very good job of showing it, I love Steve with all my heart. I'm his *wife*. I made a vow, like you said before, and I broke it. It can't happen again. I won't allow it to happen again. I hope you understand. I care about you, and I'd like us to be friends. But that's all we can ever be from here on out."

"Of course. I understand how you must feel. Steve's a good man. It was a mistake, that's all. We weren't thinking clearly, and we made a mistake. Let's just put it behind us, and pretend it never happened."

Though heartbroken, Nick was a gentleman. He never mentioned a single word of the affair to another living soul. During subsequent years, he and Steve and Deanna were assigned to the same unit on two different occasions, including the last four years together in the Norfolk office, from which Steve had retired a few years earlier.

No Faith in Justice

Nick knew in his heart that Deanna was the perfect woman for him. She still took his breath away, even after all this time. But he also knew he would never have her, barring the premature death of her husband. As luck would have it, Steve was a fitness and nutrition enthusiast, healthy as a horse. It would probably take a random accident to hasten his demise, and the odds against that were staggering. He'd occasionally fantasized about helping that process along, but that was just fantasy. He could never actually do anything like that. Probably.

In the meantime, Nick gradually became more and more isolated over the years. There'd been a series of forgettable lady-friends throughout his thirties and forties, but none could hold a candle to Deanna, and he wasn't about to make another mistake like the one he'd made with Carla. Eventually, the periods in between girlfriends became longer, and the shelf-life of the fleeting relationships grew shorter. By the time he went to Denver to investigate the Faith Cooper case, it'd been three years since his last date. And there were no good prospects anywhere on his horizons. Maybe that ship had already sailed, forever.

Chapter Fourteen
October 13th, 2010

Nick Maynard had been warned about Jill Tolliver, the U.S. Attorney in charge of the District of Colorado federal prosecutor's office. "She's got big plans, if you know what I mean," FBI Agent Miguel Herrera had said. "We call her 'The Senator' around here. If you take her a case that makes her look good in the press, you're golden. But if you do anything, no matter how small or unintentional, that can in any way even remotely reflect poorly on her public image in any way - watch out. She won't hesitate to rip your balls off and stuff 'em down your throat." So he'd double and triple checked the Mahoney file, and his notes, before sending them over for review.

"I'm going to see Judge Heyward for your search warrants before lunch. I don't see any problem, given the DNA match. And the fraud case is a slam-dunk, besides. How did you get those test results so quickly, by the way? Less than a week? We can't seem to get anything back in less than three months around here."

"I guess the sample we provided was good enough quality to make it a straight-forward process. And we had enough money in our cold-case budget to use a contractor lab to do the testing."

Tolliver nodded her head in reply, and went back to re-reading the case notes. After several minutes of reading, she closed the folder and pushed her chair back from her desk. "I hate these old cases. Lots of attention from the media whores, but too many potential pitfalls and surprises. And I don't like surprises, Maynard. I don't like surprises at all. Have you talked with the Virginia District prosecutors?"

"My boss did. I was told they'd be happy to take the lead on the prosecution, but figured you'd be in a better position to...influence the suspect since the fraud case happened here in your jurisdiction. Plus his assets are here. Mostly real estate holdings, but some cash, too."

Tolliver glanced up at the ceiling for a moment, then exhaled deeply and fixed her ice-green stare on Maynard. He'd seen eyes like hers before on many occasions. The eyes of a predator.

"Okay. See what you can find at his home and his office this afternoon, then talk to the victim's family. I understand there's a sister? Get her reaction to a deal that would send this character away for eight years. We can probably get an agreement for eight, considering the fact that I could easily get close to that sentence on the fraudulent scholarship alone. But we don't want to get her hopes too high. If she doesn't balk at the idea of eight years, then we have a baseline for negotiation, anyway. Explain how difficult it is to prosecute a case this old. The DNA only proves he was with the victim sometime the day before she was killed. There's still no motive, and no witnesses. Juries love DNA, but it would be a real crapshoot at this point. Probably a loser. Tell her eight is better than none."

"You want me to email you, or your assistant, after I talk with the sister?"

"Call my assistant. I don't like emails. And don't imply that I'm endorsing an eight year recommendation. Just float it as a hypothetical. I want to know if she's going to create any problems for us when the time comes to work out an agreement. Does he have an attorney yet?"

"Not yet. But I suspect that'll change after we execute the warrants. I'll call your assistant as soon as I know who he retains."

Chapter Fifteen
January 27th, 1981

Marty Stillwell felt so good he wanted to scream. He settled for a fist-pump and a big grin as he watched the military van drive away after dropping him near the bus stop directly outside Gate #5 at the Norfolk Naval Operating Base. It'd been more than four months since he'd last breathed air as a free man. And he aimed to enjoy himself for a day before using the Trailways bus ticket the Navy had provided as transportation back to his home of record, after telling him repeatedly that they were under no obligation to do so, given his status as a BCD low-life scumbag. Uncle Sugar's small way of saying "no hard feelings." They were probably hoping he wouldn't spread too much public ill-will, and make recruiting efforts more difficult for them than they already were. The all-volunteer Navy was kinder and gentler than the old draft-era Navy. *We even give our shitbirds bus tickets home.* He flagged down a taxi, and watched as the driver loaded his seabag into the trunk.

It was only a few minutes past 1000, or 10:00 AM as they say in the civilian world he'd officially re-entered, per the DD-214 he'd signed earlier that morning. But he knew a place nearby that was open and served cold beer and toasted submarine sandwiches - perfect for a day like this one. By the time he awoke the following morning in the Econo-Lodge on Little Creek Boulevard, he was $93 poorer, massively hungover, and ready to put Norfolk, and the Navy, in the rear-view mirror for good.

Fortunately, he still had a decent chunk of cash. He'd sold his car before the Fitz deployed for South America, and he'd left all his pay on the books during the cruise while living off poker winnings. Even after the heavy fines and the bust *"awarded"* at the Special Court-martial, he still managed to leave the brig with almost $1600 in cash. It was enough to tide him over until he could get home and land a job.

His mother was less than thrilled when he showed up on her doorstep in Liberty Missouri three days later, exhausted from a grueling and tedious bus trip.

"How long do you plan on staying?" she said soon after he'd put his seabag away in the basement, next to a large box of personal belongings he'd mailed home prior to getting underway for South America seven months before.

"Only as long as I have to, Mom. I'll be looking for a job and an apartment starting tomorrow."

His new accommodations consisted of a well-worn sofa, also in the basement, which served as the guest bed now that his old bedroom had been turned into an office.

After sleeping in until almost noon the next day, he found the Kansas City Star newspaper, conveniently opened to the "Help Wanted" section of the classifieds, on the kitchen table. She'd even circled some of the more promising leads. Within a week, she was also circling ads in the "Roommates Wanted" and "Apartments for Rent" sections. Subtlety was not high on his mother's list of priorities. She'd seen her middle-son struggle with substance abuse problems and petty criminal activities for much of his young life. She'd done her sincere best to help, to no avail, and it was now up to him to figure it all out as best as he could, on his own. Her primary concern was her youngest son, Lee, who was doing well in junior high school and rarely gave her any trouble. She was determined not to let anyone's past mistakes create any further collateral damage in the family.

No Faith in Justice

Marty bought a faded brown '73 Ford LTD with a torn and tattered white landau top for $450, and began working at a local convenience mart. He also moved in with two old party-hardy buddies from high school who were renting a house in the nearby city of Independence - former home of the late Harry Truman. Within three months time, he'd been arrested twice: Once for DWI after wrecking the LTD into a tree, and once for Drunk and Disorderly; fired from two different jobs; and finally asked to leave the shared residence after a drunken brawl over a girl one of his roommates mistakenly believed was his private stock. Marty's drinking was getting progressively more out of control, and it was likely only a matter of time before he either got himself killed, or killed someone else.

His Aunt Millie summed his situation up aptly upon bailing him out of jail after his latest arrest.

"Marty, you have the smarts and potential be anything you want to be, but potential isn't worth squat if you don't do something with it.

"You're a high school dropout, been kicked out of the military, have zero career prospects, and you're a chronic drunk, all before the ripe old age of twenty-one. Don't you think it might be time to make a few changes?"

He knew she was right. She wasn't the first person he respected who'd told him as much, straight-up. He'd thought of little else since being locked up in the brig. Yet he'd gone right back to his same old ways after release.

Something had to change, or he knew he was destined for a short, misery-filled life. He decided right then and there to do his best to quit drinking, and stop using drugs, for good. In order to have any shot at succeeding, he'd have to change his habits, his surroundings, and the company he kept.

The next morning, a genuinely contrite Marty accompanied his mother to Sunday services at the First Baptist Church of Liberty. His motives weren't entirely pure, however. He still knew how to manipulate and appease his mother. The simple act of attendance would buy him a little more time at home while he planned his next move. But his willingness to surrender a Sunday morning in return for a few weeks room and board proved unnecessary in the end. The morning's paper provided hope of an alternative solution via one especially promising ad for a painter at Green Village Apartments, a large complex in Kansas City, Kansas, where his older sister Hollie once lived a few years back. He gave her a call.

"Oh yeah, I still know the managers at Green Village. I see one of them, Mike Hartley, just about every Thursday in a pool league we're in together. He likes me, even though my team wails on his crew pretty regularly. He's always teasing me about my dimples, the jackass. You want me to give him a call for you?"

"That'd be great, sis. But I've decided to stop using the name Stillwell. Things haven't exactly worked out for me with that name. I'm giving myself a fresh start, going back to Mahoney. And that's the name that's on my social security card, anyway."

"That's great. I never thought much of the name Stillwell anyway, as you know. I'll let you know what Mike says about the job."

By that afternoon Marty had been hired. It was only fifty cents over minimum wage to start, but the job came with a heavily discounted apartment that included utilities, and he wouldn't need a car since they used golf carts to motor around the complex. And it was far enough away from the friends he grew up with that he could avoid some of the typical pitfalls that come with being young while attempting to clean up your life.

He was all set up in his new place two days later. The one-bedroom unit was small, but well-kept and clean. His mom gave him the old basement sofa and some dishes and silverware, and Aunt Millie pitched in some linens and a card table with folding chairs for the kitchen. The Salvation Army offered the other items he needed - TV, bed, cookware, etc., for less than $200 total. It wasn't exactly the Taj Mahal, but it would do.

Among the items he'd mailed home from Norfolk prior to his last deployment was a stolen VCR acquired in trade for a bag of weed. Family Discount Video was half a block away, and a well-stocked public library was only five blocks further from the apartment complex. So he quickly settled into a new routine centered around work, most of which was accomplished solo, reading, exercise, and movies. It was a boring and often lonely existence, but not unhealthy. It gave him time, and a legitimate opportunity to focus on turning his life around. He grew a little stronger and more self-confident each day.

Marty quickly became a regular at Family Discount Video. It was owned and operated by Bill and Suzy Reynolds, a jovial, good-natured married couple in their mid-fifties. Both had twisted senses of humor, and Bill was a big movie buff who loved to talk films.

"Charles Bronson again? He makes more or less the same movie over and over again, don't you think? If revenge fantasy is what you're in the mood for, you should try '*Straw Dogs*' or '*Carrie*' or even '*I Spit on Your Grave.*' All three are more interesting than watching 'Death Wish' for what, like the third time?"

"Sixth time at least if you include the times it ran at the Twin drive-in back in the day. Of course, I wasn't exactly paying attention to the screen by the third feature, if you know what I mean. Kinda hard to see a movie from the prone position in the back seat."

"Do tell...Who was the lucky guy?"

"Very funny, Reynolds. I would say 'ask your wife', but I have way too much respect for Suzy to ever imply anything so rude, crude, and socially unacceptable about her."

"You can take me to the drive-in anytime you want, sweet-cheeks," Suzy said loudly from the back of the store where she was busy re-stocking returned videos. "I've been lookin' to trade up for about twenty-five years now."

"The old bat can hear like one, too," Bill said to Marty in a hushed tone out of the side of his mouth.

"Bill just called you an old bat, Suzy."

"He'll pay for it later," she replied as she strolled back up to the counter. "You know, they say most fatal electrocutions occur inside the home, usually to the man of the house. Isn't that tragic? Fortunately, the old coot has a ton of life insurance. I would imagine it's just as easy to grieve in Hawaii as anywhere else. Ever been to Maui, Marty?"

"Just remember, Mahoney," said Bill. "You better do the job right the first time. I might be getting a little long in the tooth, but I'll never be too old to kick your little narrow behind."

Marty felt at ease with the Reynolds, and they developed a bond. They often let him take extra videos at no charge. Then they hired him to re-paint the store overnight one Friday, over-paying him for the simple chore. He arrived for the job in his standard work clothes - painter's whites, as his dad had always worn, and a USS Fitzpatrick baseball cap.

"Where the hell'd you get that hat?" asked Bill.

"I bought it at the ship's store. Why?"

"Holy shit, I didn't know you were a swabbie, Mahoney. Why didn't you ever mention it?"

"I don't know. Never came up, I guess. Why do you care?"

"Because I was in that canoe club for twenty-two years, you little knucklehead. Retired as a Senior Chief Quartermaster, almost fifteen years ago. What rating were you?"

"Signalman. Just like Jack Nicholson in '*The Last Detail*'. You know – 'Bad-Ass Badusky'.*"*

"No shit. Skivvy waiver, huh? I can't believe it. Marty Mahoney was a skivvy-wavin' tin-can sailor, just like 'Bad-Ass Badusky'. I knew there had to be *some* redeeming quality to explain why we like you. Wait till I tell Suzy. She'll shit a brick. She's always sayin' how much she misses bein' around Navy people. When did you get out?"

"Little less than a year ago."

"What were you...third class, or did you make second? SM was wide open for makin rate when I was in."

Marty hesitated for a split second. Should he tell his new friend the truth, that he'd been court-martialed, busted to Seaman Recruit, and kicked out with a BCD? In an instant, he decided instead to lie. Not because he was ashamed. He wasn't, really. He'd essentially told his family and childhood friends the truth about the circumstances of his separation from service, minus the mention of his former buddies acts of robbery and murder, which he honestly had no involvement or prior knowledge about, anyway. But he instinctively understood that if he told Bill Reynolds how his service had ended, a man who'd spent twenty-two years of his life serving proudly, a former Senior Chief Petty Officer, that he would be extremely disappointed, at the very least. And he didn't want to let his new friend down in that way. He seemed so excited to learn about their newly-discovered shared experience.

"Third class. I only did a three-year enlistment. It was one of those 'pilot programs' the brass is always trying as a way to get more suckers to sign up for critical ratings. Most of my less fortunate friends had to pull four-year hitches...losers."

"So you never even considered shipping over?"

"Naw, not really. I liked being at sea, and I loved standing watch underway on the signal bridge, and all the great liberty ports we hit. But three or four section duty in port, quarterdeck watches, and all the bullshit inspections got to me. Plus I really couldn't see myself ever hanging out in the goat locker with all you lard-ass lifers."

"Well, it was a good enough career for 'Bad Ass Badusky' and me. But it ain't for everybody. At least you did your time. That's more than many can say."

The mild twinge of guilty conscience he felt at Bill's last remark wasn't sharp enough to compel him to correct the record. It was already too late for that. A seemingly harmless lie between friends engaged in casual conversation was now in place between them for good. And the repercussions would eventually prove far-reaching.

The Reynolds soon became like family to Marty. He was a regular at their home for weekly dinners, and he began working some evening and weekend shifts at the store, routinely closing up and occasionally opening when not painting. The extra income allowed him to buy another car. Then one day, Bill suffered a heart attack while getting ready for bed, and underwent an emergency bypass procedure – a fairly new and not so common practice. His recovery would take awhile, and the doctor recommended no work or stress for at least three months. Suzy wasn't about to leave Bill alone for any extended period upon his release. Their youngest kid, Bill Jr, came home from Charleston, South Carolina where he was attending college at Charleston Southern University, to help with the video store.

"I can go full-time at the store, too, if you need, Suzy," Marty said. "I'll have to start paying full price for rent if I quit painting at Village Green, but that won't be a problem as long as I can get at least forty hours."

Suzy clasped Marty's forearm and attempted a smile while choking back tears for a moment.

"We've been thinking about asking you on as a salaried assistant manager for a while now. We only hesitated because Bill was concerned about letting business interfere with our friendship. I told him we're all level-headed enough to make it work. We could start you at eight-hundred fifty a month, with a salary review after the first six months. What do you think?"

$850 was $150 more than he was making as a painter, which would more than make up for the difference in rent. Plus he actually had a little set aside since he'd been picking up the part-time hours at the store.

"Sounds like a plan to me," Marty said as extended his hand, which Suzy brushed aside as she hugged him tightly instead.

Marty began making some changes at the store almost immediately. He'd always had a good head for figures, and he enjoyed analyzing profit margins, and reading and learning about various business concepts. While thinking through the trade-offs inherent in different scenarios, he concluded the most effective way to increase store profits was to spend less time trying to squeeze down expenses, and instead focus more on tactics intended to increase your sales volume. So he instituted a customer loyalty program, spent a little more on targeted marketing via discount mailer ads to local zip codes, and expanded their offerings to include some under-served niche segments such as foreign films and hunting & fishing nature videos, in an attempt to capture trade from the clientèle of adjacent merchants like the Bohemian Bean Coffee Shop and Hunter Joe's Sportsman's Supply Club.

By the time Bill returned to work full-time, Family Discount Video had increased monthly sales by almost 30%, with only a small concomitant increase in operating costs.

"I guess I oughta have heart attacks more often," Bill said as he and Suzy reviewed the monthly Income Statement.

"I've been saying as much for years," Suzy replied. "Marty has really done a wonderful job, hasn't he?"

"Yeah. I'm thinking we should show our gratitude with a raise and a big fat bonus. What do you think?"

"We should offer to send him to school. We discussed it before Bill Junior went back to Charleston, and he told me they don't even offer the G.I. Bill anymore. That boy's too smart not to go to college."

"Yeah, they canceled the G.I. Bill in '76, I think. Now they just have some rip-off deal called VEAP, or something like that. But I like your idea. Instead of a bonus, let's offer him a hundred dollar raise and paid tuition for some business classes at one of the local community colleges."

Though appreciative, Marty wasn't crazy about the idea at first. But after some mild yet persistent nagging from Suzy, who'd made sure all three of their kids attended university in spite of the fact that neither she nor Bill had ever so much as finished high school, he gave in and enrolled in a business program at Penn Valley Community College.

He met Melissa Kelly in Introduction to Business class. They were assigned to the same four-person team, tasked with collectively crafting and presenting a business plan for a hypothetical start-up company to a mock group of prospective investors. By the end of the term, Melissa had learned two things in the class: One – she had no interest in business, or in attending college; Two – she was going to marry Marty Mahoney.

At nineteen, Melissa had enrolled at Penn Valley because she couldn't think of a better way to get her parents off her back. Although reasonably intelligent, she'd been only a so-so student in high school, where she rarely applied herself. Her dad was a successful real estate entrepreneur who ran his own firm -- Kelly and Associates Realty -- and her mom was an executive in the finance division at Hallmark. They were both driven, highly ambitious people who were often frustrated by their only child's seeming indifference for tangible achievement.

Melissa was a late-bloomer, more shy and awkward in adolescence than most. But she grew to become a beautiful girl, and a decent athlete who preferred individual sports, such as track and tennis, over team-centered competition. She never-the-less had not so much as a date, much less a boyfriend, until senior year. She didn't know it, but her mom had also been a late-bloomer, who was well-known throughout Hallmark, and her parents' social circles, as a rare and confident beauty. The first time Marty Mahoney met Melissa's mom, he couldn't help but remember an old adage he'd learned from some old salt during his time in the Navy: "If you want to know what your girlfriend is going to look like in twenty years, check out her mother." A thrilling prospect, indeed.

Marty took charge of their group's class project when it became apparent that his three teammates weren't nearly as interested as he was in the task at hand. Apparently, PVCC wasn't exactly drawing the cream of the local academic crop. As the term progressed, he sensed that Melissa was interested in him, and he certainly reciprocated, but he'd been uncharacteristically slow to make a play. Sobriety had made him a little less bold than he'd been in the past. Without the booze as a crutch, he was substantially more risk-averse. What if he were mis-reading her signals? He didn't want to go down in flames in front of his classmates.

Then one Friday afternoon near the end of the semester, he showed up for work only to find Melissa at the counter engaged in conversation with his boss, Bill Reynolds.

"Well speak of the devil, look what the cat drug in," Bill said as Marty tried to contain his surprise. "I was just telling Melissa here what a great guy you are. I only hope the Lord doesn't strike me dead for lying."

"Hi Marty. I hope you don't mind, but I just thought I'd come in for some movie advice. I think I've already seen all the good flicks from the Blockbuster in my neighborhood. Any suggestions?"

"Of course. Mahoney's the name, and videos are my game. Allow me," he replied as he extended his bent arm and escorted her back to the 'Employee Favorites' section of the store. After helping her select several titles, he offered to check them out gratis under his own account.

"In that case, the least I can do is invite you over to watch them with me. How about tomorrow night? My parents are going downtown for a charity auction and ball. They usually end up staying at the hotel after all that champagne. But they won't mind if I have company, even if they do decide to come home early."

"Sounds intriguing. Count me in." Marty tried to sound nonchalant, but his voice caught in his throat a little as he replied. She wrote down her phone number and address, and left the store with a smile of relief on her face. She'd taken a big risk, and it had worked.

"Holy shit, Mahoney. Nice work," Bill said admiringly as he patted Marty on the shoulder. "I really did put in a good word for you. I told her what a hard worker you are, and how you served your country honorably in the Navy and all. She said her dad is a Korean War Marine Corps vet, so she really liked that you served, too. I'm surprised you hadn't told her yourself already."

Now the harmless little lie between friends had expanded to the girl who would later become his wife. He'd never set out to deceive her, but he didn't have the moral fiber, or the courage, to set the record straight, either.

Seven months after Marty and Melissa's first date, Bill Reynolds suffered a stroke. He and Suzy sold their business and moved to South Carolina to be nearer Suzy's sisters. Family Discount Video became part of the Blockbuster chain. The Reynolds gave Marty three months salary as a severance bonus, which he used to support himself while completing the courses and certification process necessary to become a licensed real estate agent.

He began work at his future father-in-law's firm, and was made partner a few years later, shortly after Melissa gave birth to their first child, Katie. The firm's insurance agent requested a copy of his DD-214 when his name went on the corporate ownership documents, in order to provide the veteran's discount on the premiums, and fortunately he still had several blank forms amongst his personal effects sent home before the court-martial. He knew how to create a passable forgery, did so, and tried to forget the matter as best he could. The ruse wasn't really hurting anyone, he rationalized. Just a formality. And it wasn't like he was making himself out a hero or anything.

He would later use the same forged document to run for office in the American Legion Post, after he and Melissa moved to Denver and began their own firm during the real estate boom of the mid-90's. And that would eventually lead to a Legion-sponsored college scholarship for his eldest daughter.

What had begun as only a harmless little lie had snowballed into something much, much bigger. And the consequences would be severe.

Chapter Sixteen
October 13th, 2010

At just after 2:00 PM, Nick Maynard led a team of four Air Force OSI investigators, borrowed from Buckley Air Force Base in Aurora, to execute the search warrant on Marty Mahoney's residence. Meanwhile, Miguel Herrera led two junior FBI colleagues in a simultaneous search on the offices at Prime Choice Properties.

"Oh my God," Janine Estrada exclaimed as the three FBI agents burst through the door, handed her copies of the warrant, and began searching the file cabinets in Marty's office, placing some files in cardboard boxes. "I need to call Mister Mahoney. He's been out sick for the last few days."

"You can call anyone you like, ma'am, just do it from the parking lot," Miguel said. "We should be finished in here in an hour or so."

Janine was completely flummoxed, but still had enough good sense to refuse comment to the Channel Six News reporter who'd been tipped off to the raid by Jill Tolliver, as an off-the-record source, of course. Federal search warrants executed against a local real estate firm was a newsworthy item in Denver, and the story would quickly be picked up by the local print press as well.

Janine called her boss, but Marty Mahoney wasn't answering his phone at that moment. He was instead sitting on his brand new custom-made couch, holding his own copy of a search warrant, wearing only a pair of sweatpants and flip-flops, bleary-eyed and hungover from a wicked bender that was now going on its fifth day. He watched as Nick Maynard and four goons in polo shirts ripped his house apart looking for God knows what. He hadn't showered or shaved in three days, and hadn't eaten a proper meal in four, but was in too much pain to care at the moment.

"You look like you've been shot at and missed, and shit at and hit, Mahoney," Maynard quipped during one pass through the great room. "Rough night?"

Marty ignored his antagonist. He was in no mood for banter. Not only had he been rudely roused from his stupor by the feds hammering at his front door, threatening to bash it in, he also hadn't seen his wife since she packed a suitcase and left the previous Sunday afternoon. She'd demanded to know why he'd suddenly begun drinking after nearly three decades of sobriety, and he'd finally come clean about his past indiscretions, and current predicament.

He told her about the court-martial. The Bad Conduct Discharge. How he'd forged the DD-214 when her father's insurance agent had asked for a copy. How he'd also used the forgery to run for the American Legion Post position, which led to the fraudulent basis for Katie's scholarship. And that the NCIS was looking at him for an old murder case, even though he'd had nothing to do with it. He left out the part about about being blackmailed by a dead man. Not because he wanted to hide it from her. But because he didn't want her to think he'd gone insane. It was just too incredible a scenario for anyone else to believe.

To say that the information hadn't been well-received would be a gross understatement. He'd seen Melissa's temper a few times over the years, but he'd never seen her this deeply enraged. Her sense of betrayal and disgust was so profound, it was beyond words. She'd not spoken, nor even glanced at Marty as she gathered her things and left their home. What he needed right now was another drink. Twenty-eight years was a long time dry. And he was suddenly very thirsty.

By the time the agents finished ransacking his home and his office, taking boxes of files and all the computers, Marty Mahoney had already begun the process of accepting the inevitable. He knew he was out of business, his marriage was probably over, and he was going to jail. Until that very moment, he'd still hung on to a sliver of hope that he could somehow wiggle out of this pickle. That he could find some way to save himself, and make it all go away. But he knew that was just a pipe-dream. The only question was how long his sentence would be. A couple years for fraud, maybe, or the rest of his life for murder. He stared at the glass of Jack Daniels he'd poured for himself immediately after Maynard and his crew had departed. Then he carried it into the kitchen and dumped it into the sink. That small act made him feel better, so he did the same with the bottle. *Alcohol abuse,* he thought to himself, and smiled. He went to the fridge and pulled out some lunch-meat. Nothing like a ham and cheese sandwich and a glass of cold milk to lift the spirits. Thirty minutes later he was clean-shaven, freshly showered, feeling almost human again, and working on his second cup of coffee.

He dialed Melissa and left her a message.

"You can come back to the house, if you want. I'm leaving this evening. The police took the computers, Kelly's desktop too, and some of my files. Tell the girls I'm sorry, and I'll talk with them soon. Kelly saw me at my worst Monday night. I hope she can forgive me. And you, too. I'm really sorry...for everything. Anyway, I'll let you know where I'm staying as soon as I get settled. We'll have to talk soon, and figure out where we're going from here."

After packing a suitcase, he stopped at a nearby Staples store and purchased a cheap laptop. He hated conducting web-based business on his iPhone. His reading glasses never seemed to be where he last put them, and the small screen was just too hard on his eyes for any length of time.

The first order of business once he got to the office was to contact his two remaining employees, and advise them that the firm was going under. Given the negative publicity from the local news reports, they both knew it was coming, anyway. Jason Kulak had been working with Marty as a salesman for a decade. He had many contacts in the business, and would have no trouble landing on his feet. He was a capable and highly regarded professional, which is precisely why he'd survived to be the last man standing while the firm downsized during the market crash.

Janine Estrada, on the other hand, had only been with the firm five months. She was headed back into a lousy job market, with few prospects. Marty felt bad for Janine, but he'd gladly trade problems with her. After breaking the bad news over the phone, he immediately drafted a glowing letter of endorsement that he knew would lift her spirits. He decided to hold off emailing it to her, however, until he'd checked all the office accounts. He'd do that on-line.

Next he emailed the fourteen clients who presently had properties listed with the firm, regretfully advising them that Prime Choice Properties was suspending operations for the foreseeable future. He'd be happy to provide recommendations for other agencies, if anyone were interested in his thoughts on the matter. He wondered how many lawsuits would be filed against him.

No Faith in Justice

Now it was time to conduct a thorough assessment of his financial status. He owned three homes, all of which were mortgaged for at least seventy percent of their estimated present value. The two rental homes he'd re-financed during the previous year when the rates had dropped, and they'd only lived in their current residence for three years. Even if he could sell all three homes right now -- an unlikely event in the current market -- he'd cash out a hundred-grand total, at best, and probably something closer to fifty-grand. He did own his office building free and clear, fortunately, but the commercial market was even more saturated than the residential. The building was forty years old, and it was situated off the main drag, giving it less appeal to businesses that rely on street traffic. He'd be lucky to get eighty-grand for it, if it would even sell.

His business checking account showed a current cash balance of $11,943.17, which was about what he expected to find. He immediately emailed the bank, advising them that Janine Estrada would no longer be conducting business on behalf of the firm.

The first big surprise came when he checked his mutual-fund investment account with Vanguard. His IRA account appeared to be in order, with a balance of $34,755. But a separate joint account he'd set up with a 500-index fund and a medical firm fund had been drawn down dramatically two days prior, on Monday. The combined balance on the accounts had gone from $107,982 to $10,000. Marty felt a chill ripple through his spine as he realized what Melissa had done. He'd betrayed her trust, and she was now looking out for her own interests. A check of their joint personal checking and savings accounts at the same local bank that managed his business account revealed a similar story. She'd left him with a total of just over

$60,000 – including the IRA and business checking account – while taking almost $250,000 for herself. And she would undoubtedly expect him to continue paying all of the bills while liquidating the remainder of their assets, in addition to the lawyer bills for his legal woes to come. All without any income.

Marty was dismayed. He'd never even considered that Melissa might raid the accounts without letting him know. Now it was his turn to feel the sting of betrayal. It'd been many years since he'd last felt any pinch on his financial status. Even with Melissa and the girls spending lavishly, he'd been bringing in more than outlays for quite a few years before the crisis. Even with the crash, they hadn't really needed the scholarship Katie had won. Her college fund was sufficient to handle most of the costs, and he could've easily swung the rest. But she'd really wanted to win the relatively insignificant three thousand dollar annual scholarship she'd been receiving for each of the past four years, and now it was going to cost him everything. If she'd never entered and won, which was of course covered as a human-interest tidbit in the local newspapers, Maynard would probably have never found out about the fraudulent DD-214 in the first place.

Of course, the real truth was he had only himself to blame. He'd set the stage for this disaster with his own duplicity. He'd only joined the Legion to help establish a foothold in the local real estate market, and to give himself an excuse to get away from Melissa and the kids now and again. In all his years as a member, he'd only gotten two listings from other members, both of which were priced too high by the seller. Neither ever sold. Not only had he not made a dime, he'd lost both time and money in the bargain.

No Faith in Justice

He sat and stared at his computer screen for a long time. What was coming next? Could things really get any worse? *Rhetorical question*, he thought. He already knew the answer. And they undoubtedly would. One thing for sure, his life was going to be very different from now on.

After sitting for what seemed like hours, numb, unmoving and staring straight ahead, he was suddenly overcome with a an overwhelming sense of fatigue. He flipped off the lights, laid down on the leather couch in his office, and immediately fell into a deep sleep.

He awoke with a start several hours later in the middle of the night, wondering for a moment where he was. He sat up, rubbed his eyes, and looked around the room. He was suddenly terrified to see a dark figure of a man standing just to the left of the office door. He sprung off the couch in the direction away from the man, toward the windows, as the shadowy figure reached over and flipped on the lights.

"*Motherfucker!*" Marty shouted as he realized the identity of the intruder. "What the hell are you doing here?"

"Calm down, Matilda," Rick Patterson replied as he held up his hands, palms out. "Man, you're really getting jumpy in your old age. Bad dream?"

Marty's heart was pounding. He glared at Patterson, fists clenched at his sides. He could feel the adrenaline coursing through his body. He glanced at his desk, considering how much damage he could do with the lamp, or the heavy three-hole punch. He wished he'd brought his pistol when he left the house.

Patterson knew what he was thinking. "Don't even think about it, cupcake," he said as he reached his right hand into his jacket pocket and pulled out a nickel-plated snubnose .38

187

caliber revolver of his own. "You'd be dead before you made it to the desk. Now sit down and behave yourself, and nobody gets hurt...tonight, anyway."

Marty's rage began to subside a little as his instincts for self-preservation kicked in high gear. "All right, but put the gun away first."

Patterson put the pistol back into his jacket pocket and motioned to the couch, where Marty sat down.

"How'd you get in here?"

"You didn't push the door all the way shut, moron. Shoulda used the deadbolt. All I had to do was put a little force against it with my shoulder and it opened right up. When I saw the ten o'clock news report about your police problems, I drove past and saw your car in the parking lot. I figured you were probably in the doghouse with the old lady. Bit of a bad luck streak I guess, huh?"

"My bad luck began the day I met you, Patterson. I just had a thirty year reprieve while you were spreading your joy all over South America."

"If I didn't know better, I'd think you aren't really all that happy to see me."

"Very perceptive. And you should probably think about going back to South America, by the way. The economy here stinks. And you blew any chance of extorting any cash outta me. My wife already beat you to the punch. Between her and whatever the lawyers are gonna bleed me for, there won't be anything left. You jumped off too quickly this time, Patterson. You ruined me before I could pay off. How did you put NCIS on my tail, anyway? Anonymous letter?"

Marty's blatant attempt to get information made Patterson smile. "You know I don't like to reveal my methods. And I'm not buying your 'I'm broke' routine, either. I know you own property. And you probably have some secret accounts your old lady doesn't know about, big time real estate mogul like you. You can come up with some cash if you want to. And I know a few ways to make you want to."

"I'm already going to jail for fraud. And they've got my DNA, which I'm sure matches whatever they took from Faith when she was killed. Which means they can already prove I had a relationship with her. Whatever pictures you have of me and her together won't tell them anything they don't already know. I'm pretty much screwed already. You should've given me a chance to pay before sicking the cops on me."

It was Patterson's turn to glare. The truth was, he knew that Marty was right. He'd given away his leverage too quickly. He hadn't realized that Faith's sister could get NCIS going so quickly on Marty's trail. He hadn't even mentioned Marty's name during their only conversation. He'd been planning to make a subsequent call to Joy Barry, and he would have brought Marty's name up as if he'd just remembered him as a former spurned boyfriend of Faith's. But the NCIS agents assigned to the case were better than he'd anticipated. The ones he'd dealt with when he was in the Navy were pathetic. They must've improved their hiring and training over the years.

Still, he was getting desperately low on funds. Nobody seemed to want to play cards for money anymore. All the easy marks did their gambling at the casinos, dumping money like zombies into slot machines. He had a couple of other schemes in mind as possibilities, but none as lucrative as he'd hoped Mahoney would be. And not nearly as much fun, either.

"If you think I don't have other means to exert pressure, you're not thinking clearly. See, the difference between you and me is that you're a family man, now. So I believe that even if you'd be hard-pressed to come up with some money in your present circumstances, you would figure something out if it was the only way to make sure your kids stayed safe."

Marty could feel the adrenaline rushing through his body once again, as the rage began to build anew. He locked his eyes on Patterson's and communicated his hatred without a word. In the back of his mind he'd wondered if it would eventually come to this, that Patterson would stoop so low as to blatantly threaten to harm innocent family members. But he'd done his best to dismiss those thoughts until this moment. The prospect had been too horrifying. A man who'd committed multiple murders -- one of them his own best friend -- was now making an overt threat of violence against his little girls.

"You might as well kill me now, motherfucker. Because if you don't, I'm going to kill you the moment I get the chance."

Patterson pulled his pistol out of his pocket again, and stared back at Marty. There was nothing in his dark eyes. Nothing at all.

"That's big talk for a guy with a gun in his face. You're lucky I'm a forgiving person. But there's a limit to my kindness. I want a down payment on that fifty grand you owe me by next Monday. Fifteen thousand dollars. That's a small price to pay, considering your alternatives. I'm sure a resourceful gent such as yourself can figure out a way to swing it. That's chump-change for a guy with your assets."

Marty wasn't going to say anther word. He had only one thought, and he'd already expressed it as powerfully as he knew how.

"I'll be in touch, Mahoney. Monday. Don't fuck with me on this. Don't even think about it. There's no reason for anyone to be stupid. Just get the money, and then you can focus on your legal problems, without any worries about the people you love. And don't even think about calling the cops right now. I think somebody may have cut the phone line to the building. I couldn't get a dial tone on the receptionist phone when I tried it before you woke up. So I'll need to borrow your cell for a few days." With that, Patterson picked up Marty's iphone from his desk, and walked calmly out of the building and disappeared into a small section of woods adjacent to a nearby apartment complex.

Marty picked up his desk phone. Sure enough, the line was dead. But he didn't trust the police, anyway. He knew what had to be done. And he was going to figure out some way to do it, if it was the last thing he ever did.

He opened his desk drawer and pulled out the microcassette recorder. He rewound the tape that was in it, and pressed 'Play'. Nothing. He fast-forwarded and stopped in several different places. It was blank. He did the same with every other tape in the drawer. None of them contained the recording he'd made of Patterson in the canyon. Had Patterson swiped the tape before he woke up? Had Marty misplaced it somehow? Nothing was going right. This was the worst streak of bad luck he'd ever had in his life. Maybe karma had been saving up for a few decades, and was dumping on him all at once. He wondered what the final tab would be.

Chapter Seventeen
October 14th, 2010

"You've got big problems, my friend," George Turnbow, attorney-at-law, said to Marty Mahoney after reading the search warrant, and listening to his prospective new client describe the events of recent days. "You should've contacted me the minute the NCIS agent first approached you. In the future, never, ever talk with the cops without an attorney present. Always a bad move. Especially with the feds."

"Got it."

"Based on what you've told me so far, and the fact that the warrant authorized a search of your financial records and computers, I wouldn't be surprised if their next move is to file a lien against your properties, and put a freeze all your financial accounts. They often do in these types of cases. They'll justify the liens by claiming that they want to ensure that the people who've been defrauded out of the scholarship funds have access to adequate recompense in the future. And they'll argue they need time to review all your property transactions for more potential fraud, and violations of the federal code."

"But you'll be countering their arguments, right?"

Turnbow hesitated before answering. "If I agree to take your case, then yes - of course. But first we need to address the matter of my retainer. I'll need a cashier's check for ten-thousand dollars delivered here before five PM today. And that's just for starters. If they decide to charge you with murder, the fees will be significantly greater if you want an adequate defense. You'll be looking at six figures easily, if that happens. Do you have any family that can assist, in the event your assets do get frozen?"

No Faith in Justice

"Not really." The conversation was unfolding about how Marty had expected. He understood the priorities of lawyers. Just like real estate agents, first and foremost - they wanted to get paid. He'd been referred to Turnbow by a former colleague, Dale Turner, who used to be in the real estate business. Turnbow had gotten Dale out of a serious drug trafficking charge for which he'd been facing a significant jail sentence. Dale had raved about his skills, but he'd warned Marty that his services were very expensive, and that he was a bit of a hard-ass.

"Very well, then. Bring the check, then set an appointment with my assistant so we can discuss all the alternatives and start mapping out a strategy," Turnbow said as he stood up and extended his hand, a signal that their brief conversation was over. Marty would have to return with some money if he wanted any more of his time. It was just past noon, and he went straight to his bank in Englewood.

He knew what had happened before the flustered teller could excuse herself. Several minutes later, she returned and asked him to accompany her to the manager's office.

"I'm very sorry, Mr. Mahoney," said the middle-aged woman named Catherine something or other, who'd introduced herself as the branch manager. "But the federal government has placed a hold on all your accounts, business and personal. We can't allow you access to any of the funds without a court order. It happened this morning, and we mailed letters of notification to your home and business addresses already."

"You could've called. I've been banking here for fifteen years."

"We have to be extra careful in sensitive matters like these. We prefer written correspondence over telephone conversations. We need an official record of communications. Again, we're very sorry for this trouble. But there isn't much we can do about it."

He drove back to the office and got on-line to check his Vanguard IRA and investment accounts, only to discover his access had been suspended. He didn't need to call them to find out why. He was screwed, and he knew it. He dialed Melissa's cell. Voicemail.

"It's me. I had to buy a new phone. I need to speak with you as soon as possible. It's extremely urgent. Call me back at this number as soon as you get this message."

He hadn't spoken to her since discovering her raid on their accounts the prior evening. He was trying to keep his anger in check. He'd been deceiving her all these years, after all. And he knew his best bet was to reason with her, and appeal to her better nature, even though he wanted to strangle her. He decided to go by the house and confront her face-to-face.

When he arrived at the house, he was mildly annoyed to find that his garage door opener didn't work. Bad battery, maybe. So he went to the front door, but when his key didn't work either, he knew what had happened. "*Godammit!*" he hissed out loud. Melissa was a woman scorned, and she was striking back at him in every way she could. He pushed the doorbell repeatedly for several minutes, until the door finally opened to reveal a sleepy-eyed Kelly.

"Dad!" she said excitedly, embracing him tightly. "I've been worried about you. You never answer my texts. What the hell is going on with you and Mom and the police? She won't tell me anything."

"It's a long story, honey. Is she here?"

"No. It's Thursday. She's got Pilates, I think. But I doubt she'll talk to you, anyway. She says she's filing for divorce, and she had all the locks and stuff changed this morning. You have to tell me what happened, Dad. You kept saying 'I didn't kill anybody' when I saw you Monday night. I've never seen you drunk like that before. Me and Katie are worried sick about all of this mess. Why did the cops search our house, and take our computers? Do they really think you killed somebody?"

"I'm sorry you saw me in that condition, Kell. But I don't want you or your sister to worry over this mess. I'm not gonna drink anymore. Everything is going to work out fine, now. I didn't kill anyone. But I did lie to your mom and your grandpa Kelly, and to the Legion about my military status. The truth is, I got kicked out of the Navy for drugs and some other minor offenses thirty years ago, and I was ashamed of myself. I was just a stupid kid. I did some really dumb things. And even though I served for more than two years honorably before getting into trouble, and completely turned my life around after my time in the service, it was wrong for me to lie about my situation. And since Katie qualified to compete for that scholarship based on my lies, the feds are calling that fraud."

Kelly looked puzzled. "Okay...but where does murder fit into any of that? Why did you keep telling me you didn't kill anybody?"

Marty took a deep breath. May as well get it all out in the open now. "Before I got booted from the Navy, I was running with a pretty rough crowd. Unfortunately, I think one of the guys I roomed with might've killed a girl we knew, and NCIS is looking at me on that case because they were never able to solve it. But I didn't have anything to do with it, so there's nothing to worry about. I may have to pay a big fine, and maybe serve a little time for fraud over the scholarship deal, but that'll be it. Everything will be okay. I promise."

"Oh, Dad...I just...It doesn't seem real. I can't believe this is happening. I haven't been able to sleep for days. I'm exhausted. You and Mom...Jail?" It was bad enough seeing one of your daughters cry. But when you know it's your own malfeasance that's causing her pain, and that there will likely be much more to come, the hurt is excruciating. He didn't dare speak as he embraced her tightly. Didn't want to sob, himself. Just held her there on the doorstep for several minutes, until her crying began to subside.

"Everything will work out, honey. It may look bleak right now, but we'll all be fine. Trust me. You and Katie will be okay. I promise."

Kelly tried her best to smile, but couldn't quite pull it off.

"Well, I'm gonna go try and catch your mom when her class lets out. Don't call her. I don't want her getting spooked. It's urgent that I speak with her. And I misplaced my phone, too, so I have a new number. Go get a pen so you can write it down. I want you to call me anytime you need anything. And tell your sister to call too."

He was waiting in his car when his wife emerged from the gym. As he watched her lithe figure glide gracefully through the strip-mall parking lot towards her car, he was suddenly hit with a sharp sting of regret and loss. The beautiful woman who'd been by his side for so long was lost to him now, forever. He'd never win her back, no matter what he did. He'd blown it. She wasn't his any more. And he would never get over it.

"Hey *Melissa*," he called out as he approached her. "We need to talk."

The look she gave him was pure contempt. She was disgusted with the man she'd once loved, and she had no intention of hiding her feelings. Marty had seen others receive "The Sicilian" treatment over the years. It was his turn in the barrel, now.

"It's over, Marty. There's nothing to talk about. I don't trust you. I don't want to be with you anymore. I'm meeting with a divorce lawyer tomorrow morning. She'll do all the talking for me from here on out, as far as you and I are concerned."

"Is that who told you to take all that money out of our accounts? Your lawyer?"

"No, actually that was someone else's suggestion. And I didn't take all of it. I left you some cash, and you can keep whatever you make from selling our properties. I think that's more than fair, considering your treachery. I just want our business together finished as soon as feasible."

"Whose suggestion was it, then?"

Melissa hesitated for a moment. "It was Bob Ellis, if you must know. He's been very helpful since I found out about all your lying and criminal activity. He suggested I protect myself in case the government comes after our assets. I don't want to be left with nothing after twenty-eight years, Marty."

"Bob Ellis?...Bob Ellis?...You've gotta be shittin' me, Melissa. Bob fucking Ellis? He's a high school Social Studies teacher, for Chrissake. What the fuck does he know about anything?"

"He's Vice-Principal now, and he knows plenty. He has a Master's degree, you know. He did a lot of research, and he has friends in government and the legal profession. I didn't know who else to turn to, with Dad gone. And thank God he was spared from all this, by the way. It would have broken his heart. He loved you like a son, Marty. Anyway, I'm very grateful to Bob for all his advice and assistance."

"Grateful? And just how do you think Bob expects you to demonstrate that gratitude, huh Melissa?"

"You're the one who's in the wrong here, Marty. Don't you *dare* try to turn this back on me. You're the one who repeatedly lied to me and the girls for our entire lives together. You chose to make us unwitting parties to your schemes. Think of the shame Katie and Kelly are experiencing, and all that's going to come. We did nothing to deserve this mess you've made for us. *Nothing.* You've destroyed our marriage and our family with your deceit, and now you're leading us to financial ruin as well. So don't you *dare*..." Melissa's voice choked, and tears welled up in her eyes.

Marty looked at his shoes, ashamed. Every word she'd spoken was true. He was solely responsible for this mess. She hadn't done anything wrong. But he was in desperate need of a lawyer. And he needed cash now to get a good one.

"You're right, Melissa. That was just jealousy getting the better of me. I'm sorry. This is all on me. And I intend to accept full responsibility for the things I've done, and try to insulate you and the girls as much as I possibly can. But they're trying to railroad me for a murder that I swear I had *nothing* to do with! And I need some money for a lawyer, fast. But they put a lien on the accounts after you made those withdrawals, and I can't get to any of the cash that's left. I need your help...*please*."

Melissa wiped the tears off her cheeks. "So Bob was right after all. They are coming after our assets. Thank God I listened to him."

No Faith in Justice

"All I need is ten thousand for the lawyer, plus enough to cover a bail bondsman if they arrest me. Will you help me? I'm the one who earned that money, after all."

As he watched the look in her eyes change quickly from hurt to anger, he knew he'd said the wrong thing. "You'll be hearing from my lawyer soon. And if you come anywhere near me or the house again until I move out, you can add a restraining order to your long list of legal problems. Goodbye, Marty."

Marty was placed under arrest ten minutes later when he pulled into his real estate office's parking lot. The charges were forgery and fraud. Nick Maynard smirked while snapping the handcuffs on his wrists as FBI special agent Miguel Estrada stood by, ready to assist.

Not a word was spoken as the trio made the short drive to the Federal Correctional Institution in nearby Littleton. Maynard sat in the back with Marty while Estrada drove. He turned on the radio while sitting at a red light a few miles from the prison. An oldies station was running its daily tribute to The King: *Elvis in the Afternoon*, they called it.

"My daddy was a green-eyed mountain jack"...he crooned. *At least it's not Jailhouse Rock,* Marty thought as they drove on to the jail.

"Not nearly as nice as your Daniels Park digs," Maynard said as they walked from the parking lot to the main entrance of the facility.

A moment later, as they walked through the door, Marty looked at Maynard and said "Elvis in the Afternoon...what a crock. Like there aren't a couple hundred better oldie singers who deserve some air-time. Elvis is wildly over-rated if you ask me. Not to mention a narc for Richard Nixon, of all people."

Chapter Eighteen
October 18th, 2010

"You know the drill," Nick Maynard said to Marty Mahoney. "Kill some trees first, then we can talk." Marty nodded and quickly scrawled his signature on the now-familiar rights waiver form. The two men were sitting in an interview room at the Federal Correction Institution in Littleton, Colorado.

"So, how are the accommodations?"

"Can I check out right now if not satisfied?"

"Sorry. No refunds, and no early checkouts."

"My arraignment is scheduled for the twenty-first. But I don't have a lawyer yet, since you guys locked up all my bank accounts, so I'll probably be here for awhile."

"Maybe a lot longer than you think. Might as well get used to being locked up, Mahoney. You're on the federal prosecutor's radar screen now. And as dirty as you are...you're going down, one way or the other. Johnny Cochran couldn't save your ass, God rest his soul. You can be sure of that."

"C'mon, Maynard. You guys can't be all that concerned about a rinky-dink scholarship lark, with all the murder and mayhem you have to worry about every day. Don't you have bigger fish to fry?"

"Like I told you before, I don't give two shits about your pathetic little scholarship scam. I'm interested in the Faith Cooper killing. But we can use the forgery and fraud beefs to lock your ass up, while we take our time and build the murder case, which -- by the way -- is strong enough to charge on right now, even if we don't ever get anything else.

"You're looking at a maximum sentence of twenty years for the fraud charge alone. Facing that kind of weight, you better start thinking about cutting a deal on all the charges if you ever want to see your family again without a wall of glass between you."

"Twenty years? Over a few lousy dollars worth of scholarship money? That's bullshit! They'd never go that far over something so minor."

Maynard shook his head in disbelief. "Are you really that stupid, Mahoney? This isn't some cheesy TV drama, where the bad guy gets off over some ridiculous technicality. This is the real world. Don't you read the news? Last year the feds in Arizona got a woman locked up for five years for lying about her address on a school enrollment form, in order to get her daughter into a better public school. Think about that. A loving mother simply trying to get her kid a better education, and she gets five years hard time for her trouble. And you think they're gonna take it easy on someone as sleazy as you, profiting off a fraudulent military career while true heroes are fighting and dying for this country? You're going up against the U.S. Government. We literally print our own money, dipshit. And we hire bloodsucking lawyers by the boatload. The prosecutor's going to squash you like a bug, and then laugh about it with her buddies over drinks and sushi afterwards. I'm sure as hell glad I'm not you, boy, cause your shit is ragged."

Neither man spoke as the words of the seasoned investigator sent cold shivers up Marty's spine. Twenty years? Could that really be true? The look in Maynard's eyes said it all. Marty could see the disgust, but there was also a glimmer of pity. He really was in some deep kimshee this time.

"What if I could help you out on more murder cases? Would that get me out of this jam?"

"More?"

"Yeah. The Bantam case. Petarsky. Maybe Faith Cooper, too."

"You know where Jimmy Petarsky is?"

"No. Petarsky's dead. I'm talking about Patterson. Rick Patterson. He lived with me and Petarsky in that apartment. I was the only one who signed the lease, which is why that investigator only called me. But Patterson was there, and he met Faith, too. And you know he killed Bantam, for sure."

"Nice try, Mahoney. But you got it backwards. Patterson is dead. Probably killed by Petarsky. I saw his burnt remains myself. The keys found on him matched Patterson's locker. And his identity was confirmed by the Navy Medical Examiners in Norfolk."

Marty locked eyes with Maynard, and held his gaze steady before replying.

"Patterson must've switched the dental x-rays and doctored the records to match. He had access, you know. After he told the Striker-Board he wanted to strike for corpsman, Doc used to let him work in sickbay once in awhile when little-doc was on leave, or when something big was going on, like flu-shots for the crew or something. You can ask anybody who knew him aboard the Fitz at that time. Everybody used to joke that Doc better have a big-ass lock on the drug cabinet whenever Patterson was around, otherwise there wouldn't be anything left for the sick people. Anyway, I think he planned the whole thing out in advance, switched the x-rays, then killed Petarsky so you guys would forever be looking for a ghost."

Maynard sat silently, an incredulous smirk his only reply. Mahoney continued, undeterred.

"I'm telling you right here and now, as God is my witness, I spoke to Rick Patterson in person on two separate occasions in the past two weeks. He's very much alive, and he's blackmailing me over the Faith Cooper case, threatening to provide you guys with information and more evidence that would implicate me in her murder. He probably already has, for all I know. Why else would you guys at NCIS have suddenly started looking at me in a case that cold, after all these years? I'll bet you got an anonymous letter pointing towards me...or a phone call, didn't you?"

The smirk faded, and Maynard remained silent for a few more moments, thinking, before he replied.

"I gotta hand it to you, Mahoney. You certainly are full of surprises. But this goes beyond the pale, even for a world-class liar like you. Do you honestly think you can convince me that your drug-addled little buddy was actually a criminal mastermind and world-class forger, who killed Faith Cooper, then faked his own death, fooling the medical examiners in the process, and subsequently eluded capture for decades? You would've been better off blaming the Cooper murder on your pal Jimmy Petarsky, instead. At least in that story, you wouldn't have had to sell the absurd 'switched identity' idea."

"You're right. If I was trying to concoct a story to get myself off the hook, I would've gone with Petarsky as the culprit. But it's not a fabrication. It's the truth. I was stunned when I saw Patterson last week. When I got the blackmail note that set up the meeting in Waterton Canyon, I assumed it was actually from Petarsky. Just like you and everyone else on the Fitz, I thought Patterson was crispy-critter dead, and Petarsky was on the lam all these years."

"Do you still have the note?"

"I don't know. Maybe. It was in my windbreaker pocket when I met with Patterson, but I haven't worn it since. I got pretty drunk that same night, so...I'm not sure. Maybe it's still in the jacket. Or I might've inadvertently thrown it away, or my wife could've. Maybe your guys took it when you searched my house and hauled out all those papers.

"But it was signed with an alias that Patterson used that I know you're familiar with, because you mentioned it to me in our first interview that day after I saw you in the park: Peter Phoenix. Phoenix, as in 'arisen from the ashes.' That's the same name you asked me about. At the time, I couldn't make sense of how you'd know the name of my blackmailer. I even wondered if you could've sent the note yourself as some kind of ruse to get me to confess, or something. But once I found out it was Patterson, I realized he probably sent you guys a letter or made a phone call using that name to get you pointed towards me in the first place. Am I right?"

Maynard thought for a moment before replying. "You're only saying this because I mentioned the name Phoenix to you myself. You're simply a desperate man, taking a stab with the only thing at hand. But it won't work, Mahoney. Even if you could produce a note, it wouldn't prove anything. It would just look like what it is...a feeble attempt to deflect blame.

"The truth is, we have your DNA recovered from the victim. A photo of you with the victim obviously involved in some kinky kind of S&M escapades, conveniently date and time stamped the same night she was killed - gotta love those old Minoltas. And also the original investigator's notes, that document your denial of knowing the victim - a blatant lie.

"We also have a necklace that we recovered from your office desk drawer which appears to be an exact match for one worn by the victim in the aforementioned photo. A little memento, perhaps? That's more than enough to indict you for murder right now, if we wanted. We can establish opportunity. And we can establish the fact that you were an alcoholic drug abuser, who could've easily snapped while playing a sexual game with the victim.

"But Jill Tolliver -- that mean bitch federal prosecutor I mentioned before -- has decided to hold off on the Cooper case, for now. There will be plenty of time for that later. After all, there's no statute of limitations on murder. Instead, you'll be going to the federal penetentiary for fraud and forgery while we put every land transaction you've ever been involved with under a microscope, so we can tack on additional years for whatever obscure federal regulations you might've violated over the years. We're also going to freeze or seize every asset you own, and completely destroy your life. The local press will have you sounding more despicable than Bernie Madoff by the time we're finished. Unless..."

"Unless?"

"I'm not making any promises -- I don't speak for Tolliver -- but she's indicated to me that she might be wiling to negotiate a deal, if you'll plead to the Cooper killing. She might even be wiling to go for manslaughter. Either way, you're looking at roughly the same amount of jail time - perhaps even less for manslaughter, with a good recommendation for leniency. It's really just a matter of whether you want to have it all over and done with, and maybe retain a few assets for your family and the chance to see your future grandkids as a free man sometime down the road, or live with a first-degree murder charge hanging over your head while you rot in jail, stripped of everything you own, for the other felonies you've committed."

Marty was flabbergasted. "Un-fucking believable. So I'm better off admitting to a murder I didn't commit, rather than simply owning up to a few thousand dollars worth of fraud - the kind of charge connected people dodge every day in this country?"

"Sucks, huh? Guess my dad was right after all...Crime really doesn't pay, unless you're in politics. Then it pays very well indeed."

"He probably also said 'you can't fight city hall.' Doesn't seem like I have much of a choice."

"You're not really a stupid guy, Mahoney. You just do stupid things. A distinction without a difference, maybe. But you're smart enough to identify the trade-offs that work to your advantage. There's only one smart choice, and that's to play ball with the prosecutor. You'll make the wise move and plead. Your lawyer, when you get one, will help you see the light, especially since he stands a much better chance of actually getting paid under a plea deal that shelters some of your assets from forfeiture."

"American justice. Land of the free and home of the brave my ass. It's all rigged."

"Always has been, my friend. You aren't the first, and you won't be the last. Try not to take it personal."

Marty couldn't help himself from chuckling at that bit of gallows humor, even at his own expense. "Still, aren't you even mildly interested in getting the guy who in all likelihood really did kill Faith, and most certainly killed Petarsky and Lieutenant Bantam, and who knows how many others? Wouldn't a case like that make you a legend in the annals of NCIS investigative history? They'd probably name a building after you. Or maybe even a destroyer. Imagine...the USS Maynard. What would your dad think about that?"

It was Maynard's turn to chuckle. "Or, I could go down in infamy as the gullible idiot who went off on a wild-goose chase based on a cockamamie story from a suspect who was desperate to avoid prosecution."

"I'm willing to take a polygraph about Patterson. And if you test that necklace, you won't find any of my DNA because it was also planted in my office. I didn't even know it existed until just now when you told me about it. But Patterson must've kept it for all these years, as a memento, like you said, then planted it as part of his scheme to implicate me."

"Look, Mahoney. Before you keep on pressing this charade - get a lawyer. Your best-case scenario is take your lumps like a man, do your time, then put it all behind you. You might even get to have some input into where you jail. Persisting in this crazy story isn't going to help you. It's only going to muddy up the waters. Like you said before, polygraphs aren't really reliable. The lack of your DNA on the necklace proves nothing. And you got the Peter Phoenix name from me during the initial interview. Your story is just a story, and it's full of holes. Let it go and get on with it."

Marty held Maynard's gaze for several moments. "I probably will take a plea. The smart thing. Whatever's the easiest way ahead. That's my style. But I never figured you for that type. Allowing a killer to get off scot-free, because the truth is just too inconvenient."

Maynard picked up his notepad and the rights waiver form, put them in his briefcase, and walked out of the interview room without another word.

Chapter Nineteen
October 26th, 2010

Nick Maynard had already read every article of even remote interest in the Sports Illustrated he'd picked up at a newsstand that morning, and was now reduced to perusing stories about soccer and NASCAR as he waited in U.S. Attorney Jill Tolliver's office reception area. Her secretary had called him the day before and instructed him to be there at 10:00 AM, which had come and gone twenty minutes earlier. He was about to get up and leave when Tolliver finally opened her office at 10:23 AM, and beckoned him to enter.

"Sorry to keep you waiting so long. Have you had coffee?"

"I'm coffeed out, thanks," Nick said as he looked curiously at the young woman sitting across the desk from the prosecutor.

"This is Rita Zimmer from the Denver Post. Rita - special agent Nick Maynard from NCIS. Nick's the crack investigator who broke the Cooper case open."

Nick tried to hide his surprise as he shook hands with the young reporter and sat down. He had no idea there would be press at the meeting.

"I've already filled Rita in on the broad strokes of the case. She's going to do an exclusive feature story for Sunday's edition, if I can get the judge to put us on the docket for Friday afternoon."

"We're going on the docket already?"

"Oh, right. I forgot to tell you. Mahoney's attorney and I finalized an agreement yesterday afternoon. He's pleading to manslaughter, with a sentencing recommendation of eight years. In return, we're dropping the forgery and fraud charges conditional on restitution of all the scholarship money received by his daughter, plus an additional fifteen thousand dollar donation to the American Legion as a means of compensating them for the time this fiasco is taking away from their charitable work, and the deprivation of benefits caused to kids who actually deserved the scholarship."

"Have you already talked to the victim's sister, or should I follow up with her?"

"I called Mrs. Barry last night. She thought it over after you spoke with her earlier this month. She understands the difficulties we face, as you explained. The risks of taking a purely circumstantial case to a jury, with no motive or witnesses...She was willing to accept an eight year sentence recommendation as at least some measure of justice for Faith. It gives her closure, and proves that her sister wasn't completely forgotten by the system. She seemed relieved, frankly, at the idea of putting it all behind her.

"She was also naturally concerned that the defense would try and use the photo, along with the statements of the victim's co-workers, to paint her sister as some kind of promiscuous, kinky slut who liked to participate in S&M role play. They would have probably argued that her death could have easily been the result of a consensual encounter gone bad. I can't blame Mrs. Barry for wanting to keep those kinds of accusations out of the public eye. She's worried about protecting her sister's memory.

"By the way, that's all background, off the record stuff, Rita, so don't put that in your story. It's not true, anyway. It's just something the defense would say if we went to trial. We have to consider the feelings of the surviving family members."

"Of course. Don't worry. This is going to be a feel-good piece. We want to let people know about all the good work you're doing here, Jill." What Rita really wanted was a favor in her pocket from a powerful public official, not to mention an ambitious, potential future DC politician. Senators need PR reps with press experience, too, didn't they?

"Wow," said Nick. "This is great news. I guess I can make my reservation to fly back home now. I thought I was looking at weeks of the exciting task of poring over real estate transaction paperwork. Thanks for the reprieve, ma'am. I owe you one!"

"Don't make your travel plans until after court Friday."

"Let me get a few pictures of the two of you," Rita said as she reached for her camera carrying case. "My editor loves pictures. And I'd also like to get thirty minutes of your time before you fly out, if I could, Nick."

Nick glanced at Tolliver, who nodded slightly, "I'll give her your cell number when we're finished."

Several awkwardly posed photographs later, Nick left for his hotel, a happy man. He had at least four more days to kill in Colorado with little work to do other than reading a couple of new case files, and he'd made his request for waiver of the mandatory retirement rules a lot stronger with another closed cold-case. The positive PR from the newspaper story wouldn't hurt, either. He'd be sure to have Full-Throttle Tottel forward a copy of the article up to the SECNAV's office, too.

He decided to go for an early lunch at a Mexican joint he'd been eyeing near his hotel. He took a seat at the otherwise empty bar, and ordered a plate of fish tacos and a bottle of Budweiser. The TV behind the bar was tuned to a local news channel, and a pretty young lady was providing a brief overview on the stories of the day for her Denver-area viewers. The Colorado Senatorial campaign was a dead-heat, apparently. *Too bad they can't both lose.* Jill Tolliver would probably be running in the next election. She'd take full advantage of the opportunity for free PR from the Faith Cooper case. Nick didn't know which party she belonged to, but it didn't much matter to him. They were all jerks in his opinion. The lowest form of crass opportunists. Not much different from many of the criminals he pursued, just better educated and more cunning.

The next story was more up his alley. The desk anchor turned the broadcast over to another pretty young field correspondent named Lucy Sifuentes, who was standing in front of a small brick home that appeared to be a 50's-era style, with a low roof, a single car garage, and not enough windows.

Lucy Sifuentes: *Thanks Lauren. I'm in Arvada today talking to a local man with a very unusual past. William Weldman is seeking help from the public in solving a mystery that spans almost four decades, at least two states, and involves two different families - possibly more.*

It all started thirty-nine years ago, when three-year old William disappeared from his front yard here in this quiet neighborhood, while playing with his Tonka trucks near this old tree, as his mom went inside to fetch some Kool-Aid. She claims to have been inside the house less than five minutes, and frantically contacted police immediately when she came back outside and discovered William missing.

Police initiated a massive search effort, to no avail. No trace of little William or his kidnapper was found, although one neighbor reported seeing a strange blue station wagon cruising the area several times that morning just prior to the disappearance.

The grief-stricken family was completely devastated by the event for more than two years, and then a miracle happened.

211

Police called William's mom and told her they believed they had located her son, abandoned, in Topeka Kansas. A witness had seen the child being let out of a blue station wagon in a grocery store parking lot before it drove off. Police in Kansas remembered the William Weldman case, and after comparing photographs, they became convinced they had the right boy, who gave his name as Willard, seemed unsure of his last name, and told police he was age four - William Weldman would have been five by that time.

The Weldmans rushed to Topeka and agreed with the police, especially after comparing close-up pictures of younger William's nose -- which was an exact match -- with the Willard who'd been abandoned in the parking lot. Sounds like a great ending, doesn't it? But there's more to this mystery. Here's Mr. Weldman explaining the situation to me earlier this afternoon.

William Weldman: *Well, Lucy, the whole thing is really bizarre. I don't really remember much of anything at all before about age six. Maybe a snippet or two regarding the police in Topeka, but that's about it. I guess I maybe kinda blocked most of it out. But I grew up believing I was the boy who'd been kidnapped, then rescued two years later, even though I always kinda felt a little different than the rest of my family. As you can see, I'm a fairly large man, and I'm quite outgoing and boisterous by nature. But both of my parents were very quiet and reserved people, same as my sister Margaret, and they are all fairly small, as are most of my cousins. And when I compare pictures of myself at age five with the baby pictures my parents had before the kidnapping, I just don't see that much of a resemblance, beyond the nose thing. And I mean, a* *lot of people have similar noses, don't they? There are only so many to go around.*

Anyway, by the time I went to college, I began to suspect there may have been some kind of mistake made, but I never voiced my concerns for fear of hurting my mom and dad. They were wonderful people, and I loved them dearly. But then last year, my parents were both killed in a car accident during that wild February snowstorm, and a few months later I decided to have my DNA checked against theirs. And unfortunately, my suspicions were proven correct. My DNA doesn't match the Weld family at all.

So now I've decided to ask the public for help. I'm just hoping there's someone out there who can help shed some light on this mystery, and help me find out who I really am, and about my biological family. Not to mention whatever may have happened to the real William Weldman.

The bartender asked Nick if he wanted a refill as the two TV reporters bantered back and forth about the case and provided details regarding where people could contact police if they had any useful information.

"Just the check. Tacos were fantastic, by the way."

"Tell me about it," the bartender said as he patted his massive belly. "Occupational hazard. I used to be just plain ol' Mike Engel when I started working here fifteen years ago. Now I'm 'Fat Mike' everywhere I go. Even some of my own family members call me Fat Mike now...rotten bastards. I mean, it's not like any of them are gonna be winning any best-body contests anytime soon, I'll tell you that."

With time to kill, Nick decided to buy some fly-fishing gear and try for some trout in one of the nearby mountain streams.

On his way into a sporting goods store at a strip mall near the restaurant, he called back to the home office to update them on the developments.

"Tottel's in a meeting with the JAG nags again," said Deanna Sherman. "But I'll give her the good news about the Cooper case. She'll be thrilled, no doubt. Nice work Nick, as usual."

"Yeah, I'm planning to send a copy of the newspaper article to SECNAV, and I'm hoping she'll put an endorsement letter with it for me. Unless they've already made a determination. You haven't heard anything, have you?"

There was a slight pause at the other end of the line before she replied. "I haven't heard anything. When are you going to be back in the office?"

"I should be back at work by Monday morning."

"Okay. I'll put you on her schedule for an early meeting. She'll want to speak with you personally."

"About the case?"

Another pause. "Yes. You know how she is. She'll want to congratulate you in person, I'm sure. And catch you up on everything that's been going on around here, too."

Now it was Nick's turn to pause. "Okay. Monday first thing, then. And one more thing. Can you order full sets of records out of the archives for me? I need everything. Service jackets and health records, including dental, on two subjects: Richard Patterson and James Petarsky. You can get their middle initials and socials out of the investigative records from the old Roy Bantam murder file. You remember that case, don't you?"

Again, a pause. "Of course I do, Nick. You think I could have forgotten...that case?"

"I guess not. That was a pretty memorable time for all of us. Can you get all those records before I get back Monday?"

"Do you really need to ask? You're well aware of my abilities, after all."

Nick had a spring in his step and a smile on his face as he filled a shopping cart with a cheap rod and reel and supplies. The brief conversation had seemed awkward at times, but there was no mistaking the flirting tone with which it ended. Was she actually giving him an opening, after all these years? He couldn't stop thinking about her the whole time the store clerk was pointing out some good streams on the map he included in his purchase.

....

Deanna called her contact at the records archive in St. Louis to put in an expedited order for the records Nick Maynard wanted, then knocked on her boss's closed office door and entered without waiting for a reply.

"In the mood for some good news?"

Claire Tottel had told Deanna that she didn't want to be disturbed for at least thirty minutes after her meeting with Brett Stevens, the second-in-command at the Norfolk JAG office, had ended. A quick glance at her watch indicated that exactly thirty two minutes had elapsed. She closed the folder full of mid-term exams she'd been grading for the night class she was teaching on Introduction to Criminology at Old Dominion University. The exam results had been far better than she'd anticipated. Maybe she wasn't such a bad teacher after all.

"Always," she said to Deanna as she placed the folder back into her in-box.

"Looks like Maynard's about to close out the Faith Cooper case. The DA has a plea deal in place and is shooting for a Friday hearing. If all goes as planned, he'll be back in the office Monday morning."

"Good. You didn't say anything, did you?"

"Of course not. I know my place better than that, boss. Besides, I don't want to be the one that has to break his heart...again."

"Again? I didn't know you two had a history. I always thought he was just another one of your many admirers that always seem to be mooning about. C'mon...dish, Sherman."

"Well, if you must know. It was a long, long time ago. Thirty years now, I guess. Wow. Am I really that old? Anyway, I felt so sorry for him after his wife died. You know about that, right?"

"I think I may have heard something about it...suicide, wasn't it?"

"Yes. It was horrible. I've never seen a man so heartbroken and depressed, and I felt so bad for him. Anyway, Steve had gone down to Rio to replace Nick on the case he'd been working when she died. And I was helping Nick move out of the apartment in Jacksonville where she did it, with one of his own guns no less, and we were going through some of her things -- he didn't really have any family or close friends around to help him do all that kind of stuff -- and it just kinda happened."

"You little slut."

Deanna chuckled. "Hey, it wasn't like that. I felt so sorry for him. He was really tore up about it. And I don't think one little mercy-fuck makes a girl a slut, does it?"

Claire guffawed. "Did Steve ever find out?"

"Hell no. And I don't want him to either, so don't mention this to anyone. You know how these people love to gossip.

Besides, I always kinda had the feeling that Steve may have stepped out of line himself while he was away in Rio. Lots of temptation down there, I'm told. He always acts a little funny whenever the subject of Rio comes up, and is quick to change the topic. So we're probably even, anyway...not that I'd even want to know at this point. Our marriage works just fine with all the biggest lies buried deep in the past, where they belong."

"Your secret's safe with me...slut's honor," Claire said as she held up three fingers, mimicking the Scout's salute. They both laughed at that one.

"Did you talk with the head-shed yet?", Deanna asked.

"Yeah, I called Bob Reichart and ripped him a new asshole this morning, but it didn't do any good. I threatened to go up there and start breaking shit in his office if he didn't get that decision reversed. But he said it wouldn't accomplish anything, no matter how scared he is of me. Apparently, his hands really are tied. There's a blanket moratorium right now on all waivers for the mandatory retirement age, and that word's coming straight from the Secretary. Across-the-board, no exceptions. So we have to say goodbye to one of our best guys, and they'll probably send us some snot-nosed know-it-all with a couple years patrol experience, straight out of grad school, as a replacement. Can you believe that shit? It's a wonder we ever solve any crimes around here. Good thing most of these criminals are so damn stupid."

"I'm putting Nick on your schedule for zero eight thirty on Monday."

"Make it zero eight hundred. Might as well get it over with early. I'd go ahead and tell him now, but I just don't wanna do it over the phone."

"Yeah, I'm sure this is gonna be quite a blow. I don't think he has much going on besides the job. A shame, because he really is a pretty great guy."

"Sounds like someone's angling for another sympathy screw."

Deanna laughed. "Not unless I can figure out a way to get Steve out of this hemisphere again for a couple of weeks. Besides, I've already done my duty. It's your turn, this time."

"Hmmm...Nick Maynard? Not bad, but really not my type." They both laughed again. Although she wasn't open about her sexuality, it was fairly common knowledge around NCIS that Claire Tottel was a lesbian. Deanna always got a sadistic kick out of watching as one of the many hotshot, macho-man line officers who routinely came through the office would make a high-speed low-level run at Claire, only to go down in flames, every time. It had become an unspoken inside joke between the two of them.

"Anything else going on I need to know about?", Claire asked as Deanna picked up the three folders in her out-box and began perusing the contents.

"Not really. It's been quiet this afternoon."

"Good." Claire smiled and pulled out the folder of exams as Deanna went back to her desk to complete her work for the day, shutting the door behind her.

Chapter Twenty
October 29th, 2010

The court proceeding that sealed Marty's fate was shockingly brief. Fourteen minutes, to be exact. Alone later in his Littleton holding cell, he tried to recall every excruciating detail, but kept coming back to the most horrifying moment, over and over again in his mind.

Right after the judge asked if he understood the ramifications of his guilty plea, he'd answered in the affirmative, then heard the piercing wail of his youngest daughter Kelly screaming "No!" from the gallery behind him in the courtroom. He turned around in time to see her red, tear-streaked face contorted in agony as she was whisked away from the proceedings by two uniformed bailiffs. He'd pleaded with her and everyone else in his family with whom he was still on speaking terms to stay away from court. This ordeal was already more than painful enough without having to witness the affects it was having on those he loved. But Kelly was nothing if not fiercely loyal, and was absolutely determined to show support for the father she adored, especially since her older sister and mother were apparently washing their hands of him forever - a sentiment she found every bit as appalling as any crime for which her dad stood accused.

His attorney, George Turnbow, had schooled him on the facts of life the previous week, just as Nick Maynard had predicted.

"They've got you by the short-hairs, my friend. The fraud and forgery beefs are just the beginning." He reached into his open briefcase and pulled out a huge, overstuffed binder and slammed it on the table for effect. "This is just one single section of the federal code. EPA regulations. That one book alone will probably net you an additional half-dozen felony charges by the time they finish ripping apart every land deal your firm has done in the past five years. And that's just for starters. Next it'll be on to the IRS tax codes, then OSHA regs, BLM regs, and about fifty other sets of obscure rules they can use as a pretext to crawl up your ass with a microscope. By the time they're finished, people will think you're worse than Jack the Ripper, and you'll never see the light of day as a free man again."

"Don't sugarcoat it for me George...tell me how awful my situation really is."

"You're not paying me to blow sunshine up your skirt. But there is some good news...you have me on your side, and you can thank your wife for that."

"So she came through with your retainer."

"Your accounts are still frozen, so I wouldn't be here otherwise. Not that she doesn't have self-serving motivations of her own. I may have intimated that you might be persuaded to be amenable to her terms on the divorce, and not make things difficult for her."

"Naturally. Prison would be so much harder to live with if I knew I was also standing in the way of her and Bob Ellis's future happiness."

"Sour grapes won't do you any good. Your best bet is to let go of the past, and move forward. You'll still have lots of good years left after your time is done. You might even have some grandchildren to dote over by then. And a little money waiting for you in the bank, if we can work the right deal. Count your blessings."

"I feel so much better now, coach. Exactly how much time in the penalty box am I looking at?"

"The prosecutor is going to recommend eight years. But I know the judge we're getting, and I think I can get it down to six. I'm going to ask for five, but I think he'll go six. No promises, but I'd be surprised if we can't get six. Their evidence is weak. They can prove you had sexual intercourse with the victim sometime during the twenty-four hour period prior to her death, but nothing else. There's no motive. No witnesses. No confession. If not for the open-and-shut nature of the other beefs to deal with, we'd easily beat them at trial on the manslaughter alone, and they know it. *And* given the fact that you've had no history of violence previous or since.

"Plus, you've had decades of sobriety since your early years of alcoholism, after growing up with an alcoholic father. Drunken, absentee dads make excellent scapegoats for youthful transgressions. And a few minor offenses notwithstanding, you've really turned your life around since the alleged incident, and made something of yourself in spite of the rough beginnings and a lack of formal education. Judge Hertzler loves the sob stories."

"Hey, I've got no problem selling out the memory of my deceased father to get some time shaved off my sentence. You can throw my mom, brothers and sisters, and anyone else I'm related to under that bus too if it'll do me any good.

"Still...six fucking years for something I didn't even do?"

Turnbow clasped his hands together on the table in front of him. "Hopefully six, maybe eight. And there's one more prosecutor's stipulation to which you must agree. She'll allow us to stipulate an 'Alford' claim as part of the deal, which allows you to plead guilty while still maintaining your factual innocence, but you have to waive all rights to appeal. Whatever sentence the judge hands down, you live with."

"When would I be up for parole if I get the six?"

"There is no parole in the federal system. But you can earn up to fifteen percent time off your sentence for good behavior, which would put your release at five years and change, if you're lucky."

Marty had stared up at the ceiling for a few moments, then closed his eyes and took a few deep breaths to calm himself. There was nothing else he could do. Turnbow was right. Take your medicine like a man and get on with it. He had only himself to blame. He'd had ample opportunities to set the record straight, but he'd taken the easy way out at every turn. He'd lied to his friend Bill Reynolds at the video store. He'd lied to Melissa and her father. He'd forged the DD-214 to get the insurance discount at his father-in-law's firm, and to join the American Legion, just to drum up business. If he'd simply been honest, then Katie would've never been in a position to win that scholarship they didn't even need.

Truth be told, he'd always kind of liked having a little bit of a dark secret from Melissa. Hiding his criminal past from her and her parents. Putting one over on the wealthy, uppity, well-connected Kelly family. Guess the Kelly's get the last laugh now. He sure as hell didn't feel like laughing.

"Okay. I don't have any other choice. I'll take the deal. Just promise me you'll do your best to save the money I have left, and the properties."

"Of course. Between selling the business office, the homes, and your other accounts, you should have a tidy little nest-egg waiting when you get released. After all, your wife already took her share. I'm assuming you'll want me to handle your divorce as well?"

"I must be a real dream come true for you, huh George? Lot's of different types of legal nightmares, and lots of assets to pick over to boot. Do I get the ultra-fucked-up loser discount?"

Turnbow stood and began putting his folders back into his briefcase, preparing to leave.

"One more thing, George, before you take off. What would you say if I told you that the guy who really killed Faith Cooper is a former associate of mine who was mistakenly declared dead by the U.S. Navy thirty years ago, but who is actually very much alive - having fooled the authorities by switching identities with another former associate whom he also murdered, and that it was his attempt at blackmailing me that has led to my current predicament?"

George hesitated for a moment, then smiled broadly and picked up his briefcase. "I'd say you've been watching too much daytime TV since your incarceration. I think that was one of the old story-lines from General Hospital. Or was that Days of Our Lives? Back in seventy-eight, I got sick of school and dropped out of CU during my junior year of under-grad studies. The only job I could find at the time was night security at a water treatment facility. Never could get used to sleeping days, and I couldn't afford cable or anything else at the time. So I ended up watching a lot of soaps. Didn't take long for me to realize that school might not be so bad after all.

"Anyway, that whole switched identity plot sounds vaguely familiar...Is there anything else?" he asked.

Marty just shook his head and muttered "That's what I figured" as Turnbow walked out the door.

Today's hearing had been a mere formality. If not for the spectacle of his daughter's dramatic display of despair, it would've been completely unremarkable. Marty had long since come to terms with his fate, and was counting days in anticipation of a five year three months total sentence - with good behavior.

His sentencing hearing had been scheduled for the following Thursday. The prosecutor had advised the judge that Faith's sister was the only surviving member of her immediate family, and she didn't plan to appear or wish to submit a victim impact statement. She was willing to accept the judgment and wisdom of the court, and was simply anxious to put the matter behind her.

George had provided Marty with a rough draft of the fairly persuasive case he'd put together in support of his argument for leniency, in preparation for the sentencing hearing. The finished document would be delivered to the judge by Tuesday, to allow time for consideration prior to passing sentence. Among the arguments George had detailed was the fact that in the three decades since the crime he was alleged by the prosecution to have committed, Marty had married, raised two successful daughters who were productive and contributing members of society, had created jobs in the community through his legitimate business endeavors, and had never been accused, much less convicted, of any other crime involving violence his entire life.

The only things left to be determined now were precisely how long his sentence would be, and where he'd serve his time. George had asked the prosecutor to solicit the prison bureau people for the Littleton facility, and Marty was anticipating transfer from the isolation of the holding cells to the general population community, who were mostly housed in dormitory-like units throughout the compound, after the sentencing hearing.

There were hard times ahead. Five years in hell, basically. But he was already thinking about his second act. There would be opportunities for education and training while locked up that could put him in line for a new career when he got out. He was tired of the real estate business, anyway. A lot of people start over in their fifties, don't they? If they could do it, so could he. Besides, he'd have to attend classes anyway in order to qualify for the good-behavior caveat needed for early release. Wonder what majors they offer here?

Tom Barkwell

Chapter Twenty One
November 01st, 2010

Nick Maynard was in a good mood as he drove to work on Monday. Colorado had been great, but it was nice to be home. It was shaping up as another pretty fall day. Upper 60's, maybe even 70 degrees by afternoon. He might throw a line in the water for an hour or so early that evening, if it wasn't too windy, then relax later in his favorite recliner and enjoy the game with a few cold drinks.

First one in as usual. Made the coffee light, the way he liked it. As Nick began clearing all the voice-mail and email messages that had been piling up during his time in Denver, Jack Porter popped in to chide his good friend of almost twenty years. They'd first met in Naples Italy, where they made a fairly big bust together. Nick had actually been assigned to Rota Spain at the time, but the Naples office needed someone not already known in Naples as NCIS to go undercover as an ex-pat. Nick volunteered for the role, and Jack was the case officer.

Nick posed as a shady American, working for a crooked Italian construction outfit. He arranged to purchase several pieces of misappropriated heavy construction equipment from a supply officer who worked logistics for the local Seabee battalion. The target in the investigation, a young Lieutenant Commander named John Bottalico, had been making hundreds of thousands of dollars through various illegal enterprises, doctoring the books and working the supply system for all it was worth. It'd been a very successful operation on a cagey, worthy adversary. Agents always enjoyed the thrill of the chase just a little bit more when going up against the smarter criminals. The run-of-the-mill losers and deviates they commonly dealt with were either pathetically stupid or so repulsive you didn't even want to be in the same room with them. But guys like Bottalico, savvy and cunning, were a challenge to be savored. He actually admired the man's moxy. No small-time games for him. He was all in for the big score, and had been living the high life with a bevvy of beautiful Italian ladies to match. Nick almost felt sorry for him when the sentence was handed down: thirteen years in Leavenworth. He wondered for a fleeting moment how Bottalico had fared, and where he was now.

"I knew you were back in town as soon as I saw that tea you always make in our coffee pot this morning. How was Colorado?"

"Fuckin' great. You shoulda seen the big rainbow I hooked last Thursday," Nick said as he gave the universal fisherman's sign by holding his palms about eighteen inches apart. "Four pounds if it was an ounce."

"Four pounds, huh? It's your story, Nick. Tell it how you want. But I'll tell you the same thing your girlfriend did last night." Jack said as he raised his hand with his thumb and forefinger about three inches apart, and said "That ain't seven inches. And your four-pound rainbow was probably a twelve ounce stocker."

His in-box was light. Maybe the paperless Navy he'd been hearing was on its way the last twenty years was finally becoming a reality after all. The service and health records he'd requested on Petarsky and Patterson were there, but not much else. Office voice-mail was loaded however, so he listened through all the messages, taking notes as he went. Mostly routine follow-ups on some dead old cold cases he'd worked and gotten nowhere on. He'd get back with the callers later in the day.

Email was next. There were literally hundreds of superfluous messages to be deleted, and he ended up saving only nine that were actually pertinent to his job, which he would also address later that day. Governmental email systems were difficult to access when away from the office, even when working from a terminal at another governmental agency, such as the FBI system. That meant first days back in the office were often spent on administrative housecleaning chores, before the real work could begin again.

He was anxious to begin a fresh look at some of the other cases on his agenda. The unsolved murder of an eighteen year old Seaman from 1986, which had taken place aboard USS Cape Canaveral, an old Destroyer Tender long since decommissioned, was especially promising. The kid had been hit in the head with a dogging wrench, then robbed on a payday night. The prime suspect in the case, another Seaman named Lester Benett, had racked up an extensive rapsheet since his discharge from the Navy in 1987, and had recently been arrested on another robbery-murder charge in Miami, for which he was facing a likely death penalty prosecution. He might be ripe for a confession in the old case if presented with the proper incentives.

At 0745, a reminder about his 0800 appointment with Claire Tottel popped up on the computer screen. He decided to show up a few minutes early, and sound on Deanna a little bit. He wanted to see if she really was giving him an opening, or had just been in a playful mood when they'd spoken the previous week on the phone. Either way, he rarely passed up any excuse to be near her. Wonder if anybody ever noticed?

No Faith in Justice

Deanna was on the telephone when he arrived five minutes early for the meeting with Claire. She smiled and raised a forefinger as an acknowledgement of his presence as she continued her conversation.

"Uh-huh...uh-huh...Really? Wow, that's kind of surprising. I thought they were always so close," she said as she swiveled her chair away from Nick's direction and lowered her voice. Still, he couldn't help but eavesdrop.

"Well, if Amanda isn't going to do more to help out, maybe it's time we start looking at some of those assisted living facilities in this area again," she said in a hushed tone. "Either that or she can move in with us.

"I know...I know...I know...Anyway honey, can I call you back? Yeah...Okay...Okay...I love you too...Try not to worry too much. We'll figure something out...Okay...Bye."

Nick pretended to be engrossed in 'The Flagship' -- the official base newspaper -- that had been lying on a table in the reception area when he sat down. He looked up at Deanna and smiled as she swiveled back around to face him.

"So how was Denver?" she said, trying -- and failing -- to look happy to see him. Nick could see the concern on her face, even though she was trying to hide it.

"Great. Good to be home though. How are things with you?"

"Well...not so great, actually. Steve's mom took a little tumble yesterday, and she's in the hospital in Dayton. Nothing serious. Just a hairline fracture in her hip, apparently. But we're thinking it might not be such a good idea for her to live alone any longer. Anyway, I guess we're getting to that stage in our lives now. Before you know it, the kids will be having the same conversations about me and Steve!"

"Yeah. I guess we're all headed to the same place."

Deanna held Nick's gaze for a few seconds, then forced a smile and said "Shit. Will you listen to us? I didn't mean to be so maudlin. Now I've got us both talking all gloom and doom. Hell, we ain't that damn old. Plenty of good years left."

Nick could tell she was troubled. She looked at her desk-phone. "Looks like Claire's off the line. I'll go in and see if she's ready to see you now."

A minute later he was sitting across from his boss as she explained the situation. His request for continuation of service had been denied. There was an across the board moratorium. No exceptions, no waivers, and no appeals. He would have to retire no later than March 01st, 2011.

Nick sat in silence, stunned. He'd never seriously entertained the possibility that his request might not be approved. After all, he'd served so faithfully, for so long. He was in great physical shape. Never had any problems, and never received anything but glowing performance evaluations, rousing endorsements, and awards for his accomplishments. He'd just assumed all along that the paperwork was little more than a formality.

"I'm sorry, Nick. I really am. You have no idea how much I'd like to keep you on. I even threatened physical violence against some people at HQ, but there's nothing anyone can do. Their hands are tied with all this budget mess from Congress, I guess. I'm really sorry."

Nick looked at the letter she'd handed him from the Secretary of the Navy's office. He could see the word *Disapproved* printed in bold-face type in the first paragraph.

"Damn. March first? That barely gives me enough time to take all the leave I have saved up on the books."

"Really? Shit. I didn't even think about that. I guess we'll have to get someone to take your case load. I was thinking about moving Jack Porter to cold-cases. What do you think?"

"Good choice. He'll crack some for you, for sure. Guess I better get all my notes and files updated. And double-check my leave balance."

He stopped in front of Deanna's desk on the way out. She looked at him with sad eyes.

"I guess you know already."

"Yes. Sorry, Nick. I see all the paperwork before the boss, even. But I couldn't say anything. Not my place."

Nick saw the pity in her eyes. Was that for him? Or was it the situation with her mother-in-law? He certainly hoped it was the latter. Otherwise, he would be angry. No man wanted to see that look on the face of a woman he wanted.

He thought about Deanna all that day as he updated his paperwork, and turned his pending files over to Jack Porter. Would he ever see her again? Did he want to? How pathetic he was. A grown man, pining after somebody else's wife for three decades. No wonder she felt sorry for him.

It turned out he had more than enough leave to cover the period until March 01st. It took less than half an hour to get his leave request approved. By 1700, he'd cleaned out his desk, and put all his personal belongings into a large cardboard box.

He glanced at the records he'd ordered on Petarsky and Patterson. "Fuck it," he muttered to himself as he placed them into the Faith Cooper case file, unexamined, along with the rest of the paperwork necessary to close the case out for good.

"I'll let you know," he'd told Claire a few minutes earlier when she'd asked about a good time to plan his retirement ceremony. They'd both known he was lying. He had no intention of participating in any type of celebration or event to mark his retirement from NCIS. He was done. He'd asked to stay, and they'd rejected him. They didn't want him anymore.

He knew their routine. Their schedules. He'd come back to turn in his badge and his gear at a time when they'd all be tied up, behind closed doors, in one of the numerous mandatory meetings they all had to attend each week. He'd make sure to avoid running into any of the key players. *I'm done with all of it*, he thought as he made the long drive home that evening. *Done with NCIS, and everybody there.*

Chapter Twenty Two
July 13th, 2012

"You're doing great, honey. I'm really proud of you."

Visiting day at the prison, and Marty was ecstatic that his daughter Kelly had come to see him. She'd just started a new job as a real estate agent with one of his former competitors, a large international firm - RE/Max. The property market had been improving significantly in recent months, but the job market was still pretty thin for newly minted college grads. She was pleased to finally have gainful employment that didn't require a hairnet, and he was pleased that she was pleased, even though he'd hoped she would find something more meaningful than real estate sales.

"I didn't want to say anything until I passed my exams, and I wasn't sure how you'd feel about it. But I figured since it put a roof over my head and clothes on my back my entire life, I might as well go with it for a few more years. I'm a third generation real estate pro, now. There are worse jobs out there."

"That's for sure. At least you're not going into politics."

They both laughed, knowing that he was alluding to the fact that Katie had recently begun working as a legislative assistant in DC, on the staff of Colorado congressman Jordan Richards.

"In all seriousness, I'm very proud of you both. You're far better daughters than I could ever expect or deserve to have."

"Has she come by to see you even once yet, Dad? In almost two years of being locked up?"

"No, but she sent a very nice card on my birthday, and I've been writing her regularly."

"That pisses me off. She's such an ungrateful little brat sometimes."

"Now, Kell. Give your sister a break. This ordeal has been very hard on her. After all, she suffered the biggest humiliation over the whole scholarship thing. She was absolutely mortified when all of her friends and classmates at CC found out about me. It's not easy having a crooked deviant killer like me for an old man, especially when you're surrounded by kids who come from prestige and money. She'll come around, eventually. I'm going to win her back with my charm and wit once I get out of here."

'You're not a killer, Dad. Don't even joke about that. You made some mistakes, but you don't deserve to be in here. And I just hate it that Katie doesn't have enough faith in you to realize that."

Marty squeezed his daughter's hand. He really was grateful to have someone like her in his corner. How bad of a person could he really be, having raised a great kid like Kelly? It was something he held on to whenever things got really tough, as they frequently did inside federal prison. Even though he knew that Melissa had far more to do with raising their two kids than he ever did. She was a great mom, and a good influence on Katie and Kelly.

"So how's Mrs. Ellis getting along?"

"Fine. Same as always. She took me out shopping to celebrate when I passed the tests. I got three new business outfits so I can look the part at my new gig."

"Do you think she'll take me out shopping when I get out in 2016? I'm way too skinny for my old wardrobe."

"You look great, Dad. You should keep working out after you get released. The ladies are gonna be all over you."

234

"You think? So what else has been going on? Anything new besides the job?"

"Oh, I almost forgot. Did you hear about Janine Estrada, your former office manager? Apparently, she's been missing for almost a week now. It was all over the news for a couple of days. I guess her daughter just woke up one morning and couldn't find her, and the authorities aren't sure what happened. She just vanished into thin air. They're looking at her ex-husband as a 'person-of-interest.' They say he just recently came back to the Denver area after being in Mexico for a few years. But they haven't arrested him or anything yet."

"Wow. That's quite a shocker. I didn't really have enough time to get to know her that well, but she seemed like a sweet lady. I know she was crazy about her little girl, so there's no way she'd willingly abandon her like that."

"Yeah, that's what all her friends and family said when they interviewed them on TV, too. But you just never know about people and their secrets...huh, Dad?

"Anyway, there's more news. Scott's been hinting around that he wants us to get married, but I told him he'd have to wait until closer to the time you're due to get released and ask me officially, cause there's no way in hell I'm walking down the aisle unless it's on my Daddy's arm."

Marty's eyes got misty, and the lump in his throat grew bigger. The next forty-two months couldn't go quickly enough.

Chapter Twenty Three
October 14th, 2013

For the second time in his life, Marty Mahoney was waylaid out of the blue by a letter from the fictitious Peter P. Phoenix. Another blow like a two by four slammed upside his head as he read it, this time even worse than the first. He instantly retched, and laid down on his bunk for several minutes until his breathing returned to normal, and the sounds of prison life -- which had faded into near-blackness when he saw one of his daughter Kelly's business card inside the envelope -- gradually came back into focus. He got up from his bunk and went to the sink to splash cold water on his face. After several cold swallows, he sat back down and re-read the letter:

Dear Mr. Mahoney,

I was terribly sorry to learn of your legal troubles, but I trust your spirits are improving as the end of your sentence grows nearer. The next few years will just fly by, I'm sure. In the meantime, life goes on. And it's to that end I'm writing you now.

I trust you'll remember the outlines of a particular Lake County property transaction upon which we reached agreement shortly before your arrest. To refresh your memory, it was a small plot of secluded land, and involved a down payment of $15,000, with the balance of $35,000 to be paid in future installments on a schedule to be determined.

I've been thinking about your predicament, and I feel it's important that we honor our agreements, even if it would be easier to just walk away. I want you to know that I have no intention of abandoning my commitment to you just because of your incarceration. And after reviewing a copy of your plea agreement (which was conveniently made available as part of the official public record), it appears that very few of your assets were seized by the government (restitution notwithstanding), so I see no reason to deprive you of this wonderful opportunity.

My proposal is that we either conclude our business via mail, or avail ourselves of the services of your lovely daughter Kelly - if you prefer the personal touch (great photo on her business card, by the way...I can really see the resemblance). But instead of a down payment followed by installments, I believe it would be more efficient to simply exchange the entire amount ($50,000 - $5000 for cash discount = $45,000 total lump sum). But you'll have to pay her commission (she'll probably give you the family discount). After all, she's a licensed professional. I notice she has many listings of currently vacant properties. I actually met her in person, and she showed me around one of the unoccupied homes she's trying to sell. And even though she's young, she certainly seems competent and knowledgeable (she reminds me of that girl we once knew, her nickname was Turtle, I believe).

I'm not sure how much your current situation impinges upon your ability to transact business, but you can either arrange to have payment forwarded to me directly at the below address (check or bank draft should be made payable to my company - F.C. Memorial Services), or provide instructions for meeting with Kelly, if you prefer to have her serve as intermediary. It's important that you do one or the other no later than October 23rd, or I'll be compelled to seek other alternatives. Trust me, you don't want to miss out on this once-in-a-lifetime chance.

You can either telephone me with the particulars as to how you'd prefer to proceed at (303)116-9099, or by mail if unable to phone.

I'll forward the notarized deed to the property immediately upon receipt of payment (you can have full faith in my intentions to follow up completely in this matter - this letter will serve as binding agreement).

On a personal note, I hope you're availing yourself of all the opportunities provided during your incarceration. Especially the chance to commune with our Lord and Savior, seek his soul cleansing redemption for your sins, and find the grace of God's salvation, as I have.

His humble servant,

Peter P. Phoenix
F.C. Memorial Services
700 N. Colorado Blvd
Denver, CO 80206

The threat was unmistakable. Pay the money, or Patterson would kill Kelly, just like he'd killed Faith and who knows how many others. And Marty was stuck behind barbed wire inside a federal prison, helpless to stop it.

"What's wrong, celly?" said Jamaal Maxwell, Marty's cellmate for the past fourteen months, as he walked into their cell after watching his Nuggets play the first half of a pre-season game against the San Antonio Spurs in the rec room. "You look even whiter than usual. You feelin' okay?"

Marty handed Jamaal the letter, then sat silent as he read it.

"Who the fuck is Peter Phoenix? Is he runnin' a game on you or somethin'?"

"He's the guy I told you about who set me up. Phoenix is an alias. His real name is Rick Patterson. He's threatening to kill my daughter unless I pay him forty-five thousand dollars. The land reference is just a farce. There is no land. It's a straight up extortion hustle."

"Forty-five thousand...that motherfucker ain't fuckin' around. What the fuck kinda shit is that?"

"Exactly. Forty-five thousand fuckin' dollars. And I'm stuck inside this shit-hole, where I can't do a fucking thing to stop him."

Jamaal sat down and mulled the situation over for a few more minutes, re-reading the letter.

"One thing fer sho', cuz...even if you pay him, and I know you got to be thinkin' on doin' that, him threatnin' Kelly and all, but even if you do pay him, he comin' back fer mo'. Most definitely."

"I know. That's the biggest problem. He won't stop until he bleeds me completely dry, then he'll either walk away, or he'll kill her anyway just for the hell of it. Just to torture me. And I have no way of knowing which way it'll go."

"Then we gotta devise a plan to stop this heinous motherfucker once and for all. Set his ass up, and take his ass down."

"Exactly. But how? He's really smart. And he's ruthless. Shit, he even killed his best friend just to throw the cops off his trail. He tricked the authorities into declaring him dead thirty years ago, while he runs around using false identities doing dirty deeds on people."

"He sounds like one o' those diabolical motherfuckers, like from one of them Quentin Taranchalino movies or some shit. Maybe we should sic Punchy-G on his ass."

"Punchy's a bad ass, for sure. He could do the job. But I think we'd have a hard time enticing Patterson into a meeting with Punchy, even if Punchy went for it. Plus, I don't wanna jeopardize Punchy's parole. I wouldn't wanna be the reason he ended up back in jail, even though it's probably gonna happen eventually, anyway.

"No. As much as I hate to do it, I might have to try and get the law to step in on this one. That NCIS cop who busted me has some history with this dude. If I can convince him that Patterson's still alive and behind this scheme, he'll take that prick down once and for all."

"I don't know, cuz...the po-lice? I mean, I ain't never been involved in any situation that wasn't made worse by the po-lice comin' on the scene. I don't trust them motherfuckers, no way, no how. Whatever you want them stupid motherfuckers to do, it'll probably blow back on you somehow, one way or the other."

"I know. I hate 'em, too. They're never a good option. But what choice do I have? it's the best play I can come up with, even though I have no idea if that dick will even help me.

"I could try to convince Kelly to go into hiding. Maybe change her name, or something. But she'd resist that idea. She's stubborn. And the letter doesn't really sound all that ominous. I'm the only person who fully understands his threat. She'd probably think I was just over-reacting. And even if I could get her to run and hide, it would only be a temporary solution. Patterson would simply find her, or target someone else in my family."

"What about one o' them private detective motherfuckers? Maybe you could hire a professional to find that motherfucker, and protect Kelly."

"Hmmm. That's a possibility. But how would I know if the guy I hired was competent enough to do the job? And what could a private dick do to solve the problem long term? He might be able to rattle Patterson's cage a little, but eventually I'd be bled dry, and Kelly would be out there on her own again, an easy target. And we'd be right back to square one."

"Damn. I never thought o' that. This one o' them conumdrums. Ain't no good answers. I guess you got to do what 'chu got to do, then. We talkin' bout yo' little baby girl. But if the po-lice won't do anything, we best get aholt o' Punchy and see if he can take this motherfucker down,"

"Yeah. Either that, or I'll try to pay this motherfucker off slowly, and string him along until I can get the fuck outta here and deal with him myself. If I ever get within pistol range, he's a dead motherfucker on sight, no questions asked."

Chapter Twenty Four
October 15th, 2013

"I'd like to speak with Nicholas Maynard, please."

"I've told you people before - I'm on the no-call list. It's my understanding that you're supposed to check that list before initiating a call. So I'd appreciate it if you'd stop calling here."

"No-call list?...Wait. Don't hang up. I'm not a telemarketer, Mr. Maynard. I'm an attorney. My name's George Turnbow. Perhaps you remember me from the Martin Mahoney trial in Denver. I was his defense attorney in the Faith Cooper case."

"Oh, right. Of course I remember. That was the last case I closed before I retired. I hope your client's enjoying his stay in prison, counselor."

"He's surviving, and paying his debt to society, as our system demands."

"He got off far too light for what he did if you ask me...eight years, wasn't it?"

"Six. But you and I both know you would've never been able to prove he killed that girl at trial. The only thing you could prove was consensual sex. He only took the plea deal to shield his assets on the other charges, for which he would've absurdly received an even lengthier prison sentence. The federal system is perverse in that way, and you know it."

"No offense, but you sound a little like a sore loser to me, counselor. Besides, Mahoney is as crooked as a dog's hind leg. You don't know the half of it. He's probably done so much dirt over the years, a six year term won't even begin to set the ledger straight. But you just wait. He'll screw up again. You'll probably have another payday coming shortly after he gets out."

"Well...at any rate. He made a frantic call to me from prison earlier today, and he's absolutely desperate to speak with you. I tried to calm him down, but he was nearly hysterical in his insistence that I find you and convince you to talk with him about a person named Rick Patterson. He's claiming that this Patterson fellow is threatening to murder his twenty-three year old daughter unless he pays extortion money. He says that Patterson manipulated the authorities into declaring him dead, and has been running amok, committing murders and mayhem ever since, using false identities. When I suggested a call to the local authorities, he was insistent that you were the only person who might be persuaded that this whole scenario wasn't some kind of elaborate, overblown hoax.

"He was in such a panicked state, I decided to take him at his word. He never struck me as anything but a rational, reasonably intelligent man. Certainly one of my better clients. I'm not exactly sure what's going on here, but I have no sense that he's anything but sincere. So I dropped everything I was doing in order to track you down. Fortunately, when I found out you were retired from NCIS, Mahoney remembered that you were originally from Blackwell Oklahoma, which led me to your listing."

Nick was surprised Mahoney was able to recall a detail like his hometown from their first interview so long ago. He often told suspects a little about himself when trying to disarm interviewees, hoping to butter them up so they might relax, and incriminate themselves during questioning. But he hadn't done that when they'd spoken in Colorado, so it must have been from the time they talked in 1980 aboard the Fitzpatrick. Impressive.

"I'm not sure what he expects me to do about his problem. I'm retired, remember? I've got better things to do with my time than help pull Marty Mahoney's chestnuts out of the fire." He looked out the window at the john boat trailered beside the house. It had belonged to his dad, who'd passed away two years ago from lung cancer. Nick hadn't done any fishing at all since early spring. He never would've thought it possible not so long ago, but he was thoroughly sick and tired of fishing and golf. He'd loved doing both when he was still working.

"He said that you worked on another murder case, with a victim named Bantam. And that since Patterson had gotten away with that murder and tricked NCIS in the process, that you might be persuaded to try and set things right on that score, if nothing else.

"Can't you at least spare a few minutes to speak with Mahoney directly? In the interest of justice, if for no other reason? You've spent a lifetime in its pursuit, after all. And don't forget - we're talking about the safety of a completely innocent young woman here. She's done nothing to deserve this threat on her life. If there's even the slightest chance that Mahoney is right...do you really want to risk doing nothing?"

"Fine. I'll talk to him. Do you have a number for the prison?"

"It's better if I forward his call to you. Attorney calls can't be monitored by prison officials. If they get wind that he's the target of an extortion attempt, they might put him in lock-down, and not let him communicate with anyone. Its such a bizarre and convoluted situation, and there's no time for delays. He's going to call me at four PM, five PM your time. So you'll be standing by at this number, then?"

"I'll be here."

"Look, Mahoney, I'll admit my bias. I'm predisposed to assume that all criminals are lying at all times, especially while in prison. And, after listening to your story, my first inclination is to wonder what kind of a game you're trying to run. Still, this is such a far-fetched tale that I'm mildly intrigued. So let me ask you a few questions.

"First off, when you consider how clever this guy would have to be to pull off the switched identity thing, get away with the big heist, and then live by his wits for decades in foreign countries and unfamiliar cultures, why does he show back up in your life now? And why risk getting caught by trying to shake you down while you're in prison?"

"I don't know why. I sure as hell wish he'd stayed wherever the hell he was. Maybe he got nostalgic for some kind of connection to the good ol' Navy days. Maybe he wants to settle an old score from a perceived slight. We were runnin' buddies for a couple of years, and did a lot of deals together. Maybe he thinks I took more than my fair share. Plus, I dogged him out on a couple of chicks he was interested in - Faith being one of them, by the way. Or maybe he's just not as good at running game as he once was, and sees me as a big fat easy target. After all, I'm a guy with a shady past who has a little money, and there are people I care about that can be used as leverage against me. He probably originally intended to blackmail me out of all my assets, then watch me go down for Faith's killing. But he jumped the gun and missed his chance at my money. Now he wants to remedy that oversight.

"But no matter the reasons, I figure he's been emboldened by all his success. He thinks he's smarter than everyone else,

245

so he's taking more risks. Nobody's looking for him. I'm in jail for something he did. So he wants to gloat a little, maybe. Kick some sand in my face after kicking my ass already."

Maynard considered the possibilities. "Maybe. Is there anyone else from back in the day that he may be in contact with? Anyone who could possibly corroborate any of this?"

"Not that I know of. Petarsky was his best friend, believe it or not. His sister Colleen in Pittsburgh, maybe. They were tight. But she wouldn't give him up in a million years. Probably wouldn't even say a word to any cop, ever. But like I told you before, you should talk to Doc Jackson from the Fitz. He'll confirm that Patterson had access to those dental records. They were always doing reports on dental screening percentages and readiness status for deployment. That's the kind of menial work Doc had his flunkies do while he was busy treating patients.

"And check out all the old records on Petarsky and Patterson. I guarantee you'll find they've been tampered with in some way. It's the only explanation that makes any sense. Unless you consider straight up incompetence by the Navy as plausible."

"Or the other obvious possibility - you're lying."

"C'mon, Maynard. I can sense you know that's not true. You said yourself that I'm not stupid. I'm more than halfway through my sentence, with good behavior, and I'll soon be able to put all this shit behind me for good. What possible reason could I have to make up a story like this now, after I've already accepted the sentence? I'm begging you...please help my daughter. *Please*."

The next thirty seconds of silence felt like an eternity to Marty.

"Okay, Mahoney. I'll talk to NCIS for you. But you have to remember, I'm retired. And retired agents who try to stick their noses into service business and stir things up are about as welcome as your monthly cold sore. So no promises."

"Thank you. All I'm asking is that you try. Nobody else would even hear me out, much less take this thing seriously."

"Exactly. So what does that say about me?"

"That you care about the job you did for all those years. That you're a loyal and dedicated public servant, even in retirement."

"Nobody likes a kiss-ass, Mahoney. I already said I'd talk to 'em. And tell your lawyer I need an email copy of that letter. Better yet, tell him to overnight express me the original, too, along with the envelope it came in. He has my address, obviously."

"Yes sir. And thanks again."

Chapter Twenty Five
October 22nd, 2013

Rick Patterson was having a good run at a Fortune Valley casino poker table when the pre-paid throwaway cell phone in his pocket began vibrating. Finally, the bastard calls. He was up over $500, and nobody seemed too upset about it. He always had to be careful, and maintain a relatively low profile. Ignoring the phone, he picked up his chips and excused himself from the table, walking out to the parking lot. When the phone started buzzing again, he answered.

"F.C. memorial services, can I help you?"

"It's me."

"Well...if it isn't my old pal 'Very-Young' Martin Stillwell. I mean Mahoney. How the hell are you, old buddy?"

"You can cut the crap, Rick. This call isn't being monitored. My lawyer transferred me through to you, and the prison can't listen in to attorney calls. Legally, anyway."

"Okay. But just so you know, this is a throwaway phone. And I'm not going to stay on the line long. As a matter of fact, I'm getting into my car now and will be driving as we talk. After we finish, I'll be removing the battery, the SIM card, and throwing it all into the nearest lake."

"Don't worry. I tried to get the cops on you, but they just think I'm either batshit-cazy, or playing some kind of game. Turns out they don't think too much of wild stories from incarcerated felons. They wouldn't do shit about it, so I had to take things into my own hands."

"Is that so?"

"Yeah. It is. I've learned a few things in prison, motherfucker. And I've made a few close friends who just live for the opportunity to fuck somebody like you up. They'd do it for free if I couldn't afford to pay. So listen up and I'll run it all down for you.

"First of all, I'm being sued. The assholes who bought my business office property are claiming that I failed to disclose a few little minor plumbing and electrical problems they say are going to set them back over fifty-grand. And they want additional compensation for lost revenues, temporary move expenses, and damage to their professional reputation. Of course their claims are total bullshit. But I'm a convicted killer, and they're nothing more than crass opportunists, trying to take advantage of my misfortune. But the judge in the case has placed a freeze on all my accounts, so I have no money to give you at the moment."

"That's most unfortunate. Especially for poor, sweet Kelly."

"I'm not finished. You'll soon realize that Kelly has disappeared. She's no longer in the Denver area, and she's living under an assumed name. Taking after her pops that way, as you might recall. Anyway, you'll never find her."

"Marty. C'mon. Is that really how you want to play this? You have another daughter. Not to mention an ex-wife I assume you still have some feelings for, even though she's fucking that Bob Ellis guy now. She's still the mother of your kids, after all. Plus brothers and sisters. Nieces and nephews. Are you gonna send everyone into hiding?"

"Interesting you should bring up nieces and nephews. Did I mention that I've been studying computer science in prison? They have me working in the I.T. section, too, troubleshooting our network. It's a pretty substantial operation, by the way. We have dozens of guys doing customer service jobs for various government agencies and private firms. Prison industry is big business. Wages are even lower than illegals get, so the profits are enormous. Anyway, I did a little on-line sleuthing in my free time, and I came across Colleen's Facebook page. See, it turns out you can look for ladies using their maiden names on a lot of these systems. And what a surprise it was to find her. I guess she's had a few different last names over the years, and gained a few pounds unfortunately, but she's got some beautiful little grandkids.

"Anyway, I saw some interesting photos of your great-niece Rae Lynn, and your great-nephew Colin, hanging out with their great-uncle Ricky in Colorado! Talk about a shocker. It looked like you were having a ball with those little yard-apes. Colin even looks a bit like you, too. Still... allowing your picture to be posted on a public forum like Facebook? Is that really wise, given your status?"

"You'd better be real careful, asshole. Do you really want to go there with me? You're way outta your league."

"Look. I just want you to understand where I'm coming from. Whatever you can do to someone I care about, can also be done to someone you care about. There's nothing like a few years in a federal penitentiary to harden a man's spirit. If you hurt someone I love, I'm going to hurt someone you love. Period. I don't want to be in a war with you, but I have the stomach to do what has to be done, if you force me.

"But, I'm also anxious to offer a way forward where *nobody* else gets hurt. I'm a deal-maker. It's my nature. You know that. And I've had more than my fill of you and your...revenge, or whatever it is you're doing with me. I don't care about payback, anymore. I just want you out of my life, and away from my family, once and for all. So here's what I'm willing to do.

No Faith in Justice

"My ex-wife is in the process of putting together twenty-five thousand dollars in cash. She doesn't want a check or traceable instrument linking her to this deal in any way, because she's really paranoid about the authorities trying to put her in jail on any pretext they can trump up - like 'aiding and abetting' or whatever. I can't really blame her after my experience. She's telling her bank that the cash will be used to bargain down the price on a used boat. All that green can be very persuasive.

"She'll have the money tomorrow, but she insists that she will only hand it over to you in person. I tried to talk her out of it, but she won't play otherwise. She's afraid of you, but she thinks she can persuade you to leave the kids alone if she can look you in the eye. It's a mother thing, I guess. Anyway, we both want your assurances that this ends now. She wants to hear it from you directly. No more threats, no more contact, and no more demands for money. This is *it*. Understand?"

Patterson was taken aback. This conversation hadn't gone at all as he'd anticipated. Was this some kind of trick?

"You know I'm going to check your story out, don't you?"

"Of course. I know you've been keeping tabs on my family, and checking the public records from my trial. I'm not trying to pull anything here. I'd never risk my family's safety in that way. I'm just doing the only thing I can think of that might send you on your way, forever. All you have to do is take the cash and forget about us. You've already ruined my life, and now you're going to get paid. Isn't that enough for you, Rick? I've lost my marriage, my business, and six years of my life because of you. That's gotta be enough. Just take the money and be done with it."

Patterson couldn't think of a good reason to disagree. He'd check it all out as best he could, and think about it over-night. Consider all the angles. His gut was telling him that Stillwell was on the level. It sounded reasonable. Maybe he *had* already put things straight. He was getting a little tired of Colorado, anyway. Hated the Broncos. Maybe it was finally time to get closer to home. He'd been gone way too long already. Nobody was looking for him. The Pirates were finally a winning franchise again. It'd be nice to get season tickets for next year. He missed being around family. And maybe he wasn't too old to start one of his own, with the right woman.

He still had one pristine identity left to use. And the name was very close to his own. He'd acquired it in Panama from an American engineer named Richard Paxton, who'd spent better than twenty years working on the canal. He'd had no immediate family left alive, never married, no kids, with a squeaky clean record. Rick had run a background check and hadn't found so much as a parking ticket. Nobody would ever come looking for Paxton, and nobody would ever find him, either. Rick wouldn't even need to get used to a different first name. It was perfect. Maybe this was the right opportunity to make one final move. Maybe even go legit. He was getting a little old for all this drifting and hustling.

"Relax, Stillwell. Don't be such a drama queen. I fully expected you to negotiate. I would've even been a little suspicious if you didn't. I don't have anything against your kids. They didn't choose to have you for a dad. This is between you and me. And I guess twenty-five thousand will put us square, once and for all."

"Good. How do you want to do the transaction?"

"Write down this number. It's another throw-away. (303)116-7270. Tell your wife to call me tomorrow at five-thirty PM, and I'll give her instructions. And let her know someone will be keeping tabs on her. She has to be alone. And no monkey business, or there will be hell to pay. Are we clear on that?"

"Absolutely. She won't do anything dumb. She's just a mother, worried about her kids. She just wants to make sure that you understand where she's coming from before she lets go of the money."

"I'll be waiting for her call."

Chapter Twenty Six
October 23rd, 2013

Clyde Kovach didn't care for Mark Bell. It wasn't just that Bell had beaten Clyde out of $20 that he couldn't afford to lose the previous week, shooting eight ball for $2 a game. There was just something about the dude that gave Clyde the creeps. The way he looked at people with those coal black eyes. He was a predator, for sure. Not someone to trifle with. Clyde would have preferred to never see Bell again after their previous encounter, but when the man came with a proposition that offered the possibility of a nice payday, he couldn't afford to pass. He was broke. He was always broke.

"So that's all I have to do?", asked Clyde as they met earlier that day in the the Blue Goose, a dive bar located in Commerce City. "Just ask for this Kelly Mahoney chick at the RE/Max office in Englewood, then watch as some other broad leaves her house later tonight in Centennial, and you'll pay me two-hundred-fifty bucks?"

"And pick up a copy of a lawsuit complaint that was supposedly filed at the county courthouse in Englewood, before you go to the RE/Max office."

"So three errands, and that's it?"

"Yep. A hundred after you go by the courthouse and realty office, then a hundred-fifty more after you keep an eye on the other broads' house between 5:15 and 5:45."

"I'll need some gas money for my bike to ride to Englewood."

Patterson, aka Mark Bell, handed Kovach a $20 bill, one of Kelly Mahoney's business cards, some instructions, and a cell-phone.

"This is for expenses. After you gas up, go directly to the courthouse and pick up a copy of the complaint I wrote down for you. They'll charge you a few bucks to make copies. It's public record. They probably won't, but if they ask why you want it, tell 'em you work for one of the plumbers who did some work on the building in question, and your boss wants to make sure his firm isn't being named in the suit. Just make up a company name.

"Then go from the courthouse to the RE/Max office, and watch how they react when you ask about the girl. If they want to know why you're asking about her, tell them an acquaintance gave you her business card a few months back and told you she was a good agent, and you were thinking about listing an old house you own. If she's there, just pretend to get a call on this phone and tell her you'll get back with her later. If they try to put you onto a different agent, just insist that you only want to deal with her, then excuse yourself as if to answer the phone, and split."

"Okay. No problem. Sounds like easy money. Should we meet back here so I can get paid?"

"Yeah. We'll meet back here at four this afternoon, then I'll give you instructions for the last errand, watching the other broad's house. Then we'll meet back here again at nine o'clock tonight, and I'll pay you the rest."

"So what's all this about, anyway? You hot for this slit?", Kovach said as he admired the picture on Kelly's card.

Patterson just stared directly in Kovach's eyes in reply.

"Okay. No offense. None of my business. As long as I ain't doin' anything illegal to violate my probation, I don't really care why. I need the money, bad."

255

When the two men met back up at 4:00 PM, Kovach reported that the RE/Max office staff told him that Kelly Mahoney had recently quit, and was no longer working in the real estate business. They naturally tried to put Kovach on to another agent, but he didn't sense anything amiss or any undue concern coming from the staff.

The lawsuit complaint also appeared legitimate. It had been filed a few days before Patterson had posted the extortion letter to Mahoney. Everything Mahoney had said was checking out.

Unbeknownst to Kovach, Patterson had followed him and watched from a safe distance as he completed both errands. He'd wanted to see if anyone tailed Kovach after leaving RE/Max or the courthouse. He'd seen no suspicious activity in either location. It appeared Mahoney was on the up-and-up. It didn't look or feel like a trap. Patterson began to relax. By 7:00 tonight, he'd have $25,000 in cash in his duffel bag, as he drove East on I-70 towards Pittsburgh. Home. Man that sounded good.

"Good work. Here's the hundred for the first two jobs. And directions to the house I want you to watch. Just pull off on the side of the road four or five houses up the street at about 5:20, and pretend you're having some mechanical problem with your bike. Pull out a screwdriver, and tinker around. But keep an eye on that house. If you see anyone come or go, call me at this number immediately. I'm expecting you to see only one woman, a good-lookin' lady with dark hair, drive away from that address by herself just after 5:30. She'll probably be in a blue Volvo. I want you to call me immediately when she leaves. Then try to catch up to her and follow from a safe distance, just for a few miles, if you can. But you can't let her know you're following, so stay back. If you lose her, don't sweat it. But if you notice anyone else following her, or if she stops and picks somebody up, pull over and call me. The most important thing is to make sure she's alone when she drives away from the house, and that nobody else follows her out."

As he rode his raggedy but reliable old '84 Yamaha 700 Virago to the Centennial subdivision, Clyde wondered again what kind of angle this asshole Mark Bell was working. Checking up on a pretty young real estate agent, then having him watch some other broad leave her house in a swanky neighborhood? Why didn't Bell pick up the lawsuit paperwork on his own, and save a few bucks? Clyde knew that Bell was bad news. But he hadn't worked more than ten days in any month for the past five years, and couldn't afford to turn down any opportunity. Carpentry work wasn't easy to get these days. Between the Mexicans and the lousy economy, competition was fierce. He barely made enough to pay the small amount of rent his grandmother charged for the basement, and his other meager living expenses. He had no idea what he'd do when his Grandma passed. At seventy-six, she was still pretty spry, fortunately. Probably had another ten years, maybe. But it wouldn't take his Uncle Jake long to give Clyde the heave-ho when that day came. He wasn't too crazy about Clyde being there for the last eight years, even though he mowed the lawn and helped his Grandma around the house.

Man, he had to stop drinking so much, and get his shit together one of these days. Thirty-three years old, and hadn't even been married yet. Hadn't even lived on his own more than eighteen months since his Mom kicked him out.

Clyde's '93 Ford Ranger needed a new exhaust system, or it wouldn't pass inspection. The tags had expired three months ago, and winter was coming. Riding a bike wasn't really feasible during much of the Colorado winters. He wondered if Bell had any more action for him. He'd gladly run errands all day every day for $250. Hell, he'd do it for half that amount.

He pulled over to the curb four houses past the designated address as instructed, on the opposite side of the street, up a slight hill, so he had a clear view of the driveway. Then he pulled the tool kit out from underneath the seat, and pretended to work on the carburetor. After a few minutes, he pulled the cell phone Bell had given him out of his jacket and checked the time - 5:23. He lit a smoke and continued to act like he was making adjustments.

At 5:36, the garage door went up on the designated house, and a blue Volvo pulled out of the driveway and drove away in the opposite direction from Clyde's location. He immediately phoned Bell.

"It's me. She just left the house in the Volvo. It didn't look like anyone else was in the car."

"Could you see what she looked like?"

"It was a little hard to tell. There's a slight tint on the windows. But it looked like a pretty lady with dark hair, just like you said. Looks like she's headed toward Arapahoe Road. And she has a bicycle in a rack on the trunk."

"Good work. Remember...not too close. I don't want her to know you're following. Call me if you see anything weird."

"Got it. See you tonight at the Goose."

"Right. Nine o'clock. I'll be there."

Clyde put his toolkit away, climbed aboard the bike, and rode off in the same direction as the lady in the blue Volvo. By the time he reached Arapahoe Rd, he'd already decided not to follow her any further. He was thirsty, and he had over a hundred bucks in his pocket. He'd say he lost her, if Bell asked what happened. As he rode back to the Blue Goose, he failed to notice the dark sedan that followed him all the way to the tavern.

While Clyde was on his way to the bar, the pretty lady in the blue Volvo was headed towards Waterton Canyon. By the time she arrived at the empty parking lot at the trailhead. It was almost dark as she pulled the bicycle from its rack and began pedaling into the canyon. She was wearing athletic pants, sneakers, a red ballcap over her dark hair, and a loose blue windbreaker.

It took just under twenty minutes of pedaling for the pretty lady to reach her destination; a bench located about a mile South of Mill Gulch Bridge. She dismounted, sat down, and checked her watch - 6:21 PM. She nervously tapped the heel of her right sneaker up and down as she continuously surveyed the area around her position, and waited. It was quiet in the canyon, except for the gentle sound of the South Platte river as it coarsed through the rocks. It was just dark; not yet pitch black. She could just make out the fly fisherman a hundred yards North of her position, who was using a green fluorescent strike indicator that could be seen in the dark, as he repeatedly cast out from the bank.

Above and behind her position, unseen from below, Rick Patterson was likewise surveying the surrounding terrain. He'd been in place since shortly after 6:00 PM, having ridden Pablo the four miles from the nearby ranch where he was staying, after giving instructions to the pretty lady over the phone. He'd seen her arrive, alone, as ordered. He'd also seen the fisherman arrive via bicycle about fifteen minutes ago, closely behind two park rangers who'd driven slowly past this location on an ATV as they headed South towards the end of the main

259

canyon trail, near Strontia Springs reservoir. Patterson knew that the rangers often did a sweep up and down the trail just after dark, chasing out the scofflaws who overstayed closing time. He wondered if the fisherman had purposely kept behind the rangers to avoid detection. Maybe that was his favorite spot. Sunset was an active time for trout.

He waited several more minutes, scanning and straining to listen in every direction, and saw nothing for concern. He put away his night vision binoculars, re-mounted Pablo the dependable Appaloosa, and they began the steep descent from their hiding spot, down to the main trail where the pretty lady awaited with his money.

After reaching the main trail, Patterson started walking Pablo slowly up the trail towards the pretty lady on the bench about a hundred feet to the North. She jumped up quickly as he approached, and stood with her feet planted firmly, spaced shoulder width apart. Odd. Had Stillwell's wife been in the military? A few more steps, and he could see the pretty lady more clearly. He'd never noticed her wearing a ballcap before. He'd followed her about town a few times, and had often marveled at Stillwell's ability to marry so far above himself. Not just a beauty, she was also a stylish dresser, classy, appearing somehow elegant even in the casual apparel she wore when going to the gym, or on routine errands. But something didn't seem quite right about her now. The hair underneath the cap. Was that a wig? And wasn't she taller than that?

At ten feet away, Patterson looked past the pretty lady and for the first time saw the silhouette of a dark SUV parked squarely in the middle of the trail, lights off, about a hundred yards to the North. It was a trap! He suddenly heard the sound of small rocks sliding down the path he'd just taken from the canyon wall above, and he wheeled Pablo around just as the pretty lady pulled out a 9mm pistol and screamed "Freeze!"

One shot whizzed past as horse and rider bolted down the trail, away from the pretty lady and past the path where he'd just descended. He knew he couldn't go back up that way. He could hear someone making their way down. He spurred Pablo on to full speed as they approached the fly fisherman, who was now in a shooter's stance -- left foot forward, left hand cupped under the butt of his pistol, held firmly in his right hand -- in the middle of the trail, screaming "Halt!" Rick saw the "park rangers" in their ATV just past the fisherman's position, also with guns drawn. His only chance now was to head for the river, and hope that the current could sweep him back past the pretty lady policewoman and her friends in the SUV quickly enough to allow him to slip away into the dark mountainous forest.

But before he could get Pablo slowed and turned toward the river, the fisherman fired three quick shots into the ground a few feet ahead of the horse. Pablo panicked, let go a shrill whinny, and abruptly stopped while bucking his hind legs and executing a complete one-eighty, throwing Patterson twenty feet through the air as he did. There was a sickening-sounding crunch as he hit the gravel and rolled off into the brush along the side of the river. There would be no further escape. Rick Patterson was not only stunned from the force of his fall, and experiencing white-hot flashes of pain that were unfathomably excruciating. He was also completely unable to move his arms or legs.

As he drifted into unconsciousness from the pain, he wished he'd never seen that asshole's picture on that real estate sign in the first place. Or that he'd just gone back home to

261

Pittsburgh as soon as he'd exacted his revenge, and the prick was in jail. But his pride just wouldn't allow him to let go of the fact that he hadn't gotten any money out of Stillwell. That pride was his downfall.

Nick Maynard stood over Rick Patterson's motionless body for a moment before holstering his weapon, and checking for a pulse.

"Is he dead?" Claire Tottel asked breathlessly as she came running up the trail, flinging the black wig aside as she stopped.

"He's got a pulse," Nick replied. "But it appears he's out cold. I don't see any obvious gunshot wounds. Better get an ambulance here, fast. And we probably shouldn't move him. He might've broken his neck. That was one helluva fall."

Claire called for an ambulance while Nick went through Patterson's pockets. He pulled a .38 snubnose from an inside pocket of the brown leather jacket he was wearing, along with a cellphone and wallet.

"The ambulance is on its way."

"Good. I'm gonna go pick up my fishing gear and put it away before I forget. You should've seen the big-ass rainbow I had on the line when that bastard bolted. It was four pounds if it was an ounce. Had to let it go in order to bring this jackass to a halt."

"Four pounds, huh? Sounds like a real whopper, Nick."

Chapter Twenty Seven
November 15th, 2013

"I was beginning to wonder if you'd forgotten about me," said Marty Mahoney.

"No such luck," replied Nick Maynard.

They were sitting once again in an interview room at the Federal Prison in Littleton.

"Well, I'm grateful for the opportunity to thank you in person, anyway. If not for you, my family would still be at risk. I don't even wanna think about what that son-of-a-bitch had in mind for Kelly..." Marty choked up slightly, and his eyes misted over as he spoke. "I owe you. Big. Nobody else would've helped."

"Can't really blame 'em. That story was pretty far-fetched. Until my NCIS colleagues pulled those military dental records and compared them to some old records Petarsky's family dentist in Chicago had in storage from before he enlisted, they thought I'd lost my mind, too. But it didn't take long to see that those Navy records had been tampered with. Luckily, the Chicago dental practice was one of those family deals. The guy running it now took it over from his Dad, and they had all the old patient files tucked away in boxes.

"Patterson was smart. He was counting on the fact that a cursory look and quick comparison would match the burnt body, and there would be no reason to look any closer. And he was right."

"Has he admitted to killing Petarsky?"

"Not yet. He hasn't admitted to killing Bantam, or anyone else, either. We think he's done a lot more. He had several stolen identities; passports, drivers licenses, multiple credit cards, even some in female names. Some of the people have been reported missing. A couple of them were ex-pat Americans who lived in South America. I have a feeling he knows where a lot of dead bodies are buried. This might end up being the biggest case I've ever worked before it's all said and done. His lawyer isn't letting us near him. But If I was him, I'd be telling all, and begging for the death penalty.

"Because he's paralyzed?"

"Yeah. He's got nothing from the neck down. Can't move his arms or legs at all. Can you imagine? He might not make it long enough to ever stand trial. But we have to investigate everything as if we're going to court...just in case. Rude bastard could've saved us all a lot of trouble if he'd just gone ahead and died. I probably should've shot him when I had the chance, but I was afraid I'd hit the horse instead. I wouldn't want that on my conscience."

"Speaking of conscience, I don't suppose there's any way you could get him to admit to the fact that he's the guy who actually killed Faith Cooper, and that he framed me, is there?"

"I doubt it. And even if he did, it wouldn't help you. You signed away your rights to appeal, remember? And there's no way you're getting a pardon. The prosecutor would just argue that you and Patterson probably did the deed together."

"I hate that bitch."

"Hey...watch it, Mahoney. She was just doing her job. And she's a district court judge now, anyway. She got the appointment after losing the primary in that Senate bid last year. But the new prosecutor is just as ruthless. So there's no way you're getting out of here before your sentence is up. You might as well forget about that."

"I knew it was a longshot. Thought I'd ask, anyway."

Maynard smirked, picked up his things, and said "Have a nice day, Mahoney" as he walked out the door.

On the way back to his temporary office at FBI Headquarters, Nick decided to stop and get some fish tacos. His phone rang as he was waiting for his lunch. It was the new federal prosecutor for Denver, Kirk Levarron.

"Just wanted to fill you in on the latest. Looks like the negotiations with Patterson's attorney will be a long drawn out process. How's your end coming?"

"The extortion charge is pretty much all written up now. I've got all the statements and evidence documented and collected. But I've got a ways to go on the big-ticket murder charges, even though we've already got the doctored records and the switched x-rays to prove pre-meditation. I'll have to get updated witness statements, and go through all the old evidence more thoroughly. I'll probably be racking up some serious flyer miles before it's all over. But NCIS has authorized me to stay on active service for a hundred and eighty days, so I should be able to see it all the way through to the end. Apparently, they can call up retirees for six-month periods without restriction. They've already said they can extend me further, too, if necessary. But we might need to get somebody else on all those potential missing persons, since the rest of this case will have me tied up for awhile."

"Okay. Sounds like you're on track. I'll see about getting one of the FBI guys to work on it with you. Maybe a newbie. Just keep forging ahead. I'm going to do my best to get him to tell us where all the bodies are. No telling how many families we can help get some closure. There has to be some way to exert some pressure, even on a quadriplegic. Maybe if we promise him the death penalty...how about that for a twist? Most of them will do anything to avoid the needle. Patterson might beg us for it, before it's all over with."

"Let's hope," said Nick. "I'd be more than happy to oblige on that front. Maybe we can use his sister for leverage. We could investigate her for aiding and abetting, and apply a little pressure that way. She surely knew he was wanted. And I think she might be his only vulnerability at this point. He's got nothing else to lose. Anyway, I'll keep you posted on whatever I can dig up from my end."

The fish tacos were even better than the last time he'd eaten at this restaurant. Best he'd ever had.

"Where's Fat Mike?" Nick asked the very friendly lady bartender with the pretty smile, who appeared to be in her late forties. He'd noticed that Colorado seemed to have more than a fair share of attractive women near his age group.

"Mike retired, and moved to Florida. I'm Karen, by the way. Can I get you another beer?"

Maybe he would move to Denver. There wasn't any reason to stay in Oklahoma anymore, now that Dad was gone. He liked the mountains. And the people out here.

After logging into his gmail account upon arriving back at the FBI building, he was surprised to see a message from Deanna Sherman:

Hey Nick,

Just checking in to see how it's going in Denver. Claire can't stop bragging about the big collar you guys made. She was really excited about getting back in the field for a couple of days. You're a big star around here, too. She's been raving about you to the brass, so you might be seeing an award soon.

Hope you don't mind I told her you prefer paper, especially green in color.

Anyway, I hope you'll be coming back this way soon for at least a few days. We really miss you around here. Let me know if there's anything I can do for you...

Hope to see you soon,
D

There was a time when an email like this from Deanna would have had him all spun up, wondering if she was encouraging him to make a move. But not anymore. It had only taken a few decades, but he'd finally learned his lesson. No more pining after someone he couldn't have. There were lots of other fish in he sea. She was out of his system for good. He had moved on.

Still...what if her and Steve were having problems? Nahh. That was silly. They'd been married forever.

Maybe he should head back to Norfolk for a few days for business, though. After all, he would have to go through all those old files personally. There were reams of notes to plow through. Someone less familiar with the case might overlook something important. And he kind of missed the ocean, anyway.